INCANTATIONS

KEIRA O'SHEA

INCANTATIONS

KEIRA O'SHEA

For my loved ones

PART ONE

TWISTED WORDS

Chapter One

Caine

A GONG FILLED the dim room, signaling a quarter to eleven. Caine had been counting the seconds until then, the clock hand ticking in the back of his head.

He had been sitting at his desk, working absentmindedly, filling tiny glass beakers with bright-green liquid, twisting their caps shut, and tying ribbons under the rims—over and over and over. The monotony of the job never took hold in his mind. A more prominent task filled the space.

At the stroke of the clock, he began to stash each item in its designated cabinet. Nagging thoughts in the back of his head reminded him that it didn't matter. He wouldn't be coming back, but he couldn't bear to leave it cluttered.

His assistant, Alice, helped him line bottles up on the shelves and eventually ushered him toward the door. "Go on. I'll finish up."

Caine adjusted the near-floor-length cloak one last time, pulling the buckles tighter and tugging his hood on. The huge archmage cloak, adorned with all its buttons and brooches, had always seemed garish, but he still wore it with pride.

Trusting Alice to keep an eye on the room, he left swiftly and made his way to the depths of the castle. The trek was quiet as he strode along the polished gray stone. Caine kept his gaze trained ahead, sidestepping hanging banners out of habit. He didn't run into anyone except a few night shift guards who only nodded to him.

Caine ducked around a corner, stopping below a painting depicting the throne room. He placed his hand against the wall, and the stone flashed a dull orange before disappearing. As he approached the old stairwell, a musty smell filled the air, and the wall reappeared behind him.

Not needing to light a candle, Caine pressed his palms together, and an orb of pale-blue light formed between them. The descent was still treacherous despite the stairs being illuminated. He walked slowly to avoid the cracks in the rotting wood.

Caine was the last to join the group at the small table, although he wasn't late. They'd all been given staggered meeting times so as not to draw attention to the rest of the staff.

He slid into the hard wooden chair and rested his elbows on the table.

King Paskal nodded to him before addressing the entire table, consisting of two advisors, the captain of the guard, the archmage, and an officer. "The town leaders have reported that all is fine, no attacks in the last month, human or otherwise. No word from my son since his last… message."

The advisor to the king's right, Joanna, raised her hand. "I know we've already spoken about this, but would it not be beneficial to send a mage there to spy on the Sophonix Kingdom?"

"I see no need for that. As long as our initial task is completed, everything will be fine."

Caine assumed the king's last comment had been aimed at him, but he let his eyes drift to the flames dancing along the wall. He had nothing to count tonight aside from the number of cracks in the stone or lines in the table.

"Blackwood," King Paskal said. "How are your preparations coming along? You haven't given us a concrete update in some time."

Caine decided that counting the wrinkles in the king's face would suffice. "I'm doing my best, Your Majesty. It's nearly finished, but I can't figure out the last ingredient to make the teleportation work."

"How long?"

He pretended to think about it. "A month at the most."

The king's words were firm but not unkind. "Can we help with anything?"

"I appreciate the offer, but there's not much you can do."

No one argued with Caine.

Joanna spoke again, her hands clenched on the table. "I apologize, Your Majesty, but I think this situation with the prince is more of an issue than you're making it out to be."

Caine sighed as the king frowned, screwing up his count. He glanced at the paper that sat in the middle of the table instead. He didn't need to be close to read. The bold letters were seared into his mind.

AS A MEMBER OF THE KING'S ASSEMBLY, WE WILL DO ALL WE CAN TO PERFORM THE ACTIONS EXPECTED OF US WITH GRACE AND SECRECY. THERE IS NO ROOM FOR MISTAKES. FAILURE OR TREASON WILL NOT BE TOLERATED AND WILL BE DISCIPLINED HARSHLY.

Blood from each person who sat at the table had dried below the letters many years ago as a constant reminder of what they'd agreed to—a warning of what was to come. Caine had sliced his finger so easily then.

A hand brushed his elbow under the table. Sparrow leaned toward him, her tan hair falling onto his shoulder. "Stop daydreaming," the captain murmured, but her eyes were heavy as well.

They both sat up straighter as the king raised his voice to counter whatever Joanna had said. "We will *not* continue this conversation. The prince and Sophonix are not threats."

Sparrow held back a smile, this time for the red-eyed officer mouthing silently to her from across the table. Caine could feel them both watching, and he found himself reading the agreement in the center once more.

~

THE GROUP STOOD and bowed before they made their way to their chambers after a long night. Caine was the last to leave. Only the king remained, rocking on his heels. The royal made no move to stop Caine.

Still, Caine paused. Anything to keep the king from visiting them later that night. "Everything will be completed. I need a little more time."

"I apologize. That wasn't meant to rush you." King Paskal rested his hand below Caine's hood. "I know you'll get it done."

"Thank you, Your Majesty." He bowed, letting the king's hand slide away. "Have a good night."

"You as well."

Sparrow waited for him as he emerged from the passageway. "Are you sure you and Alice don't need anything?"

Caine reaffirmed his claim, and she took his arm as they made their way up to their bedrooms.

"Goodnight, Sparrow," Caine said.

"Get some sleep," she teased, continuing down the hall.

He waited until he was sure she would be in her own room before heading back down a flight of stairs. He slowed on the landing to greet the princess, who was leaning on the windowsill, gazing out at the nearly full moon. She was relaxing as if she'd spent the whole night there, but he and Sparrow had just passed through.

She returned his hello. "Working late again, Mr. Blackwood?"

"As always."

She opened her mouth but only motioned for him to continue.

He got a few steps past before she whispered, "Your meeting has already adjourned, yes?"

"It has. His plan still holds."

She closed her eyes, shoulders drooping. "Okay. Thank you, Caine."

"Of course, Rilla."

Caine looked up again when he got to the bottom of the stairs. The princess was already gone.

Finally back in his office, he locked it and pressed his hand against the door until the frame briefly flashed blue.

Alice sat at his desk, now clear of everything except a bowl of water, a vial, and a silvery sphere. He uncapped the vial and let a single drop fall into the bowl. They watched the image of a sparse living room that appeared, trying to get any indication that someone was home. He had checked earlier, so hopefully she was still there and her roommate was absent.

"We don't have to do this," Alice said. "You could always go along with the king's plans."

He picked up the small glass orb and ran a finger over it. "You don't have to come. Just don't tell anyone my plans."

She tapped the water, letting the image dissipate as she pocketed the vial. "You think, after all this time, I wouldn't go?"

"Stop whining, then." Caine snapped the orb cleanly in half, placing one part in his pocket as he walked behind his desk. "*Potentia,*" he whispered over the other half sphere before laying the flat side onto the bare wall and gradually adding pressure until it cracked. As it shattered, lights of many colors ebbed onto the wall. They shuffled into unrecognizable patterns before finally melding together as one large blinding-white square.

"Ready?" He offered a hand to his partner.

Alice took it and squinted into the light. "There's no going back after this, is there?"

"Not at all."

They jumped into the portal.

The pair landed in the darkness with a thud. Caine regained his balance first and yanked Alice behind a corner as a light turned on in the hall.

He let out a breath as the woman ignored what was left of the receding portal, seemingly brushing it off as lack of sleep. He crouched down as rushing water sounded from behind the door.

He removed a dagger from its sheath along with a miniature bottle as Alice kept an eye on the hall. He drenched the blade in fluorescent-lavender liquid. It absorbed the potion, leaving only a slight glow in its place.

They waited until the woman closed the door behind herself

before moving from their hiding spot. Neither risked creating a light, and both prayed they wouldn't bump into anything.

Alice gripped the back of Caine's cloak. He cringed as one of the floorboards creaked below them. Caine stopped when they reached the door.

They both tensed as footsteps came closer. Backing away slightly, he readied his blade. Sparks flickered at the tips of Alice's fingers, and she put her hands behind her back.

Caine worried about rushing in. He had no idea how she would retaliate or if magic would aid her panic.

Alice must have recognized his hesitation and started to ask, "Should we—"

They both tensed as footsteps came to the door. Backing away slightly, Caine readied his blade.

The woman's eyes were wide as she halted in the doorway. Alice held her still with telekinesis as Caine scratched the back of the woman's neck with his dagger. She struggled for only a moment before her eyes shut and the useless weapon clanked to the floor. Only the levitation kept her from falling with it.

Chapter Two

Violet

VIOLET SHOT UP, nearly toppling off the small bed. Her pulse drummed in her ears as she realized this was not her bedroom.

Foggy memories of the previous night flashed through her mind. Hushed voices and timid footsteps, a burst of light, the searing pain that still lingered at the base of her skull. Running her fingers along the back of her neck revealed a long, thin scratch. Violet felt the chain and pendant of a necklace around her throat, and she tried to remember putting one on.

She removed a fluffy comforter and slid out of the bed. Misjudging her own steadiness, Violet toppled, landing hard on the floorboards.

The room was well lived in, with a trunk of colorful clothes spilling over the edges and a cluttered dresser next to it. Sunlight streaked across the dim room each time a cool breeze blew the curtains upward. Despite Violet's tumble from the bed, the door stayed shut. It wasn't her parents' house, and she wasn't friends with any resident students for it to be a dorm.

She combed her memory for where she could have gone at midnight, but the last thing Violet remembered was throwing her chemistry book to the side and pulling back her hair with a rubber band. She felt the back of her head for the long, dark-brown ponytail just to confirm that memory. It was messy but still in place.

Violet had another recollection of grabbing a box cutter and going to investigate a noise. That felt real too. No one besides Violet's sister could get into their shared apartment though, and Crystal was away on a work trip. Maybe someone had made it through the weak locks on her door and had been hiding in some dark corner.

She crept to the door and opened it as slowly as possible, leaving it ajar, too scared of the noise it might make. It was agonizing to tread down the hallway without making a sound. Violet held her breath every time she passed a door and nearly died when the floorboards squeaked.

Her silent walk led her to a rustic kitchen. The door to the outside was open, and her heart pounded faster as she saw a person leaning over the porch railing. A red-and-black cloak hid most of the figure. Light shone from under another door at the end of the hall, and she could hear shuffling from within.

Violet pulled herself out of view of the kitchen. *Abducted,* that was all she could think. She hadn't been tied up, but she couldn't come up with any other reason she would be in someone else's house.

She took a deep breath and peeked back around the corner. Violet moved silently again, crossing the kitchen and stopping inside the door. The person only shifted, but they would certainly feel if she stepped down onto the porch.

A large candlestand beside the doorframe caught her eye.

Glancing up at the person again, she picked up the stick, careful not to let it scrape the ground. She shifted the metal post's weight in her hands. It felt hollow, but it would do. Violet took a step forward, hoping she wasn't making a mistake in assuming that the person was dangerous.

Violet's hands shook as she hesitated. Running away wasn't possible. The dense evergreen forest surrounding the cabin foiled her getaway plan. Sneaking out would be one thing, but roaming through the forest wasn't viable until she knew her location. Even if she did run, she would either have to go down the stairs past the person or leap the guardrail. Neither seemed like a profitable choice. And the longer she looked at the hood, the surer she felt that it would cushion the blow too much.

As Violet moved forward again, her foot got caught on something. She lost her balance and fell onto the kitchen floor. She didn't have time to catch herself, and her chin smashed into the ground. The person spun around, his eyes immediately focusing on the candlestick she was still gripping. He threw his arm to the side, and the post shot out of her hand, smashing into the wall.

Violet stared at her empty hand. *He hadn't touched the...* Ignoring the impossible motion, she tried to push herself up, still hoping to make a run for it. Violet squirmed, but her legs locked into place. She glanced down and nearly screamed.

An orange light-rope snaked up and around her lower half, consuming her upper body just as fast. A woman stood in the room, the same glow around her hands. As the rope reached Violet's chest, it vanished.

Violet scooted away from the two strangers and rubbed her legs and chin. She shuddered. They were both watching her as if waiting for a reaction.

"You're up fast, sunshine," the man said.

Violet kept her mouth shut, trying to focus on anything but the tears building. The first thing that caught her attention was their eyes, which seemed to glow even in the bright sunlight.

The man's were a shade of amber, unnatural, much like Violet's purple irises. He pushed the front door shut and leaned against it. "You're not going to talk?"

The woman was playing with the glowing rope, coiling it in her hands. "Maybe you made the necklace wrong." She wore a short, hooded shawl identical to his cloak's colors. The two brooches she had pinned above her heart matched the ones on his as well. Although the woman's deep-gray eyes were startling, Violet was drawn to her curly electric-blue hair.

The man glared at the woman. "Are you doubting my craft, Alice?"

"It was a hard spell, Caine, and we didn't have time to test it. There's a good chance—"

They had given her the necklace, then. Violet cut into the conversation. "Where am I?" she asked.

The man raised an eyebrow at Alice before responding to Violet. "You're in my private home on the outskirts of the Endrel Kingdom."

"Endrel… Kingdom? Stop talking nonsense." Her voice had dropped into a hoarse whisper. She glared at him, well aware that her tears were diminishing her stern look.

"It's not nonsense, sunshine."

The woman kneeled beside Violet, the rope still in her grasp. "We're not in your world anymore."

Violet ignored her answer. "What the hell is that?" She gestured to the coil.

"It's a rope spell," Caine replied. "You act like this is your first time seeing magic, sunshine."

"Well, yeah, I—" She stumbled over her words. "What do you mean magic?"

"Magic as in magic, sunshine."

"Stop calling me that, you freak."

"Whatever you say, sunshine." Caine sat at the table in the middle of the room.

The woman stood and tried to help Violet up. "Come on. It'll be okay. I promise."

Violet stood up on her own, still considering running for the door, but she followed the woman, who gestured for Violet to sit.

"Tea or coffee?"

"Tea," Caine said.

"I know. I wasn't asking you. What would you like?"

"Coffee, I guess." Violet took her time approaching the table.

Three chairs sat on one side, and Caine sat in the middle. Violet sat on the edge of her seat, poised to run if need be.

"Thank you, Alice." Caine paged through a book and thankfully didn't look up at Violet.

The only sound was Alice's quiet humming as she heated a kettle over a fire inside the large stone hearth.

"Don't take off the necklace," Caine said. "It's a translator." He tilted his head to look over at Violet, causing a few strands of inky-black hair to spill out of his hood.

Violet played with the flat, cloudy-white jewel.

"Not talking anymore? '*Where are we? What is that?*'" Caine mocked her. "That's it?"

Violet clenched her teeth, staring down at the table. Of course she had questions. Their answers just weren't making any sense, and they were sitting around like it was any other morning.

"Well, don't ignore me." He closed the book and jabbed it into her arm.

"Hey!"

She tried to get out of her chair, but he grabbed Violet's forearms and yanked her close.

Heat flashed around Violet's hands, and she nearly fell out of her chair as Caine cursed and jumped back. She pressed a hand against her chest, breathing raggedly.

Alice ran up to them. "What happened? Caine, your hands."

Shiny red stripes were burned into his fingertips. A few small blisters had risen on his palms.

"Well then, the—" He made a noise as if cutting out a word. "*She* actually stung me. You're very special. You know that?"

Although his voice held no malice, his patronizing eyes kept Violet fixed to her seat. She swallowed as he stepped behind her chair, leaning down to whisper, "Would you like to know why we kidnapped you?"

"Yes." Violet couldn't manage to keep her voice steady.

Without moving away, he said softly, "There are two known worlds. Your Earth, where all the dear, powerless humans live, and ours, Endrel. We didn't always know about your side, but the last archmage accidentally got a glimpse into it and sensed immense power coming from a girl."

Caine crossed his arms over the back of the chair and rested his head on one hand. "Now, while none of us could explain why she was blessed with such power, we knew she couldn't stay in her world. It would be dangerous. So the king declared that he would steal her from that world and take her power as his own."

"No," Violet said. These people were crazy, making up rubbish to confuse her.

He laughed as if she had told a crude joke and slid into the chair beside her. "Yes, sunshine. The king asked the archmage to create a portal so his militia could take the girl when the time came. And so I did. What they didn't know is that I never planned to let them use it. How fair would that be to you? To have you pulled from your world, told you have this amazing power, and be forced to use this power against people you don't even know? To kill people you've never even met?"

"So you took me so you could use it instead," Violet said bluntly.

"No, I thought what they were going to do was absolutely atrocious. So I've pretended for the last few years that I was preparing a portal to help them kidnap you, and instead, last night Alice and I went and brought you here."

"So if they had gotten me, I wouldn't have had a say in anything? Do I have a say in this?"

"I really think you should stay with us and learn how to control your magic. Look, you already used it without knowing."

She grimaced as he flashed a burned palm.

"Magic can be deadly. It would be a shame if someone got hurt because you didn't know what you were doing."

"You'll teach me how to control it?"

"Precisely. You would stay in this world with us until we think you can handle your magic and protect yourself. We'll show you everything we can as we travel."

"Travel?"

"Well, I can't imagine the king is very happy right now. It's obvious who took you, and treason against the crown is punishable by death, but that's only if he catches us."

"Here." Alice placed two teacups on the table and handed a mug to Violet. "I hope it's okay."

Violet thanked Alice as she moved to pour tea for Caine then herself.

"Oh." Alice dragged a chair to the other side of the table. "We don't even know your name."

"Violet Harper. Violet or Vi is fine," she said quietly, preparing for the usual response. It was so obvious why her parents had chosen the name.

Caine was more perplexed than anything. "I suppose your eyes would be startling enough in your world that you would be named after them."

Alice beamed. "I think it's pretty."

"Thank you," Violet said hesitantly.

"Though I'm sure you've figured this out by now, I'm Caine, and this is my assistant, Alice."

"Assistant?" Violet asked.

"Well, Caine is… was archmage of our kingdom, and I suppose I'm still your assistant." Alice eyed him for a second, but he ignored the partial question.

"Which means you have pretty decent teachers," Caine said. "Two of the strongest mages in the land."

"If you've been…" Violet paused. "Studying me for this long, why didn't you know my name?"

Caine picked up his cup. "That's what we're trying to explain. You were an object to the king, a funnel for power and nothing more. It was 'the girl,' never a name."

"I can't leave my life for this." Violet squeezed her eyes shut.

When she opened them again, Caine was glaring at her over his teacup. "So, you want to go back at the risk of hurting someone?"

"I just…" Violet gripped the table, trying to focus on the coffee cup. "Can I at least have some time to think about it? Maybe go back for a few days and—"

"No. I can give you two days to decide if you want to stay here or go back for good."

"Only two days?"

"That's more than I want to offer. I'd estimate we have no more than a week until King Paskal tracks us down—or Prince Cross."

"There's a second kingdom as well," Alice clarified before Violet could ask. "Sophonix, ruled by the king's exiled son. We're expecting his army to come after you too."

Caine nodded. "We need to know if you're going to be a factor in this endeavor or not."

"Okay," Violet said, still looking for any indication of a different option.

He still didn't smile. "I'm going to finish mixing some potions. Violet, go back to the room you woke up in. Alice will be there in a minute."

Violet picked up her coffee cup, stopping the "bite me" from rolling off her tongue. If by some miracle she decided to stay, she wasn't going to let him order her around like that.

Alice

ALICE WAITED until they heard the bedroom door shut. "I know, I didn't help antagonize her." It had been one thing to talk about it, but now that she was right in front of them…

She waited for a snarky comment, but Caine only watched the hallway. "It doesn't matter. I got my reaction."

Alice stared at his burn. "She conjured heat without us even telling her she had magic. That's amazing."

"It's unbelievable. I wonder if it helped her shake off that sleeping potion too."

"Maybe we should be a little nicer." She added quickly, "At least to keep some of her energy at bay."

After taking another sip of his tea, he murmured, "Perhaps. She needs some reason to stay. I was hoping the promise of power would be enough. Go on." He grabbed the teacups and saucers. "I'll clean up."

Alice pulled him in for a one-sided hug before hurrying down the hall.

Chapter Three

Alice

ALICE STEPPED into her bedroom and pushed aside a basket of sewing materials sitting near the door. The curtains were open, sunlight illuminating the mess that had taken over during the last few days of preparation. She'd come here often over the last week, trying to prepare, while Caine was preoccupied with the king's secret meetings. That had been the most time Alice had ever spent here without him. Although Caine called it his house, he'd incorporated Alice into it from the beginning.

She had walked into the room with a pep in her step, hoping to erase some of their first impression, but Violet was lying back on the bed, sobbing. Alice grabbed a handkerchief out of a dresser drawer and handed it to Violet.

Alice sat beside Violet, stopping herself from embracing the woman in some attempt to calm her down. "I'm sorry you felt threatened. We just needed to see if you could use your magic."

"Right, magic." Violet sat up, pressing the cloth to her face. "I've lost my mind."

"No, sweetie, this is real."

"What's real? Other worlds? Magic?" Violet gripped the bedsheets.

"You saw us use it. You used it."

"You're messing with me. I don't know what you want, but I need to go home." Her voice cracked.

Alice got off the bed, occupying herself with the objects on the dresser. "Do you want other clothes? And a brush? I know we dragged you out of bed."

"Yes, that's important right now." Still, Violet examined her soft pants and frilly top with a frown.

As she looked for a comb, Alice tried not to watch Violet in the mirror. She struggled to find a way to tell someone it was okay that they were being held captive. "Well, we… I…" Alice was doing her best to stop laughing, but it continued to dribble out when she spoke. "This is terrible."

Violet murmured to herself, dabbing under her eyes again. At least she'd stopped crying.

Pulling together a decent set of words, Alice said, "I'm sorry for how we treated you to get you here. We want to help you."

Violet shrugged—not the response Alice was hoping for, but the one she expected.

"Here." Alice handed Violet a comb from the vanity table.

As Violet worked through her hair, Alice pulled out a short orange cotton shirt and denim slacks. "Are these all right?"

Violet shook her head. "I don't think they're going to fit me."

She was right. Alice was curvier, and the garments would hang loose.

"I'll fix them after you put them on."

"But…" Violet made a show of pulling at the clothes once they were on. "See? They're too big."

Alice took some of the extra fabric in her hand and focused

on the materials, letting them shrink until they formed to Violet's body. "And now they fit."

Violet tugged at the altered clothes, muttering about its absurdity again.

Alice moved her to a stool before she toppled over. She adjusted a few more shirts and pants, hoping that Violet would stay long enough to need them.

She watched Violet's shaky movements as Violet examined the clothes. Alice considered how she could ease the tension, if she should say something. *Sorry we dragged you from your world and told you about this dangerous, nonsensical power you have. Care to stay?*

Alice hadn't believed it herself when Caine had told her about a mage of that capacity—and a possible wordsmith at that. No one person had ever held that amount of magic in them. Even after they'd gotten as far as leaving their world to kidnap the woman, she'd been doubtful.

Alice answered the three sharp raps at the door.

Caine poked his head inside. "Alice, could you come help me for a second? I can't seem to… what are you doing?"

"Helping her get clothes." Alice covered her smile with a shirt.

"Well, whenever you're finished playing dress-up, come to the study."

"Yes, sir."

He sighed and pulled the door shut.

Violet hadn't looked toward the door at all during their exchange and instead examined nonexistent snarls in her hair.

Alice put the remaining clothes on top of a trunk near the vanity. "Ignoring us isn't going to get you very far."

"I'm not—"

"You are, and I understand. But it's going to be hard to make a decision if you don't get to know who you're working with. I'll be back. You can pick out some more outfits if you'd like."

Alice didn't want to be so harsh on Violet, but she feared what would happen if the poor woman said no to their offer.

Violet

VIOLET GRABBED her cold coffee off the dresser and gasped at her reflection, almost dropping the mug. Her irises were glowing brightly, just like Caine's and Alice's. Violet blinked a few times, but her eyes continued to shine.

She forced her breathing to stay level. If this wasn't some elaborate joke, she hoped her irises would return to normal once she got home. She wasn't staying or getting to know those people.

It was one thing to leave school. The two years at community college hadn't taught her as much as everyone had said they would, and she had yet to pick a major at her new school. It would be the perfect excuse to stop going. But Violet's family was what she worried about. Her sister would notice first after she came home to an empty apartment. Her mom would panic and call the school while her sister would text one of her friends. They would wait and look and call, but no one would find her. After that, the police would get involved.

Violet went off in search of the others, unable to listen to her own thoughts any longer. Although she could hear voices coming from the far end of the hall, she couldn't help but peek into the other rooms. The first door seemed to be nothing more than a small storage closet, linens lining the lower shelves and sealed wooden boxes on the top. The second wasn't lit up enough, and she stepped in to get a better look. Violet couldn't make out much and started to leave the room. Her back met something solid, and she let out a little yelp.

"Did I scare you, sunshine?" Caine leaned against the doorframe. "I do apologize. Although I'd love to know what you're doing in here."

Violet looked past him. "I was searching for you guys."

"Well, I'm sure you didn't need such a close look to figure out we weren't in the pitch-black room."

"When did my eyes start glowing and why?" Violet asked suddenly. She hoped to redirect the conversation, and the dark room had called attention to his eyes.

"They started when you used your magic. It's a trait of all mages. Your eyes are as bright as mine and Alice's." He stepped out of the doorway, no longer interested in persecuting her. "Alice and I would like to show you our magic, just to give you an idea of what you'll be working with."

Maybe it was best to stay cooperative until the two days were up. "Okay."

Violet followed him out a back door tucked in the end of the hallway and into the barren field. It went on for at least an acre before coming to the forest.

"I'm sorry about your hands," she said as they walked.

"Don't worry about that." He flashed a palm in her direction. "It's easy enough to heal myself. Although I can't say the same for your loved ones back home."

Caine ran his finger over his left wrist, tracing the triangle etched into his skin, frowning at the brand. Violet wanted to ask about it, but he covered the mark with his sleeve just as fast.

The sky was almost clear, but the sun beating on their skin wasn't unbearable. A cool breeze made sure of that.

Their worlds were strikingly similar, the evergreen trees

exactly the same. If it weren't for the magic, she would have sworn she was in a forest on Earth.

Violet thought of the days she'd spent at her parents' house, romping outside with her sister until their mom would call them in. By that time, the grass would have stained their faded jeans and the dirt would have to be scrubbed from under their fingernails.

Alice was waiting about halfway across the field. Violet sat with her back to the house, inhaling the scent of fresh earth. Alice plopped down beside her.

A little smile tugged at the corner of Caine's mouth. "Are you learning too?"

Alice laughed. "Sure, I could use a refresher."

He took a spot across from them. "Evidently, you have no knowledge of magic and how it works. Do you at least know what energy is?"

"Like electricity or power?" Violet asked.

"Power is close. Energy is a person's being. Some people can use that energy to create magic. There's physical magic, which is good to fight with as well as other things, like making seals and healing. Fire, water, anything along those lines. Sound familiar?"

"Like elements?"

"Those are the basis of some energies."

"Are those the only types?" Violet asked.

"As long as the energy exists, you can harness it. The reason certain magic isn't used is because no one's figured out how or they don't have the energy to do so." He rolled up his sleeves. "Some mages can use a little of everything, but they usually specialize in one. For example..."

He held his right palm away from the women. A tendril of snow snaked out. It coiled into a circle a little larger than Caine's hand before tapering into a point. With a flick of his wrist, he sent the fully formed icicle spiraling toward the trees. It soared through the air for about five feet before bursting into chunks.

Violet let out a shaky breath, gasping at the foggy air.

"And this is mine." Alice cupped her hands, and a little ball of orange flame popped into existence. She spread her hands apart, and a wave of fire grew. The second she clenched her fists, it disappeared.

Caine said, "I know you at least hold a fire element."

"From burning you?" Violet clarified.

"Yes." Caine picked up the sheath that lay next to him and pulled out a dagger.

Violet tried to identify the flash of panic that ran through her.

"Some objects can be enchanted. My knife absorbs potions and poisons, like a paralyzing drug, for instance." Caine smiled as Violet drew back from the blade. "Alice's weapon is hidden and lets her run fire through it."

The other mage waved her hand over her hip, and Violet saw a flash of leather. "And you saw my light-rope already." The rope coil appeared in her hand. "That takes a bit more energy to use."

She nearly screamed when she turned back to Caine, who was in the midst of running the tip of the dagger across his palm. Her breath hitched as a thin line of blood dribbled down his arm.

"Another pertinent aspect of our energies is life and restoration magic." He continued to speak as if blood weren't dripping off his elbow, simply pulling out a lavender handkerchief and running it up his arm. He scanned Violet's features. "Oh. You're not squeamish, are you, sunshine?"

She refused to acknowledge the question. "You said healing magic?"

He nodded and pressed the cloth to the wound. Once the blood had slowed, he pushed his fingers into his palm.

Violet gasped as the cut shrank behind an orange glow and new skin crawled over the gash. After a minute, nothing more than a shiny patch of skin was left.

"That does have to be used sparingly. While all magic uses up energy, those spells can drain you quickly. You'll pass out before it kills you. Certain mages are also wordsmiths. They're able to use ancient words to enhance spells." Caine paused, pulling at the grass. "I won't tell you the terms yet. We only use those if we really need to, and I don't know that you could cast them anyway."

Violet tried not to frown, hoping the words wouldn't be something she could accidentally say.

He stood up. "There's also conjuration." Caine took a few steps and put his hand out in front of him. This time he closed his eyes and spoke under his breath. A blue light came out of the ground and made an array of lines on the grass. A circle wrapped itself around the zigzags, and as it came to a close, a burst of fire shot out of the ground and flew into the sky.

Violet threw a hand over her mouth as the ball of fire spread its wings. "A phoenix?"

The giant bird circled in the air a few times before landing. It was at least three feet taller than Caine and had to bow its head so the man could pet it.

"This is Flare, my summon."

The bird's attention moved to Violet quickly, and it took a step toward her. Violet jumped up, but Alice grabbed her hand before she could run away.

"Let him smell you. You can touch him, it's not real fire."

Violet held her breath as Flare brought his beak close to her face. Hot air burned her cheek. After a few sniffs, he turned back to Caine and let out a squawk that was much less intimidating than she'd expected from such a large bird.

"I know. I know. She's new." Caine rubbed his head against the bird's beak.

Flare squawked in her direction.

Caine laughed. "Sorry, you'll have to get used to her." He swatted at Flare as the bird snapped at him. "Stop that."

"Should I be concerned that the giant flaming bird hates me?" Violet asked, taking another step back.

Alice shook her head. "That bird's a big kitten."

At Alice's words, the bird looked like he was going to call out again, but Caine scratched under the bird's neck, and he let out a chirp instead.

"See?"

"Come on. He's not going to hurt you." Caine called her over.

Violet took timid steps until she stood beside Caine.

His face lit up. "Do you want to ride him?"

"No, absolutely not!" Violet protested. "I don't do heights."

"You'll have to eventually. It'll be the fastest way for us to travel. I won't go that high."

"Bull."

Caine petted Flare's feathers, and the bird lowered himself to the ground. Violet dropped back down onto the grass, arms crossed. He eventually gave up on getting her to ride the monstrosity.

Flare's head suddenly shot up, his orange eyes searching the sky. They followed his gaze, seeing only a hawk passing overhead. Caine warned his familiar to leave it be. The bird continued to growl, and Caine eventually snapped his fingers, dismissing Flare with another flash of blue.

Violet moved closer again, prompting Alice about her own pet, but the mage had nothing to show.

"I can shape-shift into a bunny, though."

"And then immediately pass out when you turn back," Caine said.

"That's more than you can do."

Caine pulled his assistant up. "Prove it."

She shooed his hands away and put a few feet of space between them. "Vi, would you count down from five?"

Violet only got to three before Caine closed the gap, forming a few blunt icicles around himself. Alice thawed them with a wave of fire, which she whipped close to his head. Violet lost track of the flurry of colors they threw, although they stuck to their main elements for the most part. They exchanged blows for only a few minutes before Caine stumbled back. Alice shot a gust of wind at his feet, and he tumbled down completely. She smiled broadly as Caine scowled up at her.

"Fine, you caught me off guard." He let Alice pull him up, trying to hide his budding smile.

"That was cool." Violet let her shoulders relax, releasing the tension from watching their blows come so close.

"Magic is fun—and dangerous," Alice said.

"That's what makes it fun," Caine countered. "I think that's enough for the moment. I don't know how far your energy will reach, but if you do stay, we'll start you with physical magic to be safe. It's unlikely you'll accidentally create a seal, but fire can fly off your fingers in a second."

Violet only nodded, the fanciful colors still dancing through her vision. All that power they had at their fingertips, and they were so sure she could do the same.

On the way back to the cottage, she held a hand up and watched her palm, stomach twisting as she imagined flames pouring out. She would have no use for conjuring nonsense at home. It couldn't be a power she was meant to have as she trailed through everyday life.

Violet entered Alice's room and found the clothes she'd arrived in still folded neatly by the nightstand. Violet searched one of her pockets, pulling out a tightly folded paper. It was titled at the top in the neatest letters she could manage, "Future Goals."

The paper was getting too weak. She would have to rewrite it again soon. For the moment, it was the only memento she had from home. She searched Alice's desk for a writing device and picked up a thin tool filled with what she hoped was ink.

She read over the list again, grimacing at the many items still left unchecked. At the bottom, she added two more: "Learn to control my magic (maybe?)" and "go home."

On the back, Violet made one tally mark before slipping it into the pocket of her current clothes.

Chapter Four

ALICE SAT BELOW THE WINDOW, letting sunlight hit her back as she looked over her handiwork one last time before folding it neatly into the sturdy paper box. It had taken her a few months to get it right, and that was as good as it would get.

She let herself into the study, holding it behind her back. "Hi, Caine."

He barely looked up before asking, "What is that?"

Alice flitted over and dropped it on his desk. "Open it."

He pulled at the blue ribbon and took off the top. Inside was a thin navy trench coat. It was much shorter than what he was used to. Rather than an abundance of belts and buckles, it had a few large pockets.

He looked between her and the coat. "Why…?"

Alice bit the inside of her lip. "I know how much you like your mage's cloak. This isn't quite the same, but I hope it'll be a good replacement while we're traveling."

His brows furrowed. "You made this?"

"Yes. Of course." She added hurriedly, "You don't have to wear it. I thought—"

Alice gasped as Caine stood up and threw his arms around her. She quickly did the same before he could let go.

He moved away after a few seconds. "Thank you."

"Try it on!"

She had done a better job with the fitting than she'd thought. It wasn't the first time she had made clothes for him, but she'd never made a jacket like that.

"Thank you, Alice."

"Of course."

They each had plenty of work to do, but Caine was going to take the brunt of it, and since he refused to talk to her about it, at least she could give him a keepsake.

She took his cloak, her shawl, and their pins and tucked them into a chest. She pressed her hand on the top, taking a few deep breaths as the sealing spell settled into the chest. If she could preserve a little bit of their previous lives, that would be enough.

Violet

VIOLET STOOD in Alice's room, getting ready for the morning. She only had to make it through the day, and she could go home.

"Come in," Violet answered the knock at the door.

An older man and woman stepped into the room. Violet grabbed a candle holder off the dresser and took a step back.

Caine quickly replaced the stranger, as did Alice with the woman beside him. He put his hands up, and a slight blue haze surrounded them. "Don't throw it, and watch your magic! You and these candlesticks…"

Violet dropped the metal, which she had completely covered in ice.

Alice elbowed Caine. "I told you this was a stupid idea. I'm sorry, Vi," she apologized. "Caine's been working on these disguises for a while, and we wanted to make sure they were having the desired effect." She lifted the brown cloaks they both wore.

"What are they?" Violet asked, still looking at the ball of ice she had created.

"Appearance-changing cloaks." Caine walked over and dropped one on Violet's head. "It will alter how you look to anyone not wearing one."

Violet tugged it off and examined it. The cloak was made of thick, scratchy material, almost like a burlap sack. She shrugged it on over her clothes and closed the small black button at the top. Violet shivered, getting the same feeling she did when Caine performed any spells. It seemed to encase her like a skin suit, and very slowly, the cloak left her vision. She could barely feel the itchy material at all.

When she looked back up at Caine, he frowned. "Your eyes…"

"Yours and Alice's did the same," Violet said. "I guess they dull a little, but they're still pretty noticeable."

Alice reached up. "Did my hair change too?"

"Yeah, it was brown."

Caine sighed, playing with the icy candleholder. "Well, they're almost perfect… no matter. It's enough to let us get around a bit more carefully." He laid his cloak over the chair. "Maybe you can fix them once you get a better handle on your magic."

"Sure," she said, forcing a smile.

As they walked to the kitchen, Alice asked, "Do you want to try making some potions after breakfast?"

"I can try."

~

VIOLET FOLLOWED Alice to the room at the end of the hall.

It was vibrant compared to the rest of the house. The walls were a deep blue and looked as if they were covered in stars. The light from the window made them sparkle as she moved. Bookshelves lined two walls, although many were filled with glass jars and plants. The other side held a small couch, a desk, and a table.

"So, we usually do things in pairs of dry and wet." Alice made a matching set of each ingredient. "And then a few of them have to be mixed fast, or they turn toxic." Alice paused. "I'll cut down the recipe to show you first. Then you can copy me, if that works for you."

Violet sat back. "Sure."

The mage scooped into each jar with the smallest measuring spoon and placed each portion into its own dish. She lit the burner underneath a large glass bowl and mixed the ingredients slowly with a metal stirrer, adjusting the flame height as she did. Each ingredient changed the liquid to a new vibrant hue, the final color turning a deep blue.

"This is your job?" Violet asked as she began measuring with Alice's supervision.

Alice handed her another jar. "Making medicine is a big part, but King Paskal would commission us for many different projects."

Violet stirred quickly as the potion began to boil over.

"You're around our age, right?" Alice asked.

"I'm twenty-one."

"Pretty close. I'm twenty-three. Caine's twenty-four. What's your job, then?"

"Nothing yet. I'm still trying to learn." Still an undecided student.

"Oh, okay. What does your family do?"

"A lot of different things. Is everyone in your family a mage?"

Alice tugged at her blue hair. "Not really. Only my aunt uses her energy for work."

Violet wondered if it had been long enough for her extended family to be contacted yet. Her aunt and uncle lived close by. Maybe her sister would have recruited them, too, after hours of missed calls and unanswered texts.

"Violet?"

"Does your family know you're doing this?" She focused on breaking up the lumps in her mixture.

"No, we didn't want to risk their lives too. It's going to be a bit of a shock for everyone." Shaky laughter spilled from Alice. "Let's add in the blue pepper berries."

Violet pushed again. "Am I in any danger if I go home?"

"Not from us, but there's no guarantee that the king or Cross can't get you there. We *believe* that Caine is the only one who can create a portal, but King Paskal could have lied, or he could find another mage to make one." Alice squeezed her hands together, and Violet could see the tiny ball of flame she played with. "We'll be safe here. Please don't worry about that. Add that powder next."

Violet didn't ask anything else as Caine joined them, but Alice's concerns lingered in her mind. *She's just exaggerating to get me to stay.* Violet assured herself that going home would be fine as she refocused on the potion.

The mixture turned from a sticky pale blue to smooth

cobalt. Violet worried it was too dark compared to Alice's finished product, but Alice moved it to the side.

~

As the afternoon continued, Violet inquired about the brews and magic, curiosity getting the better of her. They weren't meaningful conversations, but Caine and Alice didn't seem bothered by the questions pertaining to magic. Violet hoped her next one would be answered as passively.

"Wouldn't training me be safer in my world?" Violet asked, handing Caine a green stem and avoiding Alice's gaze. "We could go somewhere secluded."

Caine tossed the ingredient into the mortar and began grinding it before answering. "Do you want to risk that? You could be explosive, Violet. You need control, or you'll get hurt or hurt someone. Magic can be far, far worse than the little burn you caused."

He passed the bowl over to Violet without another word, and she matched his silence, making herself focus on the mixture. She hadn't expected Caine to give a different answer, but he and Alice were both so sure their world was the best option.

The small wall clock chimed one o'clock. Violet saw Caine and Alice glance up, but neither spoke, and she continued stirring the brew.

"Violet." Caine waited for her to look up before asking, "Have you thought any more about staying?"

"I've been thinking."

"And?"

She looked back down, failing to keep the malice off her tongue. "I'm thinking."

"Violet!" Caine hissed suddenly.

The empty chair beside him was floating a few feet off the ground. It came crashing down. Two of the legs splintered, and it toppled backward. Violet stared at the mess, barely hearing Alice's comforting words over her pounding heart.

Caine's voice rang out clearly. "This is what I was talking about when I said you were unstable."

Violet retreated to her borrowed bed, hoping to clear her head through a nap, but each time she dozed off, she would jump up, her eyes scanning the cluttered room. She sat on her hands in an attempt to keep her magic from flying out of control again. All she wanted was a good reason to go home, and the universe was giving her the exact opposite.

Despite her having nothing to do to pass the time except stare at the wall, evening came faster than she would have liked. She sat with Alice and Caine for dinner to prove that the chair incident was a one-time thing, and to her relief, nothing happened. She could go home tomorrow morning and be fine. It had been one mishap with an inanimate object, and no one had gotten hurt. That time.

She tried and failed to keep her thoughts focused anywhere else as they cleaned the dishes. Violet said goodnight and started for her bedroom, trying to quell her nerves before she made an impulsive decision. As she reached the doorway, a droning ring sounded through the house.

Chapter Five

Violet

"WHAT'S THAT?" Violet asked as Caine went to the window.

Alice gripped the table. "We put a barrier at the edge of the forest that would tell us if the king's men came, but an animal could have—"

"They're coming." Caine pulled the curtain back. "*This* is what we're protecting you from!"

Violet looked out into the field to see at least fifteen guards, some armed with swords, others in cloaks like Caine and Alice's.

"Vi, you have to make your choice now." Alice's voice wavered. "I'm sure you don't want to think of it like this, but we stole you from the king, and he will go to any lengths to get you back."

Both mages looked panic-stricken. Caine was already running down the hall to the study. "We'll meet where we planned either way."

Violet trembled as the throng grew closer. "I'll stay." She couldn't let those people follow her home. She would stay in this world until she was sure she could keep her loved ones safe from these people and herself.

"She's with us, Caine!" Alice shouted as she ushered Violet to her room.

Violet put on the cloak Alice tossed to her and slung a rucksack over her shoulder. "I thought you said we had a week before they came."

"We thought so." Without warning, Alice shoved a bag into Violet's hands and pushed her out of the room and down to the back door.

Caine exited the study at the same time. "Got everything?"

As Alice nodded, the front door slammed open. She took Violet's hand and pointed toward the forest. "We just have to make it to the trees, okay? Run with me… now!"

Caine

"CAINE BLACKWOOD AND ALICE WILLOWFLOWER, you are under arrest by order of the king for treason against the crown," Sparrow called into the house. "You may have the chance to refute those charges if you come with the girl now."

Caine took a deep breath before stepping into the kitchen to meet Sparrow standing alone, her sword and shield drawn but hanging limply by her sides. "Where's your army, Captain?" Caine asked, leaning against the wall as if they were having a leisurely conversation.

Grief took over her features as their eyes met. He forced the smile to stay on his face.

"Outside. King Paskal ordered them to wait five minutes before they come charging in."

"Thanks. Now I know I have five minutes to deal with you."

"Caine, please. I don't want to fight you. King Paskal wants to resolve this peacefully." She glanced back at the door and lowered her voice. "We can come up with an excuse. Something went wrong with the portal, anything!"

"I haven't made a single mistake. Well, except for letting you find me." He pretended not to see her flinch.

"I thought better of you."

Caine only shrugged. "You thought wrong." His expression turned disinterested. "Are you finished? I have places to be."

"Please. I'm giving you one last chance to get her and come peacefully."

Caine threw his hand out, ice shards following its path. They grazed Sparrow's armor as a warning. She mouthed "please" again, but Caine was already conjuring a large icicle. She lifted her sword and shield.

The ice battered her shield as he rapid-fired smaller chunks. Caine leapt back as Sparrow bounded toward him. She swiped at his knees with her sword, but metal clanged against a frozen wall. While she swung low, Caine drew his own blade. He regretted not dousing it with a potion before coming out. No matter. He needed one opening.

Sparrow gasped as a gust of wind swept her off her feet. Caine had angled it wrong and sent himself stumbling as well. Ice crawled across the kitchen floor and bit at Sparrow's feet, snaking up her legs and chest.

Sparrow shivered as Caine approached and kicked her shield and weapon away. The frost grew as he stepped closer. He locked her body in place and lifted her into the air before slamming her into the wall. Dagger in hand, he slid her upward so her neck was at eye level.

She coughed, blood dribbling down her chin. He looked up at her one last time…

He tightened his grip on the knife and raised it to her collarbone.

"Damn it." Caine dropped the levitation spell. He flicked the cork off a vial on his waistband and splashed his blade with a sleeping potion, only managing to cover it partially.

Sparrow tried to pull herself up using the counter. She stared past him toward the door, her voice raspy as she tried to call for help. Caine tugged her close and dragged the tip of his blade across the back of her neck. The slightest glow of purple mixed with her blood. He dropped her unconscious body as the door flew open. His five minutes were up.

The swordsman's eyes widened as he took in Sparrow's body. "Caine Blackwood, you and Alice Willowflower have been charged with treason against the crown, and now murder." He called to the rest of the group, "Restrain him and search the house for the other two! Remember, the captive needs to be taken alive!"

Violet

As THEY SPRINTED through the forest, Violet was sure guards were following them. All she heard over her heavy breathing was "Fire?" She could see the orange glow in the trees ahead.

"Almost," Alice breathed as they stepped closer.

Flare was resting in the tiny clearing. His head popped up as they stepped closer.

"Hi, Flare." Alice extended her hand slowly. The bird examined it for a moment before affectionately butting his head against her palm. "Hi, boy." She moved toward the back of him and patted his feathers. He lowered his body once again.

Violet recognized the movement. "I am not riding him."

"It's a short trip. You'll be all right." Alice grabbed Violet's arm and hauled her onto the phoenix. Once they were both on the phoenix's back, Alice patted his head. "Let's go, Flare."

The bird squawked and flew into the air. Violet fought the urge to shriek as they barreled past treetops. She wrapped her arms tighter around Alice and prayed they would land soon. Cold air battered her face as she dared to peek down. Violet gasped and gripped Alice even tighter as she realized how high up they were.

Her stomach dropped as they plunged toward the ground. The second they touched down in a small clearing within the forest, Violet ran to the nearest bush and emptied what little food was in her stomach.

She asked, "What about Caine?"

Alice wasn't paying attention. "Hm…?"

Violet followed her eyes to where Flare was. The bird was in a frenzy. He staggered around the clearing, fluttering his wings and squawking. His feathers were fluffed up, making his wings indistinguishable from the rest of his body.

"Stop it!" Alice yelled. "We'll be heard three towns over!"

The phoenix walked over to her and screeched.

"I know. Caine's not here."

The bird squawked one last time before taking flight.

"Flare!" Alice called after him, but it was no use.

The two women were left shrouded in darkness.

Alice groaned and created a small ball of fire in her hands. "I let Caine's summon loose."

"Will Flare be all right?"

"Familiars can't die until their owners do, so he's going to fly around until Caine calls for him. I don't want him to give away our location though."

"What now?" Violet asked.

"We're going to get a room at the inn in the next town. Caine will get there as soon as he's done."

Alice looked up at the bright stars and took off. Violet followed close behind, darkness just out of reach on every side.

"What is he doing exactly?" Violet moved as close to the other woman as possible.

Alice offered her hand, which Violet gratefully took. "Since we're going to be traveling east, he's leading them west. They'll figure out we're not actually going that way eventually, but it will give us a bit more time."

Violet was still clinging to Alice as they came across a small gravel path.

Alice let out a little noise of triumph. "We're almost there!"

Sure enough, the gravel turned to cobblestone, and Violet could see the outline of buildings in the distance. Houses of all sizes lined the streets. Upon closer inspection, Violet could see some were small shops. She saw little activity in the streets, and although she hadn't had the chance to look at a clock, the moon told her the night wasn't even half over.

Alice, who was obviously familiar with the area, led her into a building. Inside, the floor was littered with tables and chairs adorned with various silverware. Whatever dinner had been going on was long over. A few people in aprons pushed in chairs and swept the floors, sending dust into Violet's nose. She held back the urge to sneeze.

At the far end of the room was a wooden gate leading into a kitchen. A stout man pushed through, balking at Violet and Alice, who hadn't gotten much farther than the first table. "No, no, ladies. We're closed for the night."

Alice shook her head. "We don't want food. Only a room."

"Ah. Rooms are ten argen." The man smiled when Alice handed him silver coins. He handed a key to one of the maids. "Judi will see you up."

They followed the maid closely as she led them up a short flight of stairs. The stairs were lit only by a few tea lights, and Violet was sure she was going to trip over an unseen object. She was grateful when the maid stopped in front of one of the many doors. It creaked as she swung it open, revealing yet another dark area.

Violet heard a clink and guessed the maid had dropped the key somewhere. As the maid and Alice bent to pick it up, Violet made her way over to the window. She wrinkled her nose at the musty smell of the curtains and opened them, creating a large cloud of dust in the process. That time she did sneeze. Every piece of furniture looked as if it had been chewed up and spit out a few times. The rancid air matched.

"Why don't you take the bed? I'll sleep… here. I guess." Alice poked at an unknown stain on the armchair.

"We can share," Violet offered.

The bed was small, but there would be enough room for the two of them. Violet couldn't be bothered to change clothes before lying down and kicking off her boots. They didn't dare see what horrors were waiting for them under the covers, instead deciding to take their chances lying on the scratchy duvet.

Caine

CAINE PRAYED Alice had done her job well and they were long gone. He dashed through the trees in the opposite direction. Teleportation spells were as draining as they were flashy, and he had only risked one to get a head start to the edge of the woods. Caine had made sure the king's men knew exactly where he was, and they were no doubt close behind.

He would give Alice three more minutes to get to their

destination before he called Flare back.

"This way!" someone shouted from behind.

It couldn't have been more than a minute since he'd started running. Thudding footsteps grew too close. He reached a clearing as a mage and a sword wielder burst through the trees.

The mage threw a torrent of water toward Caine, who almost laughed. Caine flicked his hand and sent the water to freeze around their bodies. He called on his summon before someone else found him. Flare burst out of the ground, screeching. If they didn't know where he was before…

Caine shot up into the air as the rest of the group broke into the clearing.

"Hey there." He stroked Flare's neck as they soared.

He had marked out the route a few days ago to make it seem as if their group was going in the opposite direction. Still, the king had sent men too soon. No one knew about Caine's house, besides…

"Slow down a little, Flare." He didn't want to lose them too quickly. An hour's flight, then they could head back.

For the moment, he rested against his summon, trying to block out the shouts below.

Violet

ALTHOUGH SHE COULDN'T HAVE SLEPT for more than two hours, Violet couldn't keep her eyes shut. A sob escaped her before she could stifle it. Too much had happened in such a short time.

"I want to go home," she squeaked. Violet put her head under her pillow to muffle her cries so as not to wake Alice, unwilling to deal with the mage trying to comfort her.

Eventually, the fatigue became too much, and she drifted back to sleep.

Chapter Six

Alice

ALICE WOKE and nearly rolled out of the rough bed as the sun glared into her eyes. Violet was sitting in the armchair, staring out the window. She smiled at Alice but said nothing.

Alice searched the room for any evidence that Caine had arrived, but the bags still sat where they had been dropped the night before. She took a blue incense cone out, unlocked the door, and placed it in the outside corner of the doorframe. She should have done that the night before, but leaving the marker for Caine had slipped her mind in all their rushing.

She kneeled by their packs. Alice didn't know what else she was searching for, her mind running through all the disasters that could have happened. She unwrapped a cloth and separated two sets of crackers then filled glasses with the pitcher of water the maid had left on the nightstand. She offered a glass and crackers to Violet, who accepted them without a word.

Alice silently criticized the production of the biscuits as she tried to remember if it was she or Caine who made them. She swept crumbs off the bedsheet, adding to the dust on the floor.

Violet wasn't eating her portion.

"Are you feeling okay?" Alice asked. "There are healing potions in that bag if you need."

"I'm fine." Violet finally nibbled on a cracker.

Alice lay out on the bed. Only then could she hear the clock tick beside her. It was about halfway through the ninth hour. She took a deep breath as her heart jumped again. She would give him until midday before… nothing. She had nowhere to look.

She would hear news that the archmage had been arrested—unless King Paskal was keeping everything under wraps. That was a possibility. Trying to explain Violet to the public would be a catastrophe. Only the King's Assembly knew about the other world, let alone someone with such strong energy. In their fairly peaceful kingdom, explaining why two beloved mages had suddenly gone rogue wasn't an announcement in which His Majesty would take pleasure. All for a magic user in a place that valued their non-mage beings just as much. Yes, she and Caine expected the king to stay quiet about it for as long as he could manage.

Alice glanced over as the door opened and nearly threw Caine against the door as she leapt up for a furious hug. She sat back on the bed with a huff. "I was getting worried."

"Why? It was a long way back." He looked over at Violet, and Alice couldn't tell what kind of face their student was making. "Now that we're back together, tea?"

Violet

"You led them all the way into Avarice Town?" Alice asked after they had settled down.

She and Caine sat at the top of the bed. Violet curled up at the bottom.

"Yes. I don't know how long it'll take them to figure out where we actually are, but we should have time to recuperate and plan where to go next," Caine said. "I'm going to lie down for a little bit. Violet, don't get too comfortable. We have spells to work on. Try to create some ice until then."

Violet expected him to comment on her lack of response, but thankfully, he lay down without a word.

"Hey, Vi…"

Alice trailed off as Violet slid off the bed and went to the window.

"What's wrong?" Alice asked, sitting on the arm of the chair.

"I just…" Violet pressed the heel of her hand into her forehead. "This is happening."

Caine chuckled. "Yes, sunshine. You're stuck with us now."

Violet let Alice hug her.

"We're in this together. Don't worry," the mage assured her. Alice grabbed a cloak and headed for the door. "I'll be right back."

~

"Can't you manage to create even a simple drop of water?"

Don't talk back to him. Don't talk back to him. It wouldn't help, and he wouldn't listen to her anyway. Violet closed her eyes and concentrated again.

Water, or even ice, she would have taken any form of H2O, but all that was in front of her was Caine, who looked as if he was going to strangle her at any second. Just in case, she took a step back.

She had practiced for about an hour before Caine had

woken up. How the man was so awake with so little sleep she didn't understand.

He shook his head. "How can someone with so much magic in them be unable to do such a simple task? You've done more impressive things when you weren't even trying to! You really can't figure out how you used your energy before?"

"No, I don't know!" She spoke through her teeth, unsure of how thin the walls were.

"It can't just happen." He matched her harsh tone. "You must have felt something."

"Well, it did *just happen*. I was focusing on other things. I can't recreate it."

"So, you're telling me that nothing changed at all. Your hands never got hot or cold? You didn't feel tired or achy?"

Violet thought back. "I mean I guess those things happened, but that doesn't help me now. I still can't conjure anything."

"This is absurd."

Violet wasn't going to put up with his criticism. "You're absurd! How do you expect me to do things that I have never been able to accomplish before?"

"Because you're completely capable, and you're acting like you're some—"

"I'm acting like some person who has never used magic before!"

"Hey, Caine."

They both looked up at Alice standing in the doorway. Violet hadn't heard her come in.

"What?" He glared at her.

"You know Violet's never going to learn like this, right? Would you have liked it if your parents had yelled at you every time you couldn't learn a spell?"

"This is different," Caine muttered.

"No, it's not." She walked up to Caine and wrapped herself around his arm. "You're being too harsh."

He sighed but didn't move her. "I'm not going to coddle her."

"Let's switch for a little while, then, all right?"

Caine squinted down at Violet before agreeing quietly. "Keep practicing what I showed you."

Violet rolled her eyes. "Sure thing, boss."

"I'll start now." Alice pushed Caine out of the room before he could get upset with Violet again. "Don't do that."

"What?"

"Say things to make him mad." When Violet shrugged, Alice sighed. "Endrel help me. You're as stubborn as he is."

"I'm not—"

"You are."

"I don't want to be yelled at."

"Well, I'll do my best to teach nicely." Alice suddenly hugged Violet. "Sorry, I'm excited. Okay, so how does it feel when you cast a spell?"

Violet held back a scream. "I don't know. That's what Caine and I were arguing about."

"Well, now I understand why he was upset." She placed her hand on Violet's shoulder. "Vi, you must feel something, even if it's minimal."

"Well, I don't."

"You will."

Alice pulled them both to the ground to sit cross-legged, adjacent from each other.

"Fire isn't really going to feel any different from ice. The feeling your energy creates is going to carry across all your magic. It'll be strongest with what you use the most. Caine gets cold. I get hot. Well, it's a little more personal than that. You'll know it when you feel it."

Alice reached up onto the nightstand and tore a sheet out of Caine's notebook, folding it into a thick strip about the length of her hand and handed it to Violet. "You seem to be better at transferring your energy into objects rather than air."

Violet took a good look at the paper and closed her eyes. She imagined the flame bursting out from where her fingers pinched it, but the sheet remained unchanged. Maybe she should start smaller—a brown ring singeing the paper. When she looked again, it was still clear of any blemishes.

Alice held disappointment in her eyes, although it was a lot less condescending. "That's okay." She rubbed Violet's shoulder.

"Is this how you learned?"

"Not really. Caine had lessons like this from his parents. I had to figure out a lot of stuff on my own. My parents and sisters didn't really care for their magic." Alice grimaced. "This is the best way to go about it though. Well… I don't condone this, but energy can come from strong emotions except fear. You've experienced that. To get a handle on magic, you could try using emotion, but only to start out. Continuing down that path doesn't yield good results."

"Why not?"

"Ah… control is just as important as actually being able to conjure." Alice bit her lip. "I'm sure we'll come across mages like that. Caine and I are good at creating our own energy and keeping it at bay. Mostly."

Violet closed her eyes and focused on the paper again, but she couldn't grasp at anything. "I'm not really upset right now."

Alice beamed. "Well, that's nice to hear." She nudged Violet. "Forget the emotion thing anyway. We really shouldn't practice like that, not unless we get desperate."

Violet tried again to no avail.

Alice played with a flame in her hand. "I hope you're not

averse to our magic." She moved the fire a little closer to Violet. "You burned Caine, though, so that can't be it."

"What do you mean?"

"Most mages have one type of energy that makes their own weaker. Caine can't be around electricity. I can't stand earth."

"At all?"

"I can still touch dirt and stone. It's different when someone conjures it. You should get a feeling from that too."

Violet tried to pick up on any feelings as Alice wielded the fire. "I don't think I feel anything."

"No problem. Just keep trying, then."

Caine

CAINE CAME BACK as the sun began to set. Whatever Alice and Violet had been doing, they'd finished long ago. They were sitting close together once again. Alice offered what they were eating to him, but he didn't think he could stomach it, the stress of the night before still heavy in his gut. Instead, he curled back up on the armchair.

He must have fallen asleep again. When he opened his eyes, Alice was sitting on the bed next to Violet's sleeping figure.

Alice glanced over at him. "You should eat."

"I'm not hungry," he whispered back.

"Well, at least drink a potion."

He pushed away the one she pulled from the nightstand and passed to him.

"Caine."

"We need those."

"I'll make another. Please."

He squeezed her hand before taking it. She lingered for a moment before moving over to the window.

"Are you doing okay?" Caine asked.

"Violet was so worked up all morning, and I thought you'd gotten hurt or captured." She sat on the arm of his chair, her voice cracking. "They found us so quickly."

"I'm still shocked."

"I'm scared."

"I am too." He hated to say it out loud, even to Alice, but the night before had shaken him. He could understand why she felt so panicked. "It'll be okay. If they find us again, we'll go somewhere else."

She nodded. "You think Rilla might have…?"

"She's the only one who knows about the house."

The princess hadn't known of Caine and Alice's plan to betray the king. They had struggled with the decision to tell her or not, unsure if the heir would support them. She kept plenty of secrets though, and they couldn't risk misreading the disdain Rilla showed for her father.

It wasn't worth thinking about anymore. If the princess was working against them, that was the only information she had on them. They had escaped successfully with Violet.

Caine looked over at the bed. "Did she conjure anything?"

"No. And you need to be more patient," Alice chastised. "I understand why you need to keep your distance, but you still have to be nicer to her."

He wanted to be done as fast as possible, but actually getting to know her…

"We still don't know if she's a wordsmith," Alice continued. "We should tell her a term, at least one."

"She'll accidentally kill us by setting this entire room ablaze."

Alice played with a button on his jacket. "It'll be fine. We can handle it."

"Let's give her a few more days." As much as Caine wanted to know if Violet could amplify her power, he didn't want to jump there too fast. "And just one for now."

"Sounds good."

He wasn't sure when Alice had fallen asleep, but she was slowly sliding into his chair. Caine could feel his own eyes drooping and shifted so she shared the cushion with him, her legs pulled across his lap.

Chapter Seven

Alice

ALICE THANKED the server as he placed their drinks on the table.

They had been there four days already and, until then, had barely stopped in the dining area, only pausing briefly to bring dinner back to the room. Most places didn't care about their guests so long as they got paid, but the trio showing their faces was better than having three strangers obviously trying not to be seen.

She couldn't say their stay had been relaxing though. Alice was still trying to get Violet to control any kind of magic while Caine silently watched from the side, as Alice had requested.

Despite the state of the rooms, the restaurant was packed, patrons squeezing in where they could. Many were turned away, unable to fit their whole group at a table.

"How long do you think we can stay here?" Violet asked, her voice low.

"I'm not sure," Caine answered. "But we leave at the first sign of the king's men."

Alice played with the foam on the top of her drink, tasting a spoonful of the whipped sugar. "Hopefully that won't be for a while." She tapped Violet. "Stop worrying. We're okay for now. That's the important part."

"She has a right to worry," Caine said.

Alice sighed. She wished he would at least make an attempt to comfort Violet. "This isn't going to help. We have to…" She paused as the waiter brought back food.

"To what, Alice?" Caine stabbed a piece of sausage with his fork. "Pretend everything's okay? Because it's not."

Alice grimaced but didn't push any further. Violet picked at her eggs, not adding anything more.

"Good morning." A hefty man towered over the empty seat at their table.

Alice tried to guess his profession by his clothing. The abundance of belts and buckles didn't make her think of anything but a hunter or mage.

Caine spoke up. "Good morning."

"I was hoping to join you all. The place is getting pretty packed." He played with the brown scruff on his chin, surveying the three of them.

Caine smiled, flicking his eyes over to Alice. "Of course. I never realized how busy this place could get."

"The best in town, I guess." The burly man held out his hand to Caine. "Todrick."

Caine rattled off three fake names, making half-hearted gestures toward each of them.

"It's nice to meet you," Alice said as Todrick took the seat between Violet and Caine.

"Are you new in town?" Caine asked.

"Yes, I'm stopping in for a bit. You?"

"Us as well."

Alice's smile was partially due to Violet, who flicked her eyes between the newcomer and Caine. It was a little unfair that Caine showed more courtesy to the complete stranger than to Violet.

Todrick laughed as he saw Violet squinting at his shoulder. "Ah, how could I forget?" He tapped his finger on a feathery bundle.

"An owl," Violet said.

The fluffy brown creature stretched its wings and looked around at the group. Its eyes were a startling yellow.

"Yep, this is Muto. Had this guy for a while now."

"He's very well trained," Caine commented.

Alice kicked Caine under the table. The malice in his voice was a bit too obvious.

"Thank you. I taught him myself. You can pet him if you'd like."

Todrick leaned toward Violet, who backed away for half a second before simply freezing in place.

"I..."

"Don't worry. He won't hurt ya."

Violet brought her hand up and stroked the top of the bird's head. It cooed and turned into her palm.

"See?"

Violet smiled and picked up her fork again.

Caine and Todrick continued to chat, Alice piping in occasionally. She and Caine had fabricated a story while they were still in the castle. They were mages on break from work and decided to spend a few days in town. A common enough excuse that no one would need to ask any more questions.

Todrick thanked the woman who took his empty cup. "So where are you all staying?"

"Here actually." Caine gestured to the stairs. "Fair warning, the food is better than the rooms."

Todrick laughed heartily. "Well, it was very nice meeting you all. Perhaps we'll see one another again."

"Maybe so."

They watched Todrick amble out of the dining room before they returned upstairs.

"I think that bird's a summon," Caine said accusatorily.

Violet sat on the edge of the bed. "Is there any way to tell for sure?"

"No, but you get a feel for these things after working with magic."

"It was cute—and a lot nicer than yours."

"It's not my fault he doesn't like you." Caine frowned out the window, his eyes following a target in the street.

Alice sat in the chair nearby. "You know, you could have a little bit of faith in people."

She was inclined to agree it was a summon. The bird had been uncannily quiet in the boisterous room. The only time Flare behaved was when Caine was there. The second Caine left Flame alone with someone else...

"Or"—he turned away—"I have a right to be paranoid. He passed by other tables to sit with us, Alice. And most mages are open about having a summon. Why wouldn't he just tell us? It could be a tracker."

"I know. We'll keep an eye on him if he comes back, but we have other things to do. Didn't you want to go collect some herbs?" Alice asked.

He picked up his coat. "You just want me out of the room."

"Yes, I do. Shoo." She gave him a playful shove toward the door.

"All right, I'm going."

Alice locked the door behind him. "Ready?"

Violet lifted her head. "For what?"

Alice spun her finger, and fire followed it.

"Oh. No, I'm not ready."

"Yes, you are. Come on." Alice took Violet's hands and hoisted her off the bed. "Do you remember what I was showing you last time?"

"Yeah."

They sat in the middle of the floor again. Violet took another strip of paper from Alice and held it between her fingers.

"Oh. Do you want to try using one of the ancient words? It takes more energy, but maybe it'll give you a boost. At least then you can get a sense of your magic feeling."

"Sure." It wasn't like she was even getting to the point of using her energy anyway.

"I'll show you first, then you have to be extremely careful. Only use it when you're trying to cast and when Caine or I are watching."

Alice slid away from Violet and spread her hands as far apart as she could. She took a deep breath and said, "*Ignitia*."

Violet jerked back as a ball of flame shot out of Alice's left hand, larger and faster than she had seen before.

Alice caught it in her other hand, and it took a few seconds for the fire to die out. "We don't use it with elements too much. It's not usually necessary to expel that much energy just to cast a bit more, but let's see what it does for you."

"Are you sure I should be doing that?" Violet asked, hand clenched from the idea of that much fire.

"I'll make sure it stays contained." Alice handed back the paper. "*Ignitia.* Say it right before you try to cast."

Violet stared at her fingers. "*Ignitia*," she said as flatly as Alice had and imagined fire. Nothing. She tried again. "*Ignitia.*" The word felt so foreign on her tongue.

The paper remained unlit.

"You might not be a wordsmith like Caine and I." Alice smiled. "Try again?"

Violet nodded and stared at the paper.

Caine

CAINE SLIPPED OUT THE DOOR, fighting the urge to adjust the enchanted cloak. To the bustling street, he would look crazy pawing at the air on his chest. Caine weaved through the group that passed and hoped he was blending in well. It had been a while since he'd cruised the streets of a town other than his own. They were babbling about nothing. He pretended to be interested in a food stall, but his nose scrunched at the fresh fish.

The chill in the air wouldn't be gone for another month or so, but the cold meant nothing to the plethora of folk in the street. He scanned their faces as frequently as he examined the buildings. He had come across two other inns so far, and given the size of the town, there couldn't be any more than seven in total.

Todrick hadn't mentioned anything about where he was residing. Caine almost stopped at a standalone lodge, but he doubted the reason the other man had trekked all the way to their inn was because his lodgings lacked a diner.

Staking out each place wasn't an option, and neither was inquiring about the residents. The last thing he needed was for everyone to see his eyes. That was the first feature the king's men would ask about.

Caine clenched his teeth. He had entrusted their lives to

these cloaks before they'd even been finished, and the damned things still left them vulnerable. Magic was far from uncommon, and even someone with only a smidgen of magic would have a luster to their irises. But for mages as strong as he or Alice, their eyes glowed even in the bright sunlight, and that would call attention no matter what.

As he sidestepped a horse, a bird swooped past, nearly catching his hood. Caine held back from freezing its wings as it perched on top of a light post in front of another inn. And that was eight. He added that to the list of places he would need to come back and…

He paused to watch the sparrow as it preened its gray breast feathers.

Both his and the bird's heads popped up as a passerby whistled. Caine dashed behind a building. When he peeked out again, Todrick had the fowl in his palm. It was a summon—and a shape-shifting one at that. Caine prayed the man was nothing more than a traveler.

Once Todrick had entered the building, Caine pulled himself farther into the slim alleyway. Windows lined the buildings he shimmied past. When he was mostly out of sight, he put his hand to his chest and cast an invisibility spell. He opened his mouth to strengthen it but didn't speak the ancient word. The spell on its own took too much energy as it was. He crept back toward the opening, waving his hands. No one turned in his direction.

Caine crossed the street carefully. Although unseen, his body was substantial. He waited until someone opened the door and slipped inside.

Without a restaurant attached to the inn, the floor was clear of the hustle and bustle of outside. A woman stood alone behind a counter. Caine took note of the slight pink glow in the shade of her lashes.

Caine watched as the man he'd followed in approached the counter. The woman pulled her arms closer to her chest, giggling as he talked. As Caine moved toward the stairs, she pulled out a large book. The man signed his name, and she stamped something in red ink next to it.

Caine tried to read the names, but she put the ledger away quickly.

Go away, Caine begged.

They were flirting again as the woman pressed a key into the man's hand. After a few more agonizing minutes, the man convinced the woman to follow him. As they flitted upstairs, Caine walked behind the desk.

The back of it was clean. *Where did she get the book from?* He knocked along the wood until he came across a hollow section. Caine broke the seal on the hidden compartment easily. He pushed aside some coins and took out the hefty book. A ribbon was pulled across the inside, and he opened it to that page.

Caine frowned. Todrick Wheatroar, he'd arrived yesterday evening. A swirly red rose was stamped beside his name, and under the notes section, "bird" was written.

He slammed the book shut and closed the cabinet. He considered treading upstairs, but he wouldn't be able to keep up the invisibility much longer. Hurrying back to his spot in the alley, he restored his image. Caine took a few deep breaths before striding onto the crowded street and back to their inn.

～

CAINE FOUND the pair curled up next to each other on the floor once again.

Alice shook her head as he came in. "Caine, what happened to the herbs?"

"I got distracted." He draped himself over the armchair.

"By what?"

"Our friend." He cut Alice off and gestured to Violet. "How's it going?" He still couldn't feel her magic in the room.

Violet only shrugged, and he refused to look at Alice for validation.

His assistant still asked, "Caine, where did you go?"

"He's staying in the Rosestead Inn about three streets down. The guest book has his bird listed too. It's a shape-shifter. I saw it as a sparrow just now."

"So his story matches up. Are you happy?"

"Not really, but I'll leave it be."

"Thank you, because we really don't need to be drawing more attention to ourselves. Now, what did you need from outside? We still have potions to make. And what magic did you use? You look dead."

He'd thought he'd waited long enough for some of the color to return to his face before returning. "Here."

Alice snagged the list of ingredients he held between his fingers.

"Have fun."

"Be nice," she said before leaving.

Caine pondered her last statement. Be nice to—

His and Violet's eyes met. *Be nice to each other.* Caine looked toward the window, wishing Alice would come back.

Chapter Eight

Violet

VIOLET FOCUSED on her paper as swiftly as he looked away. Alice had gone through the steps with her again. *Focus on what you want to enchant. Think about what you want to create, say the word, and make it.* So far, Violet couldn't get any further than speaking. She threw the paper aside. It fluttered harmlessly to the ground a few inches away.

Caine glanced over at her, and Violet wished she hadn't moved.

"Still can't do anything?" he asked. "No flame? Not even a spark with the term?"

"No." Violet picked up the sheet again. She refused to engage with him just so he could criticize her lack of abilities some more.

Despite her dismissal, he came and sat down in front of her. He stuck his palm out toward Violet. "Give me your hand."

She recoiled. "Why?"

"Because I want you to feel magic. Every mage gets a certain feeling when they use energy, and every experience is different.

I think if you get a sense of what it's like, it will help you grasp your own powers."

Violet searched for his usual hostility, but for once, he wasn't glowering at her. She placed her hand in his. Caine's skin was cold but not unbearable.

A hot jolt shot up her arm from where their hands were clasped. She attempted to pull away, but Caine grabbed her forearm. Violet was about to cry out when the pain began to dissipate and was slowly replaced by another feeling. The tingle crawled up her arm and into her lungs. It was cold and warm all at once.

"Oh," was all she could manage.

"How does it feel?"

"Like I'm in a cold room but also wrapped in a comforter," Violet stammered, her voice distant. "Is that how you feel?"

He laughed for a second before putting the back of his hand to his mouth. "Well, that's not how I usually describe it, but yes, it's a mix of hot and cold. 'Comforting' is what I usually boil it down to."

She was a little disappointed when he let go. The sensation started to ebb from her fingertips. "I like it."

"The sense of euphoria magic gives you will be very powerful, but as you use it, the feeling will dwindle—not completely, but enough that it's not so overbearing."

"Thank you for showing me that."

If Alice had gotten quiet when she tried to talk about the feeling from her magic, Violet could only imagine how little Caine wanted to. He was avoiding her gaze, and Violet figured their little armistice was over.

She got off the bed and wandered to the window. The sense of magic had left her chest completely, leaving a hollow spot in its place. She tried to think back to when she had used her magic, but nothing like that stuck out to her. She only remembered the fear and panic lashing out.

"Violet," Caine said. "I know you don't favor me, but for the sake of your training, can we form a bit of a truce? It's becoming a little hard to teach you with this mindset."

She faced him again. "I don't dislike you." Caine pressed his lips together as she continued, "I don't like that you haven't given me time to get used to anything."

"If you're waiting to adjust to this world and its people, it's going to be a long while, and we don't have that time."

"Well, you could help speed it up by doing things like that—showing me what you mean, rather than yelling at me about it. Those two minutes were the first time I've felt like I knew what was going on."

Caine closed his eyes, and Violet wasn't sure he was even listening to her.

After a minute, he said, "Fine, but you need to be a little more cooperative too. It's infuriating to try to teach someone who refuses to learn. If you can do that, I'll have a bit more patience with you."

"Deal."

"Wonderful. That being said"—he gestured for her to stand next to him—"try conjuring flame without the paper, and tell me how it feels. Do it without the word for now. I think it would be better if you got a feeling first."

Violet put the strip in her pocket and held out her hand, shutting her eyes.

"Don't close your eyes. It doesn't make a difference."

She looked up. The absence of loathing in his expression was jarring.

"Do you feel anything?" he asked.

"Um…" Violet ignored the twitch of his lips and looked at her empty palm. *Focus, think, and now feel.*

Sharp pain sliced through her hand. She gasped and doubled over, but Caine kept her off the ground.

As he moved her toward the bed, she asked, "That feeling can't be painful, right?"

"Not that I'm aware of, but there's no guarantee that you follow those rules."

Violet pushed herself up onto the bed. With her luck, she would be the first.

Caine leaned forward onto the mattress, a faint smile crossing his lips. "Want to try again?"

"Not really."

"Come on. Maybe that triggered your energy."

They sat with their backs against the wall. Violet stuck out her arm.

Nothing. Five minutes went by. Ten. Caine was quiet throughout. If not for his hands flexing, she would have sworn he was asleep.

He sat up, and she looked back at her palm, sneaking another glance as he grabbed his notebook off the nightstand. He paused to examine the remains of the sheet they'd ripped before flipping to the middle of the book.

Caine pushed two fingers to the page. "*Enastia.*" A seal spread out from his hands and around the sheet. As he removed his fingers, fire erupted from the page.

"Is that Flare?"

A parrot-sized version of the bird flew around the room. Caine nodded and called Flare to him. He landed on Caine's palm, cooing.

"Aw." At Violet's voice, the bird squawked and snapped in her direction.

"Stop it," Caine scolded, tapping Flare's head.

The bird hopped onto his shoulder and tugged on his ear.

"Do you think I have a summon?"

"Sunshine, I'm not even sure you have magic."

She flinched a little. His tone was cool, but she couldn't take the nickname as kindly as he had meant it. Violet cupped her hand. Maybe a different position would help. Despite only holding that pose for a few seconds, pins and needles clawed at her skin. She cried out when the feeling suddenly traveled up her arms.

"What?" Caine scooted toward her.

"My hands were going numb." It had stopped. She took a few deep breaths.

Caine laughed freely. "Try again, with the word this time."

"This isn't funny!" She pulled herself away.

"I'm laughing at you, not what happened. You're so ridiculous. Try again."

"But—"

"Just try it." His tolerant expression disappeared.

Her hands closed into fists. The same prickly feeling jabbed at her palms.

"Throw fire at me."

And in a fit of rage, she did. "*Ignitia!*"

A ball of fire shot out of her palm, and she waited for it to collide with Caine's face. Instead, he caught the orb and extinguished it.

Caine grabbed Flare, stopping the bird from yanking Violet's hair. "Watch your hands."

Violet hadn't noticed the sheets singeing below her.

"Now." He handed her back the sheet of paper. "Can you focus that on this instead of me?"

Alice

ALICE HELD a cloth bundle tightly in her hands as she returned to the musty room. She brought the bundle over to the table in the corner and began sorting the plants.

Violet was curled up on the bed, paper lying flat across her palm. Caine sat next to her, Flare settled in the space between the two.

Alice mouthed to Caine, "How's it going?"

He shrugged. "Ask her."

Alice frowned. She had been trying to let Violet concentrate.

The woman looked away from her palm, obviously paying more attention to them than Alice had thought. "I created fire."

Alice nearly squealed, "You burned the paper?"

Violet glanced sideways warily. "I threw a fireball at Caine. He egged me into it."

"I wanted to see if you could do it," Caine said. "You were so close."

Alice leaned back in her chair. "High emotions—"

"Should never motivate magic," Caine finished. "I know, but to start out—"

"No, it's not a good way to start out." She knew he didn't care as long as they had proof that Violet could use her energy, but Alice wanted to try truly teaching her.

She considered voicing her thoughts to Caine as he helped her trim stems and leaves, but it wasn't fair to put him on the spot, especially in front of Violet.

Caine pulled his chair closer to Alice. "I shared my energy feeling before I pushed her," he whispered.

Alice tried not to look too surprised as she murmured too quietly for him to hear.

"Hm?" He leaned down.

"What happened to keeping your distance?" Alice repeated.

"That has proven to be a difficult task," Caine said.

They both glanced at Violet as she crumpled the paper and cupped it in her hand, murmuring to herself.

"If this is how she'll learn, then I'll make the effort, and if not, I'll try another tactic. Whatever it takes to end this."

Alice smiled at Violet instead of answering Caine. He pushed his chair away again, and they worked in silence as they began to brew the herbs.

"Hey," Violet said. "Could I practice levitation instead? I know I was able to create fire, but I can't focus on it again. I think I might do better switching between elements."

Alice flicked her eyes toward Caine. "She's right. Trying over and over again might burn her out."

Caine nodded. "The word is *motia*."

"Thank you." Violet placed the paper ball on the ground.

They watched as she stared at the object intently, saying the term quietly. Almost immediately, the ball wiggled. Violet gasped, and it stopped.

Alice hissed, "Don't," under her breath before Caine could say anything.

He glared at her and silently stirred his brew.

Violet clenched her hands and muttered again. The paper hovered shakily an inch off the ground before falling.

"That's fantastic for the first time." Alice beamed at her.

"Not her first time," Caine said but not loud enough for Violet to hear.

Their student ran a hand down her arm. "My limbs were kind of… humming?"

"It could be your magic feeling." Alice thought about how her own magic felt.

Violet nodded to Alice and focused again, new determination in her eyes.

Alice had to calm the fire under her burner.

~

THEY MADE quick work of the elixirs, content that each one had reached its full potency. Hopefully, it would be a while before they needed more.

The group wandered down to the dining room once again, where orange light filtered in between the dinner crowd. Savory smells overpowered the sweet that had lingered from the morning. They picked a small table between the stairs and front door. The ones in the back had already filled.

They ate dinner in comfortable silence. Alice watched out the window as some people made their last rounds before nightfall. Vendors pulled out carts, laying various merchandise along the edge. Unlit multicolored lanterns hung with them, ready to be powered by magic or small candles.

"Do you want to walk around a little bit after dinner?" Alice asked.

Violet said yes as Caine declined. Alice was trying to persuade him when his eyes darkened as he watched something behind her. He closed his eyes and cursed under his breath as a large shadow consumed them.

"Back for more, huh?" Todrick eased around the table to gaze at all three of them. Muto sat on his shoulder, no longer a kind owl but a piercing hawk ready to strike at any moment.

Alice smiled, tapping Caine gently under the table so he would do the same. "Just trying to make the best of a long day."

Todrick's next sentence was cut off by a scream. A hush fell over the room except for the few people who ran in, warning of trolls. Alice leaned over to peek out the window. The huge red creatures bumbled into town, some armed with clubs and spears, others with crude maces.

The townsfolk ran down the streets, getting as many people inside as possible before slamming their doors. No soldier or mage appeared to stop the creatures as they knocked over shop stalls, crushing their contents.

"I didn't think they lived out here," Alice said.

"It is a bit odd," Caine agreed.

"Well, they're not too dangerous as long as someone stops them soon," Alice added for Violet's sake.

The woman was perched on the edge of her seat, gripping the fabric of her shirt tightly.

Two of the trolls, no longer content with the items in the road, were banging their weapons against the wooden door of a shop across the street. It would splinter quickly, and they would be inside any second.

"No one's stopping them." Todrick started for the door. "Are the three of you coming?"

Alice and Caine stared at each other. Alice tried to think of any reason they could decline, but posing as traveling mages meant it was their job to help with situations like these.

Caine turned to Violet. "You're still tired from earlier, right? Go upstairs. I don't want you getting hurt."

Alice started walking away with Todrick as Caine leaned down and whispered to Violet. She reeled back for a second before he hissed for her to go. She darted up the stairs, and Caine joined them in the doorway.

Todrick pulled a broadsword from the sheath on his back. The troll closest to them was one of the smaller ones. It eyed them for a moment before lumbering closer, club raised.

"I have this one," Alice said.

Caine walked off in the other direction, leaving Todrick to stride a bit farther down the road.

Alice jumped out of the way as the beast brought its club down. She sent a gust of wind toward it, but the wind curved around its body, leaving the monster unfazed.

The troll heaved its weapon back onto its shoulder and took a few clumsy steps toward Alice. She ran forward and dove under its legs. The troll smashed the ground again, but she was long gone. Alice aimed at its back, using the air to cut slices. The beast again stood as if nothing had hit it.

Their resistance didn't seem possible. The only explanation she could think of was that they had a spell protecting them, but they couldn't cast one themselves.

Fire itched at Alice's fingertips, but she and Caine had picked other elements as an attempt to further distance themselves from their image. She called up air again, ready to aim as much as she could at its feet. A term could help, but she didn't want to create too much of a display for their onlookers.

The troll suddenly jerked forward and collapsed onto its face, soaked from the ball of water Caine had shot at it. He thinned the liquid and sliced across the back of the beast's neck. Blood spurted from the wound.

"I said I'd take care of it," Alice called to Caine.

"Well, we don't really have time for you to play games."

"My air wasn't hurting it."

"Kill it with something else, then. The cloak changed your sword, too, didn't it?" He stepped away from her, water swirling around his arms. "Here you go. Have fun."

A larger troll came toward them. It was steadier on its feet than the last one, and it charged her, closing the distance too quickly. Its spear was aimed at her head. Alice used a gust of air to tilt the attack slightly upward. The monster continued its charge past her and crashed into a nearby stall. Alice drew her short sword and let fire run through it, just enough to heat the blade up. She jumped onto the beast's back before it could get up and drove the blade into its neck.

Caine

CAINE GLANCED BACK MOMENTARILY as he heard a crash. He drifted toward their room window. Violet's panic-stricken face peeked out from behind the curtains. He tried to catch her gaze, but she was watching Alice.

His assistant's last kill made three down. Caine had lost track of Todrick.

The next troll was a little larger than the first but not by much. He considered his options as it lifted its mace.

As he pulled more water together, a bird's call sounded nearby. The troll turned away, determined to find the source of the screeching. Caine took the opening and shot the monster, throwing it into the air with a geyser. It cried out as it came crashing back to earth.

Before Caine could make his next move, someone ran past him and jumped on top of the fallen creature. Todrick held his sword comfortably in his hands. He slashed the monster's neck, and it spasmed for a moment before lying still.

"One more," Todrick called back.

Caine nodded and pulled up some water again as the last beast closed in on them.

"Can you knock it over?" Todrick asked Caine.

Caine enlarged the liquid ball and sent it out at the feet of the troll. It fell like the last one did. Todrick was already on top of it, sword raking down its back.

Todrick sheathed his weapon. "I'm going to find who's in charge of this place." He was already walking away.

Alice tugged Caine back toward the inn before he could respond.

"One of us should have gone with him," Caine said in a hushed voice, avoiding the gawking diners as they ascended the stairs.

"Would it have made a difference?" Alice walked past their room to the window at the end of the hall. "If he's with the king or Prince Cross, we're already caught."

Caine watched the street with her. Some of the townspeople had come out of hiding and were assessing the mess left in the street. Todrick was walking back with a man who was shouting orders Caine couldn't make out. "Let's leave now."

Alice pulled her cloak tighter as they headed for the room. "Did you use a lot of energy? We're going to need invisibility to get past Todrick."

"Or I can teleport us once we're down there. I just need to rest a little bit."

Violet

Violet jumped closer to the window as they entered the room. "Are you guys okay?"

"Of course." Caine picked up one of their packs. "But we're leaving now in case Todrick is with King Paskal or Cross."

As Violet grabbed a bag, the sound of horses came from the street below, too many to be a passing buggy. The three of them approached the window, and Violet drew back at what was below. The king's men stood in front of the inn. It was twice the size of the group that had come for them before.

"Ten mages. Twelve soldiers, seven of them on horses. More coming."

Violet cringed at the number Caine counted.

She started to ask if they could handle that many people, but Alice was already backing toward the door. "Can you teleport yet?"

"No, but we're not giving them the chance to corner us up here either. I'll just have to use simpler elements to fight. Violet." Caine was in the midst of dousing his dagger with a sickly green potion. "Keep in mind what I just told you about jumping, all right?"

He was referring to the warning he'd whispered to Violet before shooing her upstairs. "If someone unlikeable ends up in the room, go to the window and shout. We'll catch you."

As soon as she nodded, they dashed out.

Chapter Nine

Alice

THEY PUSHED through the dining room, ignoring the fearful patrons. Both slowed their pace, and as Caine let his expression relax, Alice tried to do the same.

Caine had balked at something out the window, and Alice saw what had made him choose such a potent poison. Todrick stood at the head of the group, a falcon resting on his arm.

"Hello again, Todrick," Caine greeted the man as they came to a stop a few feet away. "The king sent a bounty hunter for us? I'm flattered. Although I don't know how good you could be if you had to drag his army around with you."

Todrick gritted his teeth and started his sentence twice before reciting, "Caine Blackwood and Alice Willowflower, you are under arrest by the king for—"

"Yes, yes." Caine waved him off. "Kidnapping, treason. Could you take murder off that list? I haven't killed anyone yet."

Todrick moved his arm as if he was going to let his bird loose, but Caine spread ice shards above his fingers.

"You send that bird, and I'll shoot it out of the sky."

Todrick hmphed and unfolded his arm anyway. The falcon shot into the air. True to his word, Caine flicked his wrist, and the bird cried out. Its owner watched, mouth agape, as the falcon writhed and dropped to the ground before disappearing.

Todrick began calling orders, but Caine shouted over him, a seal forming at his feet. "If you want to see a real summon…"

He called on Flare. The bird returned in his largest form and swooped over the army, knocking down a handful of their attackers with his wings.

Alice redirected a sword from the bird's head with a gust of air, giving Caine a chance to command Flare. She drew her blade and drove it into the stomach of the man she had knocked back, grimacing as he twitched on the ground.

She had no time to mourn as a mage moved to encase her in liquid. She parted the bubble and pushed the water back past her shoulders. The torrent took out someone behind her.

She glanced back and saw that Caine was engaged with Todrick, trying his best to stay in range of the window. Alice dropped to the ground as earth smacked into her back. Three soldiers rushed past her and into the diner.

She struggled to get up as a mage began to encase her feet in rock. She shot flames, and he scrambled away as they blasted his face.

Alice used her light-rope to bind Todrick's arms just long enough for Caine to remove the stone.

"Five!" Caine called to her.

Five left standing. Alice shuddered at the thought of the incapacitated people. They weren't directly responsible for most. Several of them had simply been knocked out or driven away by Flare. Another few she saw fleeing from the conflict altogether.

Alice ignored the bloodied, heaving man beside her as she imagined most of them making it back to the castle to be healed.

She jumped up and gestured frantically to the window, shouting to Caine, "Three inside!"

Violet

VIOLET PUT one bag on her back and another on her shoulder, doing her best to keep the cloaks cradled in her arms. Thinking better of it, she threw one of them over her shoulders, shuddering as the magic seeped into her.

Readjusting herself, Violet willed her tears to go away. She tried to keep herself out of view as she pushed the window all the way open. The room was two floors up. She wondered if they would start at the top and work their way down. Maybe they didn't even know the face they were searching for. She worried someone might get hurt if they mistook another for her. Violet willed her brain to quit, but awful scenarios forced their way to the front of her mind.

The sound of glass breaking came from another room. Violet edged as close as possible to the window.

Caine was actively glancing up, Todrick distracted by Alice's flame.

Violet took that as her cue and threw a leg over the windowsill. As she dangled both her legs out, one last image of death ran through her brain. Violet took another gulp of air, praying that it wouldn't be her last. Bundling the cloth in her arm, she waited until Caine was directly under and pushed herself off the building.

Violet closed her eyes as the air rushed around her. She waited for her body to slam into the cobblestone below and join the other bloodied, unconscious bodies lying in the street. Her descent slowed as quickly as it started.

Violet hovered about a foot off the ground when Caine released the levitation spell, and she fell hard on her tailbone. She ignored the pain and leapt up quickly to get out of Todrick's way. Any kindness was gone from his features as he threatened her with his blade.

Violet was nearly swept away by the gust of wind aimed at him. She dropped to the ground again, scared of toppling over. Caine moved to stand between them. Alice hovered near the door, waiting for the rest to emerge.

Violet couldn't tell who had the advantage. Caine's blade was no longer iridescent, but Todrick couldn't have fallen victim to it. Violet knew firsthand how quickly the dagger's potion took effect.

Horses thundered in the distance.

Reinforcements already?

"We can't fight anymore," Alice said.

Caine grabbed Violet, putting her behind him. As they backed away, he said quietly, "Run between those buildings and to the forest. Alice and I will be right behind you."

Violet only had to be told once. She jumped over a fallen person and fled. Her chest burned as she approached the trees, the added weight of the bags making every step heavier. She couldn't tell if people were behind her, if the others had made it out. Only the rush of her blood and her footsteps echoed in her ears.

She skidded to a halt as a blazing flash lit up the area in front of her.

Violet blinked a few times to clear her vision, relieved to find it was Alice and Caine standing before her. She ran up to them, and Alice threw her arms around Violet. Violet hesitated before returning the gesture.

They parted as Caine spoke. "We're not clear yet. Give me your hand."

Alice grabbed onto his other arm and pressed her head to his chest. He pulled Violet a little closer. Hot and cold took over her body all at once. The same flash appeared again, although being on the inside made it less glaring to her eyes.

It took Violet a second to realize they were in a different location. She stepped away from Caine as she dropped his hand.

"Where are we?" Alice asked. She was still holding onto Caine.

He gripped Alice's arm tightly, swaying slightly. "Ten miles west of where we were." He paused in between speaking to take a breath.

The same birch trees stretched in every direction, and the noise of clashing swords and screaming had completely left Violet's senses.

Caine sat with his back against a tree. He pulled a knee up to his chest, resting his head against it.

"Is he okay?" Violet asked.

Alice took two of the packs from Violet. "Teleportation spells require a lot of magic, even for us. He's better at it than I am. I can only go half a mile without passing out." Alice set a cloak and a satchel near Caine and began rummaging through the bags as they waited.

Ten or so minutes passed before he joined them. "Let's get moving." Caine gestured toward the expanse of trees. "I'm not sure what direction they'll head in, but…"

He didn't finish, sounding as unsure as Violet felt, but as her mentors started moving, she fell into step next to Alice.

Violet abandoned any doubts she'd had about the two of

them. Both Alice and Caine had put themselves in danger for a second time. Even if it was for their own preservation, Violet had come out of the ordeal mostly unscathed. That would have been their perfect moment to give up on the mission to help Violet and leave her to get captured or die.

Violet looked over at Caine. The color had returned to his cheeks, but his chest continued to rise and fall quickly.

"If spells wear you out, how come the cloaks don't bother you?" Violet asked.

"I've already given my energy to that object. If I enlarge that plant over there"—he pointed to a small yellow weed—"it will take some of my energy and grow, but I will recuperate, and the plant will stay the same. The same applies to certain ancient words."

"So if I finish the cloaks then leave, they'll stay the same?"

"Yes," Caine answered. "When you contribute your magic and go home, we'll be left with the product."

~

VIOLET DID her best to track how long they'd walked, deciding when they came to a stop that it had been about an hour. The sun was still high above them, shining through gaps in the trees and lighting their path as they trekked.

They stopped twice to fill their canteens and tend to their wounds. Caine had tried healing himself as he walked. Alice took over after the first attempt nearly made him black out. Violet helped where she could. With guidance, she applied some of the healing cream to their wounds and wrapped bandages over the salve.

She wasn't sure how much farther they'd gotten by the time the sun dipped out of sight. It must have been enough for Caine and Alice to be comfortable picking an open patch of dirt and making a small fire. Violet regarded the pit warily as smoke puffed up above the trees. Alice shook a blue powder over it, and the haze disappeared.

"Would you be able to put up a barrier like the one around the cabin?" Violet asked.

"It takes hours to recover from that spell," Alice explained. "We can't risk being weak for that long."

Instead, Alice kept watch first then Caine, but nobody came barreling through the trees as they rested. Violet was supposed to stay up last, but she slept fitfully, jumping up every so often, her breath panicky.

Alice had comforted her the first time. When she woke up again, Caine was watching instead. He glanced over but otherwise ignored her panic. After she didn't go back to sleep for an hour, he offered a potion to help her rest. She took it after a moment's hesitation. Violet knew he wouldn't poison her, but something still made her pause.

She didn't rise again until she heard Alice calling for her. The sun was up, and any evidence of a fire was gone.

Violet apologized for not waking for her post during the night.

Caine reached into the bag on his shoulder. "I knew you weren't going to wake back up after I gave you the calming potion. You can make it up to me though."

She was about to ask how when he held out a piece of paper to her. Violet almost asked to do anything else but was too afraid he would come up with a worse task.

"Try without the terms now," he continued. "You can't always rely on them."

Violet held the paper as they walked, trying to keep her mind focused.

Chapter Ten

THEY STOPPED SUDDENLY. Alice had been leading the group but halted before the thick expanse of bushes and trees. They were a much darker green than the vegetation they'd previously walked through. Violet could barely see more than a few feet in.

"Caine, are you sure?" Alice peered into the trees. "This is…"

"I know. We don't have much choice."

"But—" Alice protested.

"Do you think I want to go in?" he snapped. "Would you rather take the time to walk around so the people who want us dead can catch up?" Caine conjured a small orb of pale-blue light before adding, "This is one of the smaller areas. We'll be fine."

He ducked into the droopy trees, pulling Violet along with him before she could ask what they were talking about. Alice glanced back one last time before following.

As they ventured deeper into the forest, the branches above blocked out what little moonlight they'd had to begin with. Violet fell back to walk with Alice.

"We have to be careful," Alice said in a hushed voice.

"How come?" Violet asked.

Both of her teachers' eyes flicked around, freezing at every rustle of leaves or cracking branch that echoed near them.

"Nagas nest here," Caine answered. He continued to shine the light through the trees, as if searching.

"Nagas… the half-snake, half-people things?"

"Yes. So keep quiet," Caine said. "And tell me if you see any of their shed."

Trolls, nagas, giant flaming birds, mages… Violet was beginning to dislike the length of this list.

They continued to traverse the damp forest, Caine in the lead, Alice trailing somewhere behind. Violet couldn't quite see her. Even with the light, it was hard to make everything out. She stumbled over another branch, barely stopping herself from falling onto the mushy forest floor.

"Can't you make the light any brighter?" Violet asked Caine.

"Do you want to die?"

"No, but—"

"Then shut up, and help us."

Violet glanced back at Alice, who offered an apologetic smile.

As dawn approached, they could see the trees beginning to thin.

An orange serpent's tail shot down from the treetops, wiggling in front of Caine. Violet scrambled back as he moved to attack it, but the icy shot missed as the tail coiled around his waist, and he was lifted off the ground.

The naga slithered to the ground and brought him in front of her. "My, aren't you cute? It's a shame you're not one of my kind."

Caine shuddered as she ran her forked tongue down his

cheek. "No!" He squirmed, but it only made her wrap her tail tighter.

Alice charged forward, fire in her hands. "Let him go!"

The creature rolled her eyes and swung her tail at Alice before the mage could get close enough to attack, sending her flying into a nearby tree.

Violet stood alone a few feet from the naga. She called out to Alice, but Caine stopped her. "She's... unconscious... arg!" he cried out as the naga's tail coiled tighter. "Can you use any magic? Even a small flame."

She raised her hands and envisioned fire. "*Ignitia!*" Nothing happened. "I don't think so."

"Do *something!*"

Violet ran over to Alice in search of anything she could use to fight. She looked back to make sure the monster wasn't coming after her, but the naga was too focused on tasting her prey.

Violet rifled through the bags in search of something she didn't need magic for.

"Vi," Alice croaked. She rolled over to reveal the sheath on her hip.

Violet wasted no time yanking the blade out and running back toward the naga. Using as much strength as she could muster, she drove the blade into its scales.

The creature had been too focused on taunting Caine to see Violet charge at her. The naga screamed and loosened her grip on Caine as she grabbed at her wound. Free enough to yank his hands loose, Caine pushed icy palms on her skin. She uncoiled her tail, and Caine cried out as he fell flat on his back a couple feet away.

Her attention on Violet, the naga growled, but before she could move, a blast of fire hit her full in the face.

The creature toppled back, her human half engulfed in flames. Alice grabbed the sword from Violet's shaking hands and drove it through the naga's heart. Blood splattered them both, and Violet watched in horror as the naga floundered in agony. She stopped twitching as the flames burned on.

"Caine!" Alice kneeled beside him.

Violet hurried over too. The mage had managed to pull himself into a sitting position.

"Violet, go get our bags."

Violet did as she was asked. Alice pulled out a small bottle with thick pink liquid inside.

Caine winced as he brought his hand up to wipe the blood and tears from his eyes. He was barely audible as he groaned, "We need to get out of here."

"We will," Alice assured. "But first let me—"

"We can tend to our wounds after. Even if it wasn't another naga, someone heard us. Grab our stuff, and let's go."

"Caine—" Violet started.

"Come on." He stood up shakily, using a tree for balance.

Violet picked up a bag. Caine was determined to make it out, and it would be futile trying to convince him otherwise.

Despite their injuries, it only took a few minutes to escape the forest. To get caught so close to the edge was frustrating. Tree-covered cliffs stood beside a more inviting forest ahead of them.

Caine looked up. "Do you see any type of alcove? Someplace high?"

They scanned the cliffs.

Alice pointed to an opening to the left. "Do you have enough energy to get us up there?"

Caine muttered his teleportation spell, and there was a flash of light. They appeared at the mouth of the cave. As soon as it was clear they weren't sharing it with any creatures, Caine collapsed.

Alice shook her head. "You're going to kill yourself."

"Help me so that doesn't happen. I can't die yet."

Alice let out a sigh. "Take off your shirt. Actually, take off your trousers too. They're nearly in shreds anyway."

He glanced down at himself. The naga's scales had ripped up most of the cloth. Blood seeped from the cuts.

"You're wearing shorts under there, aren't you?" Alice asked when he hesitated.

"That's not the point."

She waved the vial of medicine. "I can't help you unless I can get to your wounds."

He glared at her for a moment before finally stripping out of his clothes.

Violet distanced herself from the squabble, keeping busy reorganizing their bags on the opposite side of the cave.

"Vi, could you finish with him? I want to get firewood before it gets dark," Alice asked.

Violet took the vials from her and kneeled behind Caine.

"Scream if something tries to eat you," he called after Alice.

Violet soaked a rag in water and ran it over Caine's back, pausing at a set of long, ragged marks. "These scars look the same as your fresh wounds."

"Another naga's teeth scraped me," Caine said, "the first time I encountered one. I can't believe I even have to explain that."

Violet pressed her lips together as she dabbed the newly torn skin. Pink water dripped into a little pool between them.

Caine

THE WATER WAS GROWING COOL, but Caine didn't have the energy to heat it, and he didn't bother asking Violet to attempt any kind of magic.

Her breath hitched as he cringed, the cloth pressing too hard into his back.

"You don't need to do that," Caine said, trying to sway her from finishing.

But Violet dipped the cloth again. "I can't leave you covered in blood."

She finished cleaning his back as he did his front and legs. She picked up the pink goop, haphazardly rubbing it over his wounds. He let her be, the gentle motions mildly soothing.

Caine examined the new marks on his chest. They weren't too deep. Alice had chosen a salve that wasn't as potent, but it would prevent any scarring.

Violet peeked around, and he handed her the roll of thin cloth bandage. She gave him the end to hold as she pulled it around his lower back.

"Thank you," Caine finally managed to get out.

"I'm just bandaging—"

"For stabbing that thing."

She paused. "Oh."

"I panicked when I shouldn't have. So, thank you."

"I'm sure if that happened to you once before, you had a reason to panic. I couldn't do anything with my magic though," Violet said.

"Don't worry about it too much." Fear was the one emotion that didn't trigger magic.

"Do you want to talk about it?" Violet asked.

"I don't need you to console me." He snatched the roll and continued wrapping himself, the movement making him wince.

She took it back. "I'm only asking."

"I'll tell you the story if that's what you want." He reached for the roll again.

"Stop. Let me wrap it." She unwound the loose bandage and started over. "Tell it, then."

"About two years after I'd been appointed archmage, Alice, another mage, and I were looking for an herb. It only grew in damp, dark places. We knew about the nagas, but since the woods were so close to the main city, most of them had been driven away. The first day, we didn't find anything. The next time, I foolishly split off from the two of them, figuring we could cover more ground that way. We would meet back up at the edge of the forest by nightfall.

"Nagas dwell in places where the ground is wet and it's easy for them to slither quietly. The forest would have to be impossibly quiet for you to hear one coming up. As I was heading back, one snuck up and grabbed me. He wasted no time in crushing me and throwing my half-dead body into his nest. I stayed there for two full days. I was barely able to use enough magic to keep myself alive."

"Weren't people out looking for you?" Violet asked.

"Of course, but it wasn't worth losing other lives over, so they searched slowly and carefully. One dead man is better than ten. And of course, right before they found me, the naga got hungry. When they found and killed the beast, I was halfway down his throat." He shivered despite the warm air surrounding them. Caine rubbed his cheek. "I can still feel her licking me."

"Well, apparently you taste good," Violet joked.

He didn't laugh. "I suppose so."

Alice slipped back into the cave, dropping her collected supplies in a pile. "However you taste, you don't learn from your previous mistakes."

"I thought being in a group would make it okay." Caine

shrugged. "That was obviously a lapse in judgment, and I didn't think about them climbing trees."

"They're snakes, Caine. They do that." Alice helped the flames grow a bit. "Lie down."

"One of you needs to sleep too. I know we aren't well rested, but someone has to keep guard. Wake me up in an hour so I can switch with you."

Alice made him sit closer to the fire. "I'll watch for nagas."

"Nagas are the least of our problems," he mumbled. Caine looked them over one last time before facing the wall.

Violet

"I'LL KEEP WATCH. You got hurt too," Violet insisted. "I barely have any scratches."

"If you're sure." Alice curled up on the ground. "Thank you."

Violet settled by the entrance of the cave, leaving her injured friends to rest. She angled herself into the shadows as the sun dipped past the trees. Violet scanned the terrain below, but like the night before, no one came after them.

Although she had planned to wait out the night, Caine woke up a few hours later and made her rest. The moon was above their heads when she moved away from the opening.

When she woke again, Alice sat watch at the front, although Caine was too restless to be asleep.

Chapter Eleven

Violet

BY MORNING, they had each moved on to their own tasks. Caine restored their elixirs while Alice finished repairing the shredded mess that was his clothes. Violet watched her work magic over the cloth, the threads crawling together cleanly. Eventually, she shifted away to play with a bowl of water.

Violet was getting a better feeling for where her magic came from. It always started right below her chest. The numbness spread through her arms and up to her fingertips until…

"*Aqutia.*" The third word in her new vocabulary. A little bubble rose to the top of the water before separating itself and floating above the surface.

"Freeze it," Caine said. "*Glacitia.*"

"How?" It wasn't like the words had done anything for her so far.

"You created fire out of nothing. The element is already in front of you. Just change what it is."

He always spoke as if it were so easy to—

Violet scrambled back as a geyser of water shot up out of the bowl, the electrical feeling flashing though her for just a second. Buckets of water came back down at them as the geyser hit the ceiling. Violet tried to take control of the frenzy of water, but the pang in her chest was gone.

Caine jumped up and shot his hand out at the water. It condensed into one large bubble, which he promptly chucked out of the cave.

Violet scooted against the wall and murmured, "I'm sorry." She didn't look at Alice as the woman came to sit beside her.

Caine's tone was calmer than she had anticipated. "I don't care what damage you do with your magic. At least you're using it. I just wish you could control these bursts of energy."

Alice agreed quietly, her voice encouraging. Violet still looked at the back of the cave.

"Come on." Alice tugged Violet up. "Let's go walk outside a bit."

"Will you get some more firewood while you're out?" Caine asked.

"No problem," Alice said as they exited the cave.

They clung to the wooded area near to their temporary hideout as they walked. "We can collect wood on the way back," Alice said, taking Violet's hand. "Are you doing all right, Vi?"

Am I?

Caine and Alice were the ones experiencing most of the attacks, not her, but being so close to the battles with the king's men then the naga…

"I wish I were learning my magic faster." The sooner she did, the sooner she would get home.

"You'll get there. Look, you created a geyser today!"

"I was mad."

"It happens to all of us. Like I said, it's not the ideal way to learn, but you've done things when you're calm too. It takes practice." Alice squeezed her hand. "I think you're doing great. And so does Caine, even if he won't say it. It's only been three weeks, right?"

"Right." Violet had accomplished less in a semester of classes than she had in the last few weeks. She would try to push away her discouragement for at least a little while longer.

"Good." Alice pointed to a boulder up ahead. "Let's go that far then head back."

Violet stopped herself from asking again if she could go home and check in with her family. Her sister had surely found her empty apartment by then. Caine and Alice had to have a reason they thought it was better to stay in their world, even with the king so close.

"Is there any way I can look in on my family? Not to go back but check in on them?" Violet asked.

Alice shook her head. "We were able to see into your world because we'd anchored a potion to your energy. When we use that same potion now, it comes up blank."

"Oh."

"They're okay, Vi. Like I said, you'll learn your magic and be back before you know it."

Violet tried to have faith in that thought.

"You're really close to them?"

"My family? Yes, of course. My sister lives with me, and everyone else is only an hour away, so I see them a lot." Violet's voice cracked, and Alice hugged her.

"Sorry, that was a terrible time to ask."

"No, it's okay." Violet wanted to keep her family's faces in her head, remind herself why it was so important to gain control of her magic.

~

THEY SLEPT DURING THE AFTERNOON, planning to travel again with the cover of night. Violet had chosen to stay up last, although she didn't really know if it mattered. Her sleep was still fitful.

Violet kept her eyes on the path that led out of the forest. She waited for an army to come charging through the trees. Or a monster. Maybe she would be introduced to a new creature. Violet stared a little harder into the woods. As her eyes veered off, something darted out from behind a rock, a person dressed in dark green.

Violet wanted to assume they were a regular traveler, but the way they ran between the large stones, peeking out before sprinting to the next one, made her uneasy.

"Hey," Violet called back to the group, her voice low enough that it wouldn't echo.

"What?" Caine grumbled. He'd barely been lying down for ten minutes.

"There's someone sneaking around down there."

He picked up his head. "Is it Todrick?"

"No." The person was thinner than the bounty hunter. "They're gone now. He went into the forest."

"Well then, he isn't our problem."

"But shouldn't we—"

"Leave it alone. Call me when he climbs up here."

Violet dug her nails into her legs. After everything, he was going to dismiss her. She held a ball of water in front of her and changed its shape, doing her best not to "accidentally" throw it at his head.

About an hour passed, and she still saw no sign of the stranger or anyone else. Although she didn't want anything to happen, she felt the need to prove that she wasn't being paranoid.

Violet squinted at the trees ahead. Small tendrils of smoke rose from different areas, growing into billowing plumes. Although they were in too many spots to be a single campfire, they didn't seem to be spreading quickly.

Violet grabbed a knife from one of their packs and took her post again. It would likely be useless if a mage reached their hideout, but a blade was more reliable than her magic. She inched closer to the mouth of the cave, trying to make anything out.

A hand suddenly jerked her back. "Where are you going?" Caine's whisper was harsh in her ear. "You mean to get yourself killed? To leave Alice and me unguarded?"

"I wasn't leaving!" Violet said, yanking herself away. "But I think we should check what that smoke is. What if it draws the king's men here too?"

Caine sat back on his heels, glaring at her for a moment. He walked back into the cave and gently woke Alice. "There's smoke in the forest. We're going to go check it out. It should take about fifteen minutes. Come if we're not back by then."

Alice rubbed her eyes. "You're still hurt. Let me go instead."

"I'll be fine." He squeezed her shoulder.

She sighed, only handing him his jacket and two cloaks. Caine pulled them over the bandages alone, speaking too quietly for Violet to hear. His assistant shook her head and yawned. Caine grabbed his dagger as well, and Violet pulled her hood up before following him down the cliffside.

They ran toward the smoke in the middle of the forest until they reached the fire clinging to lower branches of the towering evergreen trees. Caine stopped at the edge, pulling some of the flame into his hand. "This is someone's magic."

Violet started to ask if he could tell whose when a woman's scream rang out from very close by. "Should we?"

"This is a setup. The flames are too controlled," Caine said as he cleared their path.

They slipped into a clearing only a few feet ahead. A large tree sat at the other end, two children and a woman tied to its trunk, each wearing a crudely cut blindfold. They dashed toward the family.

Caine tried to use his dagger to shear the rope. "It's enchanted." Caine found a knot toward the back and cast a pink glow around it.

Violet stood to the side, watching his back and the trees ahead. The fire began to clear.

"Someone's coming," Violet whispered.

"I need a minute. If they attack, we're leaving," Caine said bluntly, making sure he was completely hidden behind the tree.

Violet held her knife tightly and tried to grasp at what little magic she could as the tall man in green stepped out.

"Well, this worked better than I expected." Golden eyes searched the clearing. "Where are the mages?"

Violet shook her head. "I don't know what you mean."

"Don't. Change your appearance all you want. I know who you are." He took slow steps forward. "I don't know what they told you, but I promise you'll be safer with me than with them."

"Are you with the king?" she asked.

He paused before laughing. "Yes, I am one of King Paskal's, and I'll give you one more chance. Come with me." When Violet said nothing, he said, "If I must, then."

His hand shot out. Violet was sure her heart would leap out of her chest as a streak of white-hot lightning cracked from above and struck the ground beside her, sending charred dirt and grass into the air. Caine had mentioned other in-between energies. Besides his own ice, none of their previous attackers had shown any proof, and despite the damage she'd seen done with it, frost seemed much more docile than electricity.

She tried her best not to look back, pleading silently for Caine to come out. As soon as her attacker moved again, Violet focused on the fire in the trees.

"*Ignitia.*" She spoke softly without moving her lips, hoping the man wouldn't pick up on her attempt to shoot some toward him. She couldn't tell if the term had made the fire stronger, but she was able to launch it at her target.

The man deflected it easily and grinned at her. "So you do have energy."

Violet glanced back then. The family had been freed, but Caine still hadn't emerged.

Another bolt of lightning shot down beside her, and dirt flecks stung her cheek. Violet stood up and charged forward, blade in front of her, hoping to catch him off guard. She cleared the distance quickly, but he was still ready when her blade came at him.

He knocked the wind out of Violet as he threw an arm into her stomach. Vision blurring, she tried to lift herself up off the ground while attempting to throw the knife in his direction with telekinesis. The man sidestepped the blade and pulled her up the rest of the way, throwing Violet over his shoulder.

"Young lady, I asked you nicely. Twice."

Violet wiggled, but he only gripped her waist tighter.

In a moment of frustration, she found an exposed area of his skin and pushed her palms against it. "*Glacia,*" she hissed under her breath.

The man roared in pain as she forced ice into his skin. He tossed Violet to the ground and cleared the frost burn from his back. She struggled to get up after landing headfirst. Her weapon was so close… she tried to lift it again from afar, but the knife wobbled uselessly in the dirt.

The man had her by the legs before she could attempt to crawl away.

"Good morning, Your Highness."

Violet let herself breathe a little, hearing Caine's voice. Alice stood with him as well.

"Blackwood." The man—*no, the self-made king*—stood quickly to greet the others. "And Miss Willowflower."

Caine sauntered forward. "Do we really need the formalities, Your Highness?"

"No, I suppose not. Though after years of working in a castle, you should know how to address your betters." His eyes flicked between the mages as he got into a better stance. "You seem to be confused, Caine."

"How so, Cross?"

"You've stolen from me."

Violet watched Alice and tested her wobbly footing, only managing to kneel. Alice met her gaze but made no move.

Caine narrowed his eyes. "I have stolen from no one. Go away. I have things to do." He made a shooing motion, and a gust of wind followed. It slid Violet across the ground and nearly toppled Cross.

The prince shot a lightning bolt at Caine's head. Alice lunged forward and redirected it toward the sky. She caught a second one as Caine ducked out of the way again.

The prince's hands crackled as he spread his fingers apart. "Letting your assistant fight your battles, Caine?"

"She's a pretty great mage and better than you, but I can play too." Even before he finished talking, icicles had formed around Caine and flew at Cross.

One caught his shoulder. The others melted before they got

close. Violet could only press herself to the ground, unsure of her ability to walk.

Alice charged forward. Cross redirected some of her fire but couldn't manage all of it as ice came flying from Caine. Cross jumped back, clearing the flames surrounding him. He turned and darted into the trees.

Violet finally stood up as he disappeared from view. She turned on Caine. "I thought you said we were leaving if something happened."

"I recognized his voice. I knew he wouldn't kill you." He ignored Violet's next accusation and said to Alice, "It's been less than fifteen minutes."

"Well, it's a good thing I don't listen to you very often, sir." The fire Alice still had in her palms grew steadily.

Violet looked past them as the woman Caine had freed came back into the clearing.

"Thank you so much. I was sure we were going to die in that fire," the woman said.

"Are the kids okay?" Violet asked.

"They're safe at home, thank you."

Caine asked her a question, but Violet didn't hear it. The last thing she saw was three distraught faces as she dropped to her knees and her vision went black.

Chapter Twelve

Alice

ALICE GASPED and grabbed Violet before she hit the ground. Caine and the other woman kneeled with her.

"She's breathing," Caine said quietly.

Alice could feel the shallow rise and fall of Violet's chest. She held two fingers to Violet's wrist. Her energy fluctuated, rising too slowly back to normal levels.

"Would you like to come to my home?" the woman offered.

Alice looked at Caine and nodded. She could hear the discontent in his voice as he accepted and thanked the woman. They both pulled their cloaks tighter when the woman turned around and Alice made sure Violet's was still hiding her identity as well.

Alice did her best to keep Violet steady with levitation. Caine offered to carry her, but he was still weak as it was. Alice held onto Violet's wrist during the short walk to the cabin.

The woman, Ms. Brambill, brought them to a closet-sized guest room in the back of the house. By the time they got Violet onto the bed, her pulse and energy had stabilized once again.

They waited for Ms. Brambill to leave before doing their own healing. While they appreciated the woman's attempt at an herb mixture, which sat on the nightstand, a damp cloth with a revival potion on her head was going to do a lot more.

Alice sat near the top of the bed, Caine across from her. He was still watching Violet when Alice asked, "Were you planning on intervening before I showed up?"

He shrugged. "Cross wouldn't have killed her."

"You should have helped!"

"I wanted to see what she would do, and it's not like I could have defended myself against his lightning."

Alice lit a fire in her hand, letting it grow to the size of her fist. "Are your bandages okay?"

He leaned away from her. "They're fine."

Alice stared him down, but his eyes had already drifted back to Violet. "Are you sure?"

Caine gave half a nod. After a few moments, he murmured, "Cross is after us. He knew where we were."

She let out a breath and dismissed the flames. "We might be better off staying in the towns after all. At least we can blend in a bit better."

"Todrick was quick to find us too. Would you rather face the king's army or Cross's?"

Alice couldn't answer. Even if he was alone today, Cross likely had his troops close by. Todrick would know well enough not to hesitate the next time they met, and it wouldn't take much to convince the king he needed more soldiers. They could take a lot, but it was just Alice and Caine fighting. Even if Violet did get enough of a grasp on her magic, three against two armies was pushing their luck.

A new horror crossed Alice's mind. "Do you think the king is working with Cross?"

"Not a chance," Caine said. "His son forcefully established another kingdom and nearly killed half the population, but King Paskal wouldn't even bother sending a spy to Sophonix."

"Unless he lied about that too."

Caine's grimace matched her own.

Alice checked their student one last time before sliding off the bed, assuring Caine she would be back soon. Only their cloaks and weapons had made it out of the cave. It had been an hour. Cross or Todrick could have gotten to their camp by then, and without knowing when it would be safe to go back into a city, they needed to preserve as many of their supplies as possible.

Violet

VIOLET JOLTED UP, crying out at the sharp pain running between her temple and chest.

A hand on her shoulder kept her from lying back down too quickly. "Stupid—don't..."

Violet took a few short breaths and closed her eyes again.

"No, we already did this. Look at me."

Violet glanced up through her lashes, only aggravating her headache. She pulled away, and the hand fell. She opened her eyes again when she was lying down. Sun shone through a window above her. Caine sat on the edge of the small bed, a half smile on his face.

Violet groaned into the bedsheet. She attempted to speak, but her voice was stuck behind a layer of dust in her throat.

Caine coaxed her up again with a glass of water in hand, although she didn't remember him leaving to get it. Violet shook her head at the foul taste, but Caine pushed it back into her palm. "There's medicine in it. Drink it quickly."

Violet gulped down the powdery liquid, motivated only by the thought of making the throbbing in her head disappear.

"I passed out." Her voice was still harsh.

Caine nodded. "I'm still not sure why. It could have been because of the magic you used or physical trauma."

"How long?"

"Two months."

Her mouth dropped open, but he snickered.

"I'm joking. Two days."

Violet couldn't do anything more than glare.

"We're staying with the family we saved," he continued, answering her unasked question. "Cross didn't come back." He glanced at the door suddenly, although she hadn't heard anything.

"You let him hurt me," Violet said.

"I gave you the chance to defend yourself, and you did an okay job. I wasn't going to let you die. You know that."

Violet's mouth set in a hard line. He had stepped in eventually, but she hadn't been completely unharmed. Violet moved up so she was resting on one of the pillows and tried to keep herself calm, too afraid of accidentally using her magic. She waited for Caine to leave, but he made himself comfortable at the bottom of her bed, book in hand.

He caught her stare. "What?"

"You're staying?" She hadn't meant to be so curt, but the question spilled from her lips.

"I was only going to make sure you didn't pass out again. I'll leave."

"I wasn't sure. You're fine, thanks."

He continued frowning but sat back down on the bed. Violet closed her eyes and stretched out, accidentally kicking Caine. She almost apologized, but he gave her calf a playful flick.

~

"Sorry, I didn't mean to wake you." Alice stood over the bed.

Caine was absent from the room.

Violet accepted the mage's hug.

"Are you hungry? I was leaving this for you." Alice gestured to a plate of pasta and green vegetables on the nightstand.

Violet was able to sit up without the room spinning, and they ate together.

"Do you want to go out with everyone else yet?" Alice asked.

"Maybe in a bit." Violet wanted to make sure she was feeling okay.

Alice cozied up next to her. "Okay."

Violet grabbed a comb out of their bag just to give herself something normal to focus on.

"I should cut this while we're here," Alice said, pulling a ringlet of her own hair past her nose.

"Is your hair blue because of your magic? Like our eyes?" Violet hadn't seen anyone else with neon-blue hair or any other unnatural color like it while they were in town, and although it had obviously grown, the color still went all the way to her roots.

Alice laughed. "No, I changed it myself with magic. The first time I did it was an accident when I was a kid. I couldn't get it to change back for a week until my aunt came by and fixed it. Then I kept doing it on purpose after that. My parents hated it." She giggled again.

Violet chuckled too. "Just being rebellious?"

"Kind of. I think I wanted to use my magic for more than farming."

Violet wanted to ask more, but as reserved as Caine acted, he still seemed more willing to talk about his life than Alice was. "I think I'm okay to go out now," she said instead.

~

Ms. Brambill thanked Violet over and over for saving them, and the little boy and girl were grateful too. The children begged her and Alice to stay and play in the living room. They moved metal pegs across a colorful board game that Violet could only equate to a far-removed version of chutes and ladders. She joined for a few turns before going back to the room, the ache in her chest causing her breathing to turn shallow.

Caine returned some time later, giving her a new concoction to drink. He pressed his fingers below her neck. "*Santia,*" he said, letting a blue glow settle there for a moment. "I don't understand," Caine said, pausing to catch his own breath. "I'm losing energy healing you, but nothing is changing."

"Did Cross do this to me?" Violet asked.

"No, I would feel that. This is where you sense your magic?"

Violet nodded. It was a mild pulse all along her sternum and exactly where the pain was climbing up to her head.

"We can't stay past tonight. Ms. Brambill plans on heading into town tomorrow. I don't know if we're news to the common folk yet, but the town directors must have been notified by now."

They had kept their cloaks on the whole time, but if Ms. Brambill heard about three runaway mages like the ones she just happened to be harboring in her house…

Caine knocked his knuckles against the bed frame, sighing. "Nothing's going the way it was supposed to. Oh, here." He handed her something from their packs—the knife she'd taken, as if she'd be able to defend herself at point-blank range, or at all.

Caine tossed her a sheath too. "You may as well hold onto it."

Violet couldn't see herself trying anything like that again but took it anyway. She made it hover in her hand for a second, gasping as pain stung her chest.

"Careful," Caine said, but a smile pulled at the corner of his mouth as he watched the knife float again.

~

ALICE NUDGED Violet awake as the sun barely peeked into the sky. Head heavy, Violet slipped out of the house with only a silent goodbye to their host.

Chapter Thirteen

Caine

CAINE GLANCED BACK, trying to distinguish the wind from the sounds of small creatures rustling in the trees. The stirring grew louder, sending a torrent of dried leaves across their campground. He cupped the flame in his palm as it danced wildly. The night always brought a chill to the air, although it never got too cold.

He blinked as purple filled the corner of his vision.

Violet groaned and rubbed her sternum, her following breaths coming out in wheezes. She whispered, "The cold air…"

Caine went over the ingredients for an airway clearer. *Is that even her ailment?* He boiled the new mixture anyway, cooling the liquid before handing it to Violet to drink. He ushered her back to sleep before tapping Alice on the shoulder.

Alice tried to give up her blanket, but he tossed it back over to her. He sat down away from her but continued staring at the shaky rise and fall of Violet's chest.

"What's wrong?" Alice asked.

"She's so sick." They had only been in the open for two days.

Violet couldn't use any magic, the pain nearly knocking her out anytime she tried.

"We could—"

"No."

"Are you really going to be petty?"

"Excuse me?"

"Push your ego aside for a bit."

He gritted his teeth and lay down, forcing both women out of his head.

~

"Could I have something to practice?" Violet asked as they prepared to travel the next morning.

Caine ignored her, and she didn't ask again.

He wiped frost off his fingertips as Alice unfolded their map, taking too long to retrace their new path. Alice dropped the pointer as Violet grabbed her arm, jerking into another coughing fit. Caine's assistant glared at him. He wanted them to start moving, but Alice wouldn't budge.

"You would rather we put ourselves through all this?" she asked. "With what we have to do?"

Violet

"Violet." Caine's voice was soft. "Can I have your necklace?"

She knitted her brow. "My necklace?"

"Alice and I need to have a… personal conversation."

Slowly, Violet undid the clasp and placed the tiny chain in Caine's open palm. He spoke, and she could only assume it was a "thank you" of some kind.

She walked away and sat at the base of a tree. Her hand

brushed across her bare neck. That little jewel had become her safety net so quickly. Violet was lost enough with the introduction of monsters and magic. She couldn't take a language barrier as well.

Despite not being able to understand, Violet still didn't want to watch the two of them argue. Flames danced around Alice's fists, and ice grew on Caine's jacket where he crossed his arms.

Violet closed her eyes, failing to block out their shouts as she leaned back against the tree. Hearing them talk in their own language, Violet could pick up on a slight accent they each had. Alice's was a little heavier than Caine's. She tried to place it in her own world, but nothing came to mind. Maybe it was unique to theirs.

Violet pulled out her list, marking five more days. They had been chased out of three different places, and she'd been able to use four energies, all in half a month.

Her family must be in a frenzy. She doubted Caine and Alice had left any evidence in her apartment. Even if they had, it wouldn't lead the police anywhere helpful.

She laughed a little, imagining a Keep Out poster outside the police station door with her mom and sister's faces on it. She was certain they were in there every day, asking if the police had found any leads. The poster in her mind morphed into one with her own face plastered across the town they lived in and at the university.

Violet rubbed her forearm across her stomach, as if it would get rid of the pit that was forming there. She could go home in maybe two months—as soon as she got a handle on her power. She really needed to start coming up with a story. Violet would never show her magic to anyone except maybe her sister, but she would need a reason for her disappearance.

Violet glanced up, hearing footsteps in the dirt.

Caine dropped the necklace into her lap. "Change of plans." He picked up one of their bags. "We're making a stop a little closer."

"How come?" Violet grabbed the other bags, handing one over to Alice, who was smiling again.

"My brother lives close by," Caine said.

"You have a brother?"

"Yes, Violet. I have a family, like most people."

"I figured since you acted so spoiled, you must be an only child."

Alice muffled a giggle as Violet dodged a tendril of frost.

~

VIOLET BEGAN to see signs of civilization—trees chopped down, dirt where stone had once rested. Alice had picked a few flowers from beside what looked like an herb garden.

A cough made Violet dig her heels into the dirt just to stop herself from falling over. She stayed upright, but Alice linked their arms together anyway, letting Violet lean against her shoulder as they walked.

"We're still about an hour away." Caine looked at the map one last time before folding it back into its cube. His gaze lingered on Violet for a moment, shifting back to the forest just as fast.

Violet's head jerked up suddenly as the bushes quivered.

"What?" Caine asked. He followed her eyes to the trees on their left.

"I thought I saw something. Maybe I'm being paranoid."

Caine didn't add anything, but his hand moved to his sheath.

She tried to force herself to focus ahead but still peeked at the forest every five seconds. She swore she could feel energy pulsing from the trees. An inhuman screech from the forest made her hands clench.

They were all watching the woods. Caine formed a few icicles and held the pieces above their heads, ready to bombard whatever creature had chosen them as a target.

"I don't know what that was," Alice murmured. She looked to Caine, but he seemed just as unsure.

An animal flew past their heads. Violet whipped around, but the creature had flown too far into the sky. It screeched again and dove toward the group. Before any of them could move to attack it, a ring of green fire knocked into the animal, sending it to the ground. It tried to stand, but Caine shot ice at its head, effectively taking it down.

The fox creature was about the size of a housecat with the wings of a hawk. The green fire had left burn marks on its fur.

Violet ducked as another flying fox flew out of the trees. Caine aimed another ice chunk, but the animal dodged it easily and bared its teeth, a hiss escaping its curled lips. Alice yanked Violet to the side as another one flew their way. That one was a full-grown fox. It howled, and a dozen more swarmed around them.

The creature backed off slightly as Alice played with a ball of fire. "Caine, we killed its baby."

"I noticed." He changed his own magic to flames.

Alice shrank her fire a little. "I don't want to kill them."

"They're only fox sprites."

"Maybe if we walk slowly?"

He kept the fire in his hand. Violet stayed close to Alice as they inched away. The swarm's eyes followed them with piercing gazes. The largest called out again, and the rest dove toward them. Alice and Caine immediately sent a conjoined wave of fire out. It pushed only a handful back.

Four raced toward Violet, teeth aimed at her neck. She tried to conjure her own flame, and a painful shock engulfed her body, fire never coming to her palms. She collapsed, throwing her hands over the back of her neck as she swallowed a cough.

From behind her someone called, "Don't get up!"

Despite not recognizing the man's voice, Violet kept herself pinned to the dirt, only lifting her eyes to keep the creatures in her vision. A wave of heat moved over her, and the fox sprites dropped, their wings engulfed in colorful flames.

She sat up cautiously. The creatures no longer hung in the air.

"I think we killed an entire family." Alice tapped one with her foot.

"That wasn't even a quarter of them."

Violet hadn't heard the stranger get closer, but he was only a foot or two behind her. Violet stood and prepared to run, but neither of her companions looked panicked. They took off their hoods, and she did the same. Alice was still glancing around the clearing, her shoulders slumped a bit.

Caine squinted at the man. "Violet, this is my brother, Felix."

The man held his hand out to Violet, and she shook it hesitantly. She could see the resemblance in their faces. Although Felix's eyes glowed navy blue, his hair matched Caine's tar black.

Alice leaned against Caine. "I feel awful."

"I noticed, and I'm not sure why."

"We can't leave them like this."

"Why don't you and I stay and move them out of the path?" Felix offered to Alice. To Caine he said, "We probably shouldn't all go back at once. Unless, of course, you were planning on heading somewhere else?"

Caine said nothing, taking the pouch of herbs Felix had slung over his shoulder. He gestured for Violet to follow him.

They made it to the town quickly. It was a bit cozier than the last with quaint houses lining curvy paths and bountiful gardens or trees filling the empty spaces. Caine led her to a small house and knocked on the door.

A petite woman answered. Her curly dirty-blond hair was pulled into a neat bun. "May I help you?"

Caine looked over his shoulder before taking down the hood. She gasped and pulled him and Violet inside.

"Are you—" She looked back at the door. "Where's Alice?"

Caine motioned for her to calm down. "She's with Felix. They'll be here soon."

She hugged him quickly before turning to Violet. "Hello, dear. I'm Holly, Felix's fiancée."

"Violet," she said, smiling a little. "Or Vi."

"It's nice to meet you." Holly turned suddenly. "The rice— wait." Holly stalked back to Caine, fierce orange eyes glaring up at him. "What are you doing?"

"What do you mean?"

"The king's men have tramped through the town twice searching for the three of you!"

"Ah, that."

The door opened again. Felix came in with Alice, the bounce back in her step.

Holly threw her arms around Alice. "Is this all Caine, or did you cause this mess too?"

"Well, don't just blame me," Caine said.

Despite the worry in her eyes, Holly was smiling at all of them. She and Alice made their way to the kitchen, leaving Violet with the brothers.

Felix was watching her. "Are you trying to get yourself killed, Caine?"

Their faces were so strikingly similar now that they stood next to each other. Although Felix's gaze was somehow softer.

"Make yourself at home," Felix continued when he didn't get an answer. "You'll have to excuse the mess. I wasn't expecting guests. Actually, Caine, could you help me set up the extra bedroom?"

They walked off into the hallway, leaving Violet in the small living room. She wandered toward the kitchen doorway, stopping to cough again.

Holly ushered her to the table. "Oh no, please sit. I'll get you some hot tea. I know Felix has some with soothing agents."

"Thank you." Violet leaned back in the chair.

A bird landed on the windowsill, and her heart thudded, but its eyes were a dull brown. The smell of broth filled her senses, and the knots in her stomach slowly undid themselves. The warm air alone soothed her thoughts.

Caine

"You're crazy!" Felix scowled at him from the other side of the bed, the sheet balled up in his fists. "Being archmage wasn't enough?" he asked, glancing over at the door.

It was bolted and sealed. Caine had made sure of that.

"Oh, is that what this is about?" Caine asked, eyes narrowing.

"No, it's not—" his brother sputtered. "I can't believe you would go to this extent for magic."

"What else was I supposed to do, leave her for the king?"

"Yes." He threw the sheet to the side, the cloth singed from the teal fire he had cupped in his hands. "That's exactly what you should have done."

"Why don't you get Alice in here so you can yell at her too?" Caine slid onto the bed, refusing to look at him. "It's me you have a problem with, not what I'm doing."

"It's both!" Felix paced, swirling the fire in his palms. "Do you know how worried Mom and Dad are? They were here a week ago, praying that we had any news so they could tell Alice's aunt too. Do you even care?"

"Stop it." Caine waved his hand, snuffing out his brother's magic. "Of course I care about them. I've explained everything now, so tell everyone that Alice and I are okay." When Felix didn't argue further, Caine glanced over. "Can we stay for a little while?"

"Of course. Holly wouldn't let you leave anyway." He picked the blanket up off the floor, yanking the other one from under Caine.

"Since we're going to stay, would you care to teach Violet your magic?" Caine cut off his brother's protest. "Come on. You may as well."

"I am not fueling this anymore." Felix paused. "How strong is she anyway?"

Caine chuckled. He could quibble all he wanted, but Felix was just as enticed by the sudden appearance of Violet's magic as Caine was. "She can't always use it, but it's pretty damn powerful when she does. She's a wordsmith too."

He knew what was making Felix hesitant about adding his energy to the mix. "I want to make sure she touches base with as many types of magic as she can. There's a chance she'll develop it anyway, so at least it'll be familiar to her."

"Shut up. We both know that's not the reason. But—" Felix broke the door's seal. "Let's pretend it's for her sake, all right? It'll make me feel better."

"I'm taking that as a yes," Caine called after Felix shut the door.

It was for Violet. Being around Felix would cause her body to start trying to pick up his magic. The only reason she wasn't accidentally conjuring every spell they'd used was because she was focused on three elements. And his brother's magic wasn't something anyone wanted to accidentally wield.

"Caine." Holly's airy voice carried through the house. "Dinner's finished!"

He folded his cloak, placing it neatly inside the dresser drawer before heading to the kitchen. It was already strange not having to constantly make sure it was near his person.

Chapter Fourteen

VIOLET SNUGGLED the heavy woolen blanket around her, careful not to pull too much of it away from Alice.

"You two planning on getting up?"

The foreign voice made her jump. She lay back after seeing it was only Felix in the doorway. She must have drifted back off before he knocked.

He knocked on the frame again. "Come on. It's nearly ten."

She tapped Alice a few times, but Alice refused to move.

Violet changed into the clothes someone had left for her and Alice on the dresser before heading to the living room. "Does your family have a problem with sleeping?" Violet wasn't sure which brother she was directing the question to.

They were sitting at opposite ends of a couch. She plopped down into the chair across from them. Caine only continued to read. Felix didn't answer either, instead directing her to the kitchen for breakfast. Alice joined them shortly after. Holly had gone out for the morning, but she'd left them food and clothes, which Violet had been more than happy to accept.

"Violet," Felix said. "Want to learn something new?"

"What do you mean?" Violet asked.

He held out his hand, and a swirl of blue rose from it.

Of course. "No thank you." Violet didn't think she needed to add another energy to fail at.

He pouted. "Come on. My magic is more fun than Caine's."

Then again, how much of a difference will one more element make? She glanced over at Caine, but he never moved to contribute to her decision. "Fine."

She followed him down to an area like Caine's potion room. Most of the shelves, however, were filled with tiny potted plants. Some were contained in glass jars. Others had vines reaching the floor.

"What magic have you picked up so far?" Felix sat at a small wooden table and gestured for Violet to join him. "Caine didn't tell me too much."

"Fire, water, ice, levitation. Heat, I think. I've burned a few things without fire," she listed off. "That's about it. What's the colorful thing you've been doing?"

"It's a branch of the fire element called spectral magic." He moved his hand, and the air marbled with various shades of shimmering green. A small wave of heat wiggled above.

"So, colors not ghosts," Violet clarified.

He flinched. "No, no. That would be along the lines of phantom magic. Spectral is really hot, colorful fire. It leaves a nasty burn."

"Caine didn't tell me about that." Not even Alice had mentioned it, and she was the firebug.

Felix snickered, a coy grin creeping onto his face. "Well, he probably doesn't like talking about the things he can't use."

"How many different forms of the elements are there?" she asked.

"Too many for one mage to have. Caine, Alice, and I all have the main elements and a few different denominations. Obviously, he has the most control and strength, but he can't do everything."

"It's really pretty," Violet said. She was trying not to focus too much on the comment he had made. If their kingdom's best mage didn't have control over everything, why should she?

"Thank you. It's not the most useful as far as magework, but it has its benefits. Plant magic is a little more helpful. Pick one to start with."

"Plant magic." She wasn't completely sure what that entailed, but it had to be easier than trying to make her already-weak fire more complicated.

Felix asked a few more questions about her own magic before showing Violet how he repaired broken leaves and helped seeds grow. He held his hand over the pointed leaves of an herb. They curled and turned brown, a few breaking off. Felix pushed it toward her with a simple "fix it."

"Wait, I can't even heal people yet."

"Neither can I. So, find your energy, and do it."

She moved her fingers quickly, trying not to overthink it. She mimicked what he'd done, pinching a leaf gently between her thumb and middle finger.

She gasped as she let go. There was a pale-green circle where her finger had been. Violet continued, and within a few minutes, the leaf was healthy once again. It took her no more than twenty minutes to restore the entire plant.

"I…" She couldn't do anything but stare at the little plant. "I've never done anything that fast."

Felix was inspecting the leaves, tugging and shaking them to find any weak spots, but they didn't budge. He looked as shocked as she felt. "Are you tired?"

She shook her head. The pain in Violet's sternum was still there, but her cough was barley a tickle in her throat now.

"Rest anyway. We can try another energy in a bit."

"Is there a term to go along with this too?" Violet asked.

Felix's face darkened. "The word for grow and heal. You'll have to ask Caine or Alice for it."

"Okay." Violet rested her cheek on the table.

Felix's sleeve slid back, revealing a little black triangle on his wrist as he played with the plant's leaves again.

"Caine has the same brand there too," Violet said. "I thought it had something to do with him being archmage."

"It's the symbol for brothers," Felix said. "We've had them awhile now."

"Who's older?" Violet had tried to refrain from asking questions since Caine was so quiet about his family, but maybe his brother would be a little more willing.

"Caine, only by two years. Unfortunately, I've had to deal with him all my life."

"You don't like him?"

"He's not my favorite person. I'll help him, of course. He is family." He swallowed and stopped.

Violet was about to apologize for prying, but a plume of blue fire suddenly shot up from the plant.

Felix moved his hand away. "Put it out."

By the time she was done, the table was covered with water, the poor plant left smoking.

Someone knocked at the door.

"Come in," Felix answered.

Caine stepped in, cocking his head at the scene. "How's it going?"

"Well." Felix lifted the excess water and dropped it into a

nearby watering can. "Violet, try to heal that one." He muttered to Caine, and they left.

Violet ran her finger over the broken plant. "Sorry," she whispered.

Alice

ALICE SHOVED the needle through the pink fabric. Holly would be back soon, and she'd barely finished stitching the first part. Maybe the dress would have to be a wedding present. It would go faster with her magic, of course, but the needle and thread felt more intimate for a gift, and the repetition of sewing was soothing.

The front door opened, and Alice jumped up, hiding the material and sewing kit carefully under the bed.

Holly knocked on the bedroom door and stuck her head in. "Hi there! Where is everyone?"

"Violet's practicing magic. The boys are out."

The brothers had crept away a little while ago. Violet was playing with a plant in Felix's study. She'd seemed a little distraught but had denied Alice's attempt to stay with her.

Holly sat on the bed. "And how are you doing?"

"I'm fine."

"The king is on your tail, and you're 'fine'?"

Alice stretched out across the mattress. "Well, I've been better, but things are okay right now."

It wasn't going perfectly. They had factored in a few hiccups with the king and assumed Cross would get involved eventually. There had always been the question of whether the prince had spies in Endrel, but with how quickly he'd arrived, there must have been some truth to it. Or worse, he and King Paskal had pushed aside their grievances and were working together.

As long as things kept going the way they were, they would be okay. Violet was more than comfortable with them, and Caine had warmed up to her as well. He really shouldn't have, but Alice wasn't going to be the one to remind him of their original plight.

Holly wrapped her arms around herself. "Promise me all three of you will keep each other safe. I'm sure you guys are doing what you feel is right. I don't want any of you dying."

"Of course, Holly." Alice had made that promise to herself long ago.

PART TWO

IGNIGHTING ATROCITIES

Chapter Fifteen

VIOLET JUMPED BACK, her breath coming in pants. She leaned against a tree, her eyes never leaving the clearing, her mind racing as fast as her heart. She couldn't keep throwing attacks. It was only wearing her out.

Caine stood in front of her, his breath as ragged. Frost still licked his fingertips. He was giving her a chance to rest, but she wished he would knock her down already.

Violet created a wall of fire behind him, but her gaze gave away its location. He doused it and looked back at her, disapproval on his face.

She couldn't think of anything else to do. She didn't have anything he didn't know about, and they had steered her away from using the terms as a crutch. She considered the knife sitting comfortably on her hip, but he wouldn't let her get close enough to use it. She had nothing to levitate but twigs.

A wicked thought flashed into her brain. She found what she was looking for and moved so he would back up. The vines pulled themselves off the tree. She tried to stay focused elsewhere as one snaked over Caine's foot and up his ankle, the other around his waist.

He cursed and jumped back, tripping over the rest of the vine. Violet took her chance and threw a new wave of fire. It flashed blue, only for a moment. Despite fighting with the tightening vines, he was able to cut through the flames. The plant shriveled away as he burned it.

He threw his hand out, and ice shot up behind her. Violet stumbled forward, barely dodging an icicle, although it could have been Alice or Felix redirecting the blow. They hovered on the sidelines, watching to make sure none of the attacks got too close.

As more ice moved toward her, Violet called, "I forfeit!" She was tired, and their battle was going nowhere.

Caine dropped his hand. "Don't do that."

"What, the vine?" She leaned back, the wall of ice refreshing on her hot skin.

His lip twitched. He walked toward their onlookers, waving his hand as he turned. She squeaked and fell back as the ice melted instantly, the frigid water dropping onto her.

"Hey!" she sputtered, water dripping out her nose.

"Whoops," he called back.

Violet tried to pull the water from her clothes but only managed to get a quarter of it off. Alice came over to help, elbowing Caine as he walked past her.

They returned to the house in twos. Felix walked with Violet, leading her down the path she had yet to memorize. It was an hour's walk, but they needed to practice as far away from Felix and Holly's home as possible. They had found someplace fairly hidden and hoped it was enough to keep Caine's family protected.

"That was better than last time," Violet said.

"You certainly lasted longer. I don't know how much stronger you'll be than us, but you're learning faster than any mage I've seen."

Violet sighed and pulled her sleeves up. Spring had come in nicely—or at least what she thought was spring. She had been kidnapped in January, and yet when she'd arrived in Endrel, the trees still had leaves. Only the bitter air had reminded her that it was supposed to be winter.

But each time they walked to the secluded clearing to practice, more and more growth had taken over the path. There was still a slight chill when the wind blew, but besides that, she would have to wear short sleeves soon.

Holly greeted them at the door, checking for some of the many bruises they'd come back with over the last two months. It was always two fighting and two watching, but every once in a while, they would come back with a burn or scrape.

"We're fine, Holly." Felix held her hands. "Thank you."

"I still have to check." She kissed his cheek. "I made dinner."

Is it already that time? Violet glanced up at the clock.

Holly called the two of them to the kitchen. They waited to eat until everyone had arrived.

Violet pulled some peas across her plate. She'd missed what had been said, but Alice held a napkin to her mouth, trying to prevent any food from coming out in her laughter. Even Caine's shoulders were shaking. All the while, Holly scolded Felix for whatever he must have said, her voice still tender.

Violet chuckled, too, feeling a small pang in her chest. They had sat like this nearly every night. Each time Violet found herself contributing more, no longer feeling like an outsider to their little group.

"Violet?" She looked up at Alice's voice. "Are you all right?"

They were all watching her.

She quickly wiped away the tears that were blurring her vision. She wondered how long she had sat there with her eyes welling up. "I'm fine," Violet whispered, her smile growing.

Alice handed her a napkin as Holly rubbed her shoulder. They continued to eat, but Violet could feel Caine watching her out of the corner of his eye. His expression was uncertain, and when she met his stare, he looked the other way. She waited a few seconds before turning back to her plate.

~

Violet let Caine in as he knocked on her door. He didn't say anything at first, only leaned against the doorframe.

"You're doing well," he finally muttered. "I wasn't sure you'd get this much done, but you've actually gained some control." He moved to close the door.

Violet stopped him. "Wait."

"What?"

"Thank you. I didn't think I could do any of this. It's still crazy to me that I'm here."

Caine opened his mouth, but whatever he had to say was lost on his tongue. He glanced over at the window so suddenly Violet expected to see something there.

"It's nice outside."

Violet finished the question for him. "Do you want to go out for a bit?"

Caine nodded, and she followed him out to the edge of the woods. As they entered the trees, he created a light orb. It shone brightly, illuminating their path completely.

Violet tied her jacket around her waist, the air nearly as warm as it had been earlier.

"Where are we going?" she asked.

The path was not their usual one.

She found herself matching his impish grin as he said, "I don't know."

It was the fourth late-night jaunt they'd gone on. The first time had been after training, the second week after they'd arrived. Caine had wandered off to collect herbs for his brother, and Violet had tagged along. They had come back empty-handed after venturing into a less-than-ideal area of the forest—a few of those flying foxes still seemed out to get them. Their attempt the next time was much more successful.

The first couple walks had been silent, Violet only talking when she was unsure of what plants they needed to collect. By the third time, he was the one asking her to come along, light conversation filling the space as he poked into her personal life and revealed some of his own.

He and Felix had the same spiteful mindset about their relationship. He spoke more fondly of his parents and Alice. Violet had only good things to say about her own parents and siblings, but none of her friends had been quite as close as Caine and Alice, except for her older sister.

They walked in comfortable silence tonight, only the rustle of leaves filling the air. Violet watched as Caine rolled the light orb in his hand, creating shadows every once in a while.

"How do you make that?" Violet asked.

"I put my palms together, think about light, and pull them apart." He demonstrated.

Violet copied his movements, but nothing appeared.

"Here." Caine held the light toward her. "Hold it so you can get an idea of what it's like."

Violet reached up carefully, but the burn she expected didn't come as she cupped the blue glow.

"Ah." She shivered. "I can feel your magic." Although not as powerful, she could feel the icy calm course through her.

They walked for a few more minutes before choosing a tree to rest near. Violet still cradled the orb against herself as Caine sat down. She tried to return the light, but he pushed it back.

Violet ran her finger over it. The ball was squishy, and she could almost push her finger into it. She gasped when the spot turned green. Caine urged her to keep going, and she spread the new glow to the rest of the sphere. He took it back, sucking in a breath as it touched his hand.

Caine

HE WAITED for discomfort to come, but only a slight hum echoed through him. It didn't make him jittery despite the electricity he knew was there.

He ignored Violet's questioning stare as he ran his palm over the orb, his pulse erratic as a larger jolt of energy grazed his insides. Caine destroyed the light, the sound of broken glass echoing through the trees.

Violet's eyes were frantic. She had pressed herself closer to him in some futile attempt to get away from the dark.

He recreated the light, illuminating her concerned expression.

"Are you okay?" she asked.

A chuckle slipped from him. "I'm fine. We should go back."

She still walked close to him, gripping his coat when an animal ran through the bushes.

Everyone was already tucked away in their rooms when they arrived. Felix had known where Caine was going, anyway. Violet said goodnight, still searching his face for whatever she thought was wrong.

Caine watched her closed door for a few seconds. His hands still shook as he turned away.

Alice

ALICE HOISTED herself up on the desk in front of Caine, turning so the sunlight streaming into Felix's study wasn't blinding her.

Caine was going through their bags, meticulously lining up little vials. "Did you talk to Violet about leaving?" he asked, wrapping a cloth around a bundle and placing it gently in the bag.

"She's all right with it." Alice had expected more of a fight, but Violet had agreed with their reasoning. A "messenger" from the king had already shown up once during their stay. Although they were safely hidden under all three mages' cloaking energies, it wasn't fair to keep intruding on Felix and Holly.

Alice tapped Caine. "Are you okay?"

He nodded. "It's difficult to leave safety."

She slipped off the desk, picking up another pack to occupy herself.

~

THEY RESTED for one last day, waiting until the early hours of the morning to leave.

Holly sat in the living room with Caine, checking over their bags one last time. Felix tossed a small pouch over to them. "Here, in case you need to grow a plant quickly."

Caine grumbled about the bags already being packed but found a place for it anyway.

They crammed as much conversation in as possible, but too

soon, they were standing by the door, Holly going down the line and pulling them each into an embrace.

Alice squeezed her tightly. "Thank you, thank you, thank you."

"You're always welcome here."

Alice couldn't help but smile as Caine hugged his brother, thanking him quietly. Holly reassured Violet that everything was going to be okay and that she would be great. Tears welled up in both their eyes. Alice pulled her cloak's hood over her head, sunlight on their heels as they slipped into the trees.

Chapter Sixteen

Violet

ALTHOUGH IT LACKED its own dining area, the inn's lodgings were more put together than the last. Both were small, but this one had both a bedroom and a living room. Faded floral wallpaper cracked in a few places. Besides that, it was dirt and dust free. Violet had no problem burying herself in the couch.

"Don't get too comfy." Caine took off his cloak and gestured for Violet to do the same.

"Already?" It was barely past noon.

"Yes. You have plenty left to do, sunshine."

Violet sat up, not amused by his mischievous smile as he tried coaxing her over to the table. "No," she protested. "You come over here."

She pulled her legs up, and he took the space next to her.

Alice still had her cloak on. She hovered near the door. "Please don't blow up anything while I'm gone."

Caine waved her away. "Alice, you have no faith in me."

"Of course, sir. I do apologize." She rolled her eyes. "I'll be back."

Violet flinched as Caine made a small incision on his palm. They had moved on to healing magic, and her fear of hurting someone had returned. He healed himself only enough to stop the bleeding and wiped away the rest.

She took his hand in both of hers and ran her finger over the cut. Violet swallowed and tried to focus on what he was telling her. *Imagine the skin healing itself, like everything else.* The word was *Santia.* She would use it the first time for a jump start.

Violet rested her fingers against his wound, letting her electrical hum surface. "*Santia.*"

The spot remained unchanged.

Caine frowned with her. "Try again."

She tried aiming her magic to no avail. "I can feel my energy, but it's not doing anything."

He pulled his hand away. "Take a few minutes, then we can try again."

Alice

ALICE RUSHED UP THE STAIRS, her breaths coming out in pants by the time she made it back to their room. She tried to calm her breathing, but the heaviness lingered in her chest. She could barely open the door. The tremors running through her body made her miss the door handle.

"What's wrong?" Caine asked as she shut the door.

He started to move, but she urged him to sit back down. "Alice?"

She uncurled the newsletter she wished weren't in her clenched hands. Tears were already blurring the words, and she read aloud, "As of two days ago, a house in Bellen Town was completely taken by a fire. Although it is unconfirmed if this was an act of aggression from the king due to—" She paused to take a shaky breath. "Due to the resident being in relation to the former archmage, the fire was magically fueled, and neither Felix Blackwood nor Holly Kappel was able to escape."

Caine took the pamphlet. He scanned the page frantically. Alice waited for him to say something, but he stood up without a word.

"Caine."

"Excuse me."

Alice barely heard the whisper as he walked to the bedroom, clicking the door shut behind him. Alice sat in his spot, tears freely falling. She leaned into Violet, who held her in a sideways embrace.

They had been so careful. There was no way the king had figured out where they were hiding. *Was it Cross? Was his hatred for Caine enough for him to be that cruel?*

She needed to go check on him, but her body wouldn't shift from its hunched position. Alice pulled herself farther onto the couch as Violet left her side to go fiddle with the teakettle in their makeshift kitchen.

Alice lost track of how much time had gone by before she thanked Violet for the cup on the end table. Violet hugged her before picking up a second cup and heading for the bedroom. Alice made an attempt to drink, but every time the cup was in her hands, the liquid inside began to boil.

Alice tried to focus her emotions elsewhere, but all she could see were the faces of her aunt, parents, and sisters—so many people they could target, and she had no safe way to warn them.

Hopefully her family would already be on guard. Caine and Alice's crimes were no longer a secret, and after what happened to Caine's family, they would be even more watchful.

Alice bubbled a bit of the tea in front of her and brought it to a boil, watching it until the liquid was nothing more than steam.

Violet came back and sat next to her. "He wouldn't talk to me."

Alice shook her head. "He won't."

Violet let out a deep breath. Her face was red, but she wasn't crying. "I'm so sorry. I didn't know them that long, but they were family to you guys. I know that's not easy."

Her voice caught, and Alice's heart sank more. Violet had found out recently what it was like to be separated from family. Maybe they weren't dead, but the feeling had to be there.

Alice tried again not to picture her loved ones trapped in fire.

"Are you worried about your family?" Violet asked, as if reading Alice's thoughts.

"Kind of. My immediate family is on the outskirts of the towns. I never interacted with them much after I was hired at the castle, so I don't think the king will go there, but I lived with my aunt right in the capital." She swallowed back a sob. "Do you mind grabbing my sewing kit?" Alice wasn't sure if she could stop shaking enough to hold a needle, but she needed to get away from her own thoughts.

Chapter Seventeen

CAINE SLAMMED his book shut and shoved it to the floor. His temples pounded enough without him trying to focus on the stupid words. He really needed a remedy for his head, but none of their bags had made it to the bedroom, and he wasn't going out. Both of his companions had visited once, and that was enough for him. He continued to ignore the hollow feeling in his stomach.

Is it late enough that they would have gone to sleep already? The sun had set long ago. He would stand by the door and see if he could hear them.

Caine immediately leaned forward onto the bed after rising, spots filling his vision. He waited for someone to knock on the door, but it stayed shut. He moved too soon again and ended up leaning against the wall.

Both women were sound asleep, curled up together on the couch. Maybe he wasn't stumbling around as much as he'd thought.

Caine wandered over to their mini kitchen and cocked his head at the neatly wrapped plate, the cup, and a teensy vial of medicine. A scrap of paper with two little hearts on it lay next to the package.

He folded the paper and slipped it into his pocket. Unsure of how much food he could stomach, Caine took the items back to the room, only pausing to blow out the candle by the couch.

~

CAINE WASN'T sure why he'd even bothered trying to sleep. By the time the sun rose, he was about halfway through his second book. At some point, he'd stopped paying attention to the stories. By the afternoon, he should have gone out, should have made some attempt to train Violet. Instead, he ignored the knock at the door and turned away completely when someone poked her head in.

One. Two. Three. Four. Fi—

"Alice, go away." Despite his dry eyes, Caine couldn't keep his voice from wavering.

"No." Violet sat at the end of the bed.

"Well, like I told her, I'm not going to—"

"How does the necklace work?"

"What?"

"How does it translate?"

That's what she wants to know? "Well… our language comes from Latin—"

"From Latin?"

"Yes. That's why it was so easy to make. I pinpointed the similarity and channeled both languages into the crystal."

"Channeled how?"

"Lexicons of both our languages. We were able to transfer small objects from your world, so I used them to fuel the spell along with another ancient word, sort of." Making sure that their lips wouldn't move out of sync when it translated was an issue too. "It was a long process."

Realization spread across her features. "You stole my dictionary! I thought I was crazy."

"Not me, the previous archmage. Was there something else you wanted?" He couldn't even tell if she was listening. Maybe it was his thoughts that were distant.

Violet pulled herself up next to him. "Why a necklace?"

"No, that's not… Violet." He shook his head. "The stone needed to touch you to work."

"Why not a ring?"

"I didn't have time to do anything but throw a piece of wire and chain around it." He scoffed. "I apologize, sunshine. Next time I'll get you a ring."

Violet chuckled. "I'd probably lose it."

A smile barely touched his lips. "Probably."

His heart lost what little steadiness it had regained when she pressed herself against his side. He wished the action had been as calming as she had meant it to be. At least he had something else to focus on. Caine turned and rested his head on top of hers, and she shifted a little to try to look up at him. She sighed and leaned back again.

"Here," Violet whispered as she took two of his fingers and placed them on her wrist. "Try and match your pulse with mine."

Caine wasn't sure if he ever accomplished that, but he kept her wrist in his hand anyway. She had goosebumps. *Has the room really become that cold?*

Violet

IT DIDN'T TAKE TOO LONG for Caine to fall asleep. Violet shifted only to pull some of the comforter around them. The room was freezing, and his skin was no better, but at least it was starting to warm.

Maybe he was like her when it came to stuff like this. She had only just started getting a full night's sleep, and that was probably due to exhaustion. Their conversation seemed to have calmed him enough. He was passionate about his magic, and it was easy enough to distract him with the topic.

Violet began moving away slowly, but Caine stirred. Not willing to wake him, she reached across for the book he'd been reading. The pale-pink cover and golden lettering looked familiar despite the lack of illustration. Its soft pages and faded words made it obvious it was a well-loved story. It was a light book. She could probably finish it in the next couple of hours if she tried.

The story was miraculously similar to her own situation. A young girl lost her parents and was on a journey to discover her magic. Violet felt her heart tightening as she read. The character wasn't being chased or beaten, but the lost feeling she expressed on the pages was too close.

"Violet?"

She looked up at the sound of Caine's groggy voice. "Hi." She kept her own tone light.

"How long was I asleep?" He searched the wall for a clock.

"Only a few hours."

"Oh." That didn't ease the worry in his eyes.

"I'm hungry. Do you want to go out and get food?" He had to be starving as well.

"Okay. How is Alice doing?"

"She's good."

The other mage had come in to check on them about an hour before.

She looked relieved to see them emerge from the room together. Alice's tears had dried since the night before. Still, Caine stopped before they left, pulling his friend into a long hug, causing Alice to well up again.

The evening air was warmer than Violet had expected, although it might have been due to the lingering cold from Caine. They had to walk a little while to get to the shops. The streets were brightly lit as people bustled around, finishing their business for the evening.

Violet and Caine walked quickly, Violet veering them away from anything that looked like a newsstand. They picked a stall selling pale creamy soup using tiny round squash as bowls and escaped to the forest, unable to get comfortable with so many people.

Caine glanced up. "It's still early."

The moon was somewhere behind the trees, but it couldn't have been any later than nine o'clock.

"Do you want to stay out longer?" he asked.

"It's up to you."

They discarded their bowls and wandered deeper into the woods. Violet attempted to light the path but gave up after the orb flickered out for a third time.

They sat near a small river, although Caine worried about their hearing being obscured by the gushing stream. He played with the water, freezing bits and pieces of it, watching the water build up before letting it go in one torrent.

Violet lifted a few of the rocks and let them splash back

down, allowing the calm humming to engulf her skin. She felt like she had to keep using her energy to prove that she was accomplishing something. It followed her movements whenever she wanted now.

"I had…" Caine ran his thumb over his wrist. "I started feeling like we could get better. I'd hated him. I thought the differences in our magic would always be a barrier, but we talked so much over those two months. I actually hugged him."

He jumped a little, as if his own sob had scared him. Violet squeezed his hand.

"Damn it. I'm sorry. I've never cried like this." A wry laugh escaped through his tears.

Violet stayed quiet, afraid he would go silent again.

Caine tugged at his handkerchief. "I'm sorry."

"Stop apologizing. You can be sad." His misty eyes tugged at her heart. Their amber glow looked dull even in the dark.

He took in another shaky breath. "We should really go back."

"In a moment." Violet sidled closer again, pulling him back to lie on the damp grass. They stared up into the cloudless night as the moon made its way across the sky.

~

ALICE GREETED them when they returned, and Violet left the two on the couch, positioning herself under the bedroom window.

They wouldn't get better in a night. If their enemies were willing to strike down their families without question, then Violet could only imagine who would be next. Even if it wasn't her family, people still didn't deserve to die because of something they had nothing to do with.

Violet despised that she was one of the things stopping Alice and Caine from keeping everyone safe. If she could pick up on her magic faster and leave their world, everything would be fine. For the first time since the news of Felix and Holly's deaths, tears rolled down Violet's cheeks. She shut her eyes, curling herself farther into a ball.

Chapter Eighteen

THE GRASS SQUISHED below their feet as they trekked through a boggy area, the morning fog still lingering. Their trip so far had been a quieter one. Alice hadn't been sure they were ready to travel again. Caine was quick to point out that they couldn't mourn if they were dead.

Violet played with the mist, swirling it as it moved across their path.

Caine watched her warily. "You can't just do the stuff you're good at."

"I'm practicing," Violet said, moving on to freezing it instead.

Alice couldn't place the look on his face, or maybe she didn't want to.

Their student whipped her head to the side suddenly, stumbling back. The water she had been playing with turned into razor-sharp needles.

Alice grabbed her arm as Caine asked, "What happened?"

"You don't feel that?" Violet's voice shook.

"Feel what?" Alice held Violet closer, keeping an eye on the ice shards hanging dangerously close.

Caine melted them. "Watch your energy. There's nothing there."

They continued for another hour before Violet stopped. The plant she had been growing burst into green flames. "I can feel it again."

Caine doused her hands, his jaw clenching.

She looked frantically between him and the trees. "Caine, I swear—"

"Fine, maybe I'm being an ass here," he snapped. "Alice have *you* felt anything?"

Alice shook her head. "Are you sure, Vi?"

"Yes, it's so strong." She faced the woods. "I lost it. It's not there anymore."

Alice stood with Violet, holding her hands and using a calming spell while Caine checked the area. He came back after finding nothing, and Violet looked near to tears.

Their student took a shaky breath. "I'm so—"

Alice cut off her apology, "Don't worry about it." She shot Caine a warning glance, and he thankfully stayed silent.

Alice and Violet walked the rest of the way hand in hand, Violet not bothering with her magic again.

~

"Caine, do we really need to add this to our list of crimes?" Alice asked, pressing a hand to her forehead.

Two more days had gone by since they'd left the last town, and they were craving some type of shelter after being stuck in the woods, but this was not a solution.

Violet was less apprehensive. "Can we get worse than murder?"

Their student had been taking Caine's side more often, but Alice was happy to see them do anything besides be at each other's throats.

He stepped up to the door. "It's only for a few nights. Help me check the entrances."

They were outside a small cottage, dusty lace curtains covered the windows, and intricately painted flowers decorated the peeling yellow siding. It was equal distance between the town they'd just left and the next one, buried amidst thick pine trees. If it weren't for the neatly written note pinned to the door, Alice would have assumed it was abandoned:

PLEASE CONTACT WILLIAM IN MY ABSENCE. WILL RETURN BY THE END OF THE MONTH.

Alice stepped over some overgrowth and ran her hand along the window. "What if they come back?"

"I'm not scared of the idiot who can't bother to put proper locks on their doors and advertises how long they'll be gone," Caine called from the other side of the cottage.

"What are you two doing?"

Violet hung back, and Alice realized she and Caine probably looked crazy feeling up the house.

"Checking for any alarms or seals," Caine answered. "I can't believe there's nothing here. Maybe inside?"

Alice was a bit skeptical, too, but she couldn't sense anything. "We would have felt that from here."

They decided to risk it, and Caine teleported them into the house, unwilling to open any of the doors until they checked within. The house itself was neat enough. Alice relaxed a bit when they confirmed the cottage really was unprotected. She opened a window, airing the musty smell out a bit.

Violet went to bed immediately. Despite Alice's efforts, Violet had stayed uneasy the rest of their trip. She'd stopped voicing it, but Alice could see every time she flinched, eyes darting to the bushes. She hated ignoring Violet's concerns, but she and Caine really couldn't feel whatever it was.

Alice sat with their bags, reorganizing their already-neat supplies. Caine counted their potions and started working on a few healing elixirs. She leaned back as he reached over her for an herb, keeping her focus on the supplies in her lap.

Caine began picking the leaves off a stem. "Alice, you're avoiding me."

Evidently, she wasn't hiding it as well as she'd thought. "Are you okay?"

"We've spoken about that."

"I know. I mean other than that."

They had talked about Felix and Holly. Of course, she still expected him to ache, but he'd stopped being vocal about it after the night they'd talked.

He didn't answer right away, glowering at the floor. "I've been wondering something."

Alice put down the canteen she'd been fidgeting with. "Caine?"

Her stomach twisted at the hostility in his features. "Let's go outside for a minute."

Violet

VIOLET STRETCHED AND SAT UP. Moonlight still lit the room, so she couldn't have been asleep that long. Her vision no longer spun, but hunger gnawed at her stomach.

She panicked when she found the rest of the house empty but quickly spotted Caine and Alice through the window. Neither looked happy, and Violet could have sworn she saw tears glistening in Alice's eyes. Violet continued preparing her food, trying to ignore the few words that drifted in.

"All the support… how close…" Alice was definitely crying.

Violet went back to the bedroom quickly, not wanting to eavesdrop too much.

~

VIOLET JUMPED UP. She looked to the side first, forgetting that she had slept alone that night. Alice occupied the second bedroom, and Caine was on the couch.

She squinted into the dark, barely making out an amber glow. "Caine?"

His voice was raw. "You woke up."

"Yeah. What's wrong?"

Violet screamed as she was thrown out of bed, the sheets ripped off her and tossed to the floor. She could feel magic pressing her back against the wall. Only when he stepped up to her did she see the dagger illuminated by a slight green glow.

She tried to catch her breath, but Caine held the blade up near her throat. The slightest cut would absorb whatever poison it was. He gritted his teeth and pressed the dagger closer. Caine braced it there for a few seconds before his hand fell back down to his side. He took a deep breath, twisting the knife in his hands but not raising it.

Violet pulled herself out of his levitation spell and pushed off the wall, knocking them both onto the ground. Caine lost hold of the weapon as his head hit the floor. She rolled off him quickly, crawling for the knife. She pointed it toward him as soon as it was in her shaky grasp.

Holding up her other hand, Violet forced him against the opposite wall, pinning him there with telekinesis. Caine struggled against her magic, his eyes wide as she tightened her grip and stilled his movement.

"Why?" Violet's voice was as steady as her hand.

Caine gritted his teeth, fighting to pull away from the wall. "Your powers can be transferred through your death."

Violet nearly dropped the blade. "What?"

"That was always the plan—train you until your magic developed enough, and kill you for it."

She stared past his head. "You lied about helping me."

"Your fate would have been to come here anyway. The king wasn't going to let you stay in your world. Alice and I would have trained you at the castle, and who knows what they would have used you for there?"

"So everything you said about finding his plan atrocious… does Alice know?"

He nodded. Of course she did.

Violet's breaths came in shallow gulps. She was slowly losing hold of the knife, her other palm pressed against her chest in some attempt to keep herself calm.

She wasn't going home. The only people who could get her there had never even planned to help her in the first place. Violet's family would be endlessly searching while her body was thrown to the side, deprived of whatever strength she'd been so happy to gain.

Violet aimed a clunky ball of ice at his head before she could process her movement. He cut off the spell holding him to the wall and redirected her attack to the ground. The ice splintered.

He grabbed Violet's arm as she swung it up toward him, and

the knife grazed his shoulder. Caine let her go to check if the poisonous slash had gone any farther than his clothes.

Violet sprinted out of the room and through the front door. She paused at the end of the front yard, hardly putting any distance between herself and the house. The breeze stung her cheeks where tears had streaked down. The cool air made her already-ragged breaths shallow.

She saw no point in running. It wasn't like she could walk home. Violet wept as she sat out in the open. Leaving herself vulnerable, in clear view of the house, wasn't helping, but Violet couldn't decide what action she should take next. Every thought was met with the same issue.

She should have faced the house. She could feel their gazes on her already. Both of them would be coming this time, and she could only catch Caine off guard like that once.

Her throat continued to burn, although Violet wasn't sure if magic or cool air caused it. A bold feeling crossed over her. If Caine wanted her dead, he would kill her. There was no stopping that. At least she felt better knowing she would fight until she died.

"Well, hello."

Violet jumped up. It wasn't their eyes she was feeling. Todrick stood at the end of the clearing. She opened her mouth to call for help, but their names wouldn't come out.

"Where are your friends?" Todrick walked cautiously, his eyes searching as he gripped his blade tighter.

Violet did call out then. At the least, she knew they weren't going to let her die at the hands of someone else.

Todrick moved quickly, tackling Violet. Her fire singed the grass as he grabbed her arms. He tied a leathery pouch around her hands and pulled Violet to a stand.

"Todrick."

Violet wished relief was all she felt when she heard Caine.

"Good evening, Blackwood and Willowflower." Todrick wrapped an arm around Violet's waist and held her against his chest.

"Where's your army?" Caine readied a spell but didn't aim it.

Alice held her blade, flames dancing along the edge.

"Close by."

"You're lying."

Violet wanted them to quit with the nattering, but neither party moved. It wasn't like them to hesitate.

She felt Todrick shrug. "You're not going to hit her."

Violet chuckled. She was being used as a shield.

Alice grimaced at her laughter. Caine only stepped forward and aimed icicles toward her captor's legs. But before he could launch it, a hooded figure appeared in front of him. Caine had to redirect his ice as the person lunged at him. Alice froze.

She started to move toward Caine, but he shouted, "Go for Todrick!"

She ran closer but couldn't aim her blade without hitting the wrong person.

"No!" Violet couldn't stop herself from yelling as Caine's assailant brought down a small ivory dagger.

Todrick seemed a little put out at the newcomer, taking a few steps away from them. It wasn't one of the king's men.

Caine cried out as the attacker pulled their blade from his shoulder.

Alice swung at Todrick's vulnerable side, but the bounty hunter kicked her chest. She dropped to her knees, the fire on her blade flickering out.

Violet screamed and tried to create anything, but whatever was on her hands sent a stinging sensation up her arms. Todrick walked toward the forest, and Violet wished he would finish her. He hadn't been bluffing about the king's men. Two horse-drawn carts and a few dozen soldiers and mages had emerged from the trees. A mage walked up to her, a lavender glow on their fingertips. Violet could do nothing as he pushed the little orb into her neck.

"Violet, don't let them see what magic you have!"

She vaguely recognized Caine's voice as her head swelled, dark spots dancing in her vision. Violet struggled to stay awake, but as Todrick placed her on a wooden cart, her eyes drifted shut.

Chapter Nineteen

AS SUDDENLY AS their new masked attacker appeared, they vanished with no flash of a teleportation spell. Alice held Caine steady as he applied pressure to his wound. Blood stained his clothes too quickly.

She glanced back at the army approaching. King Paskal had learned and made sure to send more than they could handle.

"Our stuff," was all Caine got out.

Alice glanced up at Violet, who lay unconscious in the back of a wagon, Endrel's lunar emblem clearly embellished on its side.

"Alice," Caine hissed.

A mage was already flinging fire toward them.

They hurried back into the house, and Alice placed a seal over the door. Their things were still strewn around from earlier, and they only managed to grab their weapons, cloaks, and one bag before the door slammed open, four mages rushing in with plenty more behind them.

Caine yanked her close, and with a flash, they appeared in

the forest. He gripped Alice, pressing his head into her shoulder. "We're not far enough away." He teetered slightly.

"Flare?" Alice suggested.

As the bird screeched into existence, someone shouted behind them. They barely had time to grab hold as he flew off.

They needed new shelter quickly. Caine had to be conscious for Flare to exist, and Alice wasn't sure how much longer that would last. Alice searched for someplace safe to land, eventually settling on a plateau about ten minutes away. Unless Todrick and the king's men had a similar summon, it would be safe for a little while.

Caine leaned against one of the large rocks, his breath coming in heaves. "It hurts."

Alice cut away the cloth quickly, inspecting his shoulder. Only then did she realize why he was reacting so viscerally to a simple wound.

"Caine, was there a potion on that knife?"

His breath shook as she cleaned the area. "I didn't see anything." There would have been some kind of gleam, like his own dagger.

"It looks poisoned." The normal signs were there—the skin red and swelling, but a strange white glow covered the edges of the torn flesh as well. "I can't tell with what."

He glanced down, his heavy-lidded eyes just as confused.

"*Santia,*" she said, pressing her hand over it. When it remained unchanged, Alice applied an antitoxin, but the white glow wouldn't leave. "I don't think we've ever had to cure something like this."

"And we don't really have the time."

It wasn't only their own safety. Violet could already be in the grasp of King Paskal. They could only hope that she wouldn't be killed outright.

"We have to get to the castle." Caine tried to heal the wound himself, but although the bleeding had stopped, the opening itself would not close.

"How?"

"I don't know! Ugh." He moved too much, and blood started to rise again. "She probably won't even come with us. Who knows what they're going to tell her?"

"Did you tell her anything?"

They'd barely had time to talk between Caine's fiasco of a murder attempt and Violet's scream. After Violet had rushed out, Alice had found Caine still standing in the room. Luckily, the poison had stained nothing but his clothes.

"That she would be in as much danger with the king as she was with us."

"Was?"

"Well… we can't make any decisions until we're back together."

Alice was unconvinced. "You shouldn't have tried anything in the first place. I told you not to act on impulse." She smacked his uninjured shoulder.

"I know." He lay down on the cold stone.

"Go to sleep. I'll wake you if anything happens."

Caine

CAINE JOLTED UP, disoriented as he searched for two pairs of eyes. Only gray ones stared back, ushering him to sleep. He fell in and out of slumber before giving up on resting anymore.

Alice informed him of the soldiers that passed below a few times during the night, but no one had bothered to check their hiding spot. Then again, the king had what he wanted. Their capture would just be an extra victory.

His shoulder hadn't improved by morning. Every movement sent little jolts of pain down his arm. Caine continued to try to pick up on the magic, but nothing lingered on the surface. He drank another antidote on an empty stomach despite its null effects.

The mystery attacker hadn't shown themselves again. Their energy was as concealed as their identity. Caine kept going over the mask in his head—pale wooden mouthless face and hollow black eyes.

They were on foot for the time being. Caine needed to recover for a bit longer before they could make any real strides toward Endrel Castle. He teased Alice gently about her lack of ability to teleport, although the fact that he got the spell right every time was a feat in itself, and it was one of the few energies that did not have a term associated with it.

Any normal conversations they started trailed off too quickly. Alice tried to bring up Violet, but he cut her off before the name even left Alice's mouth. Caine wouldn't know how to answer any questions she had.

They shouldn't have been in their situation in the first place. He could have killed Violet at any point the night before, as she'd unearthed much of her power. Todrick using her as armor meant nothing. It should have been a straight shot through both their chests, but he'd backed off again.

It doesn't matter now, he kept telling himself. *One issue at a time.*

Alice tapped him as a small camp came into view. A fire died down in the center of two tents. A horse whinnied in the distance. They crouched down behind some bushes, not quite prepared to deal with anyone yet, as its hooves got closer.

Caine couldn't pick up anything meaningful from the conversation going on, just regular travelers they didn't need to waste time with. He started pulling Alice in the other direction until a new voice broke in.

"Did you find their location?"

One of the others answered, "Yes, Your Majesty. They're about halfway back and will probably arrive tomorrow morning. As far as we can tell, King Paskal is still not anticipating your arrival."

Cross's voice was clear now. "Good. Let's hope she's not stupid enough to get herself killed yet. And the other two?"

"They seem to have escaped relatively unscathed."

Cross tutted. "That doesn't bode well. No matter. Gather the others, and have them meet us by Habsha City. We'll ride from there."

"At least he's not working with King Paskal," Alice said once the clearing had emptied. "But he's going to get there first."

And that would be the end of it. Cross wouldn't hesitate. He knew Violet had magic even if he'd only seen it when it was still blossoming.

"No, he won't," Caine said. They weren't going to lose to Cross of all people.

Alice threw her arms up. "Caine Blackwood, how do you plan on getting there without them knowing?"

Caine picked up his bag, smiling despite Alice's scowl. "Why be subtle?"

Violet

Violet jumped up, blurry eyes searching around her as quickly as possible.

She was no longer in the tiny cart but instead a covered wagon led by two horses. Todrick as well as two mages sat on the cushions strewn along the back. Whatever conversation they had been having turned to silence as they watched her.

Violet turned away from their degrading stares and played with the restraints that still concealed her hands. Her palms sweated against the leathery material. They hadn't bothered tying her legs, and she wondered what type of reaction she would get from jumping through the wagon's opening. It wasn't like she would die going at their speed.

She pushed away the inane thought and continued twisting her wrists in any attempt to loosen the rope. She was unsure if she could use magic without her hands. She had done it once while fighting Cross and another time with Caine.

Had Caine and Alice gotten captured too? Violet couldn't decide if she cared about their fate. Neither side was helpful to her survival.

She lifted her head to look out the flap behind the driver. A gigantic gray castle loomed in the distance. She tried to take in the surrounding area before they crossed the bridge leading to its giant wooden doors. All she could grasp was that the structure was fairly isolated from the busy town before it and was surrounded by a dense forest.

As they came to a halt, Todrick attempted to help her stand, but she shimmied out of the back and landed hard on her feet. He strode down the path with another guard, and she walked as steadily as possible between them.

The stone walls were lined with blue banners, small moons embroidered along the edges. Two guards stood at attention, nodding to her captors as they passed. She ignored the whispers about the dangerous girl that had caused their poor army so much trouble.

Violet paused at two vibrantly painted pictures at the end of the hall.

One depicted the four members of the royal family, a woman, a man, and a young Cross hugging a girl. The adults looked down at them with loving smiles, their eyes lit up. They were such a sweet-looking family, and yet here she was.

The other painting was a bit smaller despite containing at least ten more people. Violet immediately picked out Caine and Alice, side by side, adorned in a red-and-black mage's cloak and a shawl over a blue dress, respectively. Todrick gave Violet a push, and she didn't have time to get a good look at the rest. She swallowed whatever ache was trying to claw its way up her throat as they continued on.

Despite her efforts, Violet lost track of all the turns along the way, only knowing they hadn't left the ground floor. They slowed in a vast room covered in the same flowing tapestries. Her shoulder brushed some of the thin material drooping down across the middle of the room. They walked up to a throne at the top of the shimmering marble stairs, the sun shining down on them from a glass ceiling.

Both men bowed as they approached a stout man with a crown adorning his head. He watched Violet expectantly, and she almost snorted. She had no respect left for anyone in their world.

The king had gained many more wrinkles along his brow since that painting had been done. Full bronze hair had been replaced with wispy gray. As dull as his eyes were, Violet could still see a brown glow.

He cleared his throat, and the men straightened. "I'd heard you'd accomplished your task, but I had to see for myself."

Todrick bowed his head. "Yes, Your Majesty. Alive and unharmed."

"And the two mages?"

"No, Your Majesty. They escaped before we could subdue them."

The king sighed. "Very well. I'll supply your reward in time. Until then, you're welcome to take a room here."

"Thank you, Your Majesty."

The king dismissed them both, apparently confident he would have no issue leaving Violet unguarded. She was trying to think of any way to prove him wrong. If he was attempting to make her feel more comfortable, it was much too late. Todrick checked her bindings before leaving, pulling the ropes tighter despite her inability to loosen them in the first place.

"Good morning, Miss…"

"Harper," she said, her tone curt.

"Miss Harper. I am King Paskal, ruler of Endrel Kingdom." He led her over to a small table and offered her a chair. "I would like to apologize first."

She wanted to stand as an act of defiance, but her wobbly legs wouldn't allow it.

"I know you've been through a lot."

Violet snickered as he spoke. His calm demeanor faltered for a second before he continued.

"I'm not sure what information our former mages disclosed, but no one here wants to hurt you."

"Send me home, then," Violet said.

He grimaced. "We cannot do that, Miss Harper."

"Well then, you want to hurt me."

"No. Magic is dangerous. We want to help you."

"Yeah, I realized. You all are *very* unsafe." Violet knew she was in no position to keep making jabs, but it was getting hard to keep her mouth shut when everyone acted like they were the heroes.

The king paused, seemingly trying to regain the

conversation. "Have you been able to use your magic, Miss Harper?"

Violet pressed her lips together. Of everything Caine had told her, his last shout was the only thing she truly believed. These people knowing about any magic she had would be a death sentence. He rubbed his fingers together, and Violet searched for any sign of magic between them.

"I would like to make this as easy as possible. All I need to know is if you have magic."

Violet stayed silent again, focusing on keeping herself calm. She didn't know to what extent the material on her hands worked, but she couldn't risk letting emotion trigger her energy.

The king nodded. "Very well." He stood and left the room.

Two mages entered in his place and were quick to grab her arms and yank her out of her seat. The sudden movement made her head spin.

Another maze of hallways and staircases brought them to a musty hall. They stopped in front of a dimly lit alcove where a woman waited. Violet struggled as the mage conjured a purple glow in her palm, but Violet only managed to get her arm twisted. The mages forced her knees onto the rough stone.

Violet gasped for air as a hand closed around her neck, pushing magic into her skin once again.

Chapter Twenty

Violet

THE STONE WALLS around her had become significantly narrower. It was a windowless box big enough for her to stretch out with some space by her feet and head. The only light was from the lone torch on the wall across from her cell.

As Violet used the bars to pull herself up, a pink glow encased her hands. She let go quickly but realized the shimmer had spread around where she sat too. A quick brush against the walls confirmed that the barrier covered the entire enclosure. It didn't hurt. She could reach through the bars all the way up to her elbows. Even outside her cell, the magic coated her skin.

She stretched her fingers, which were no longer constrained by the strange bag. They hadn't even bothered keeping her arms tied. The glow had to be a magical barrier, then. She wasn't willing to test her theory, afraid of who would walk out of the shadows. Violet peeked down each direction of the hallway, but she only saw cracked stone until it was swallowed by darkness. She was tempted to shout but thought better of it. The less time she spent with her newest captors, the better.

Violet kept preparing for tears that never fell. Her stomach was in knots. Her arms and legs ached. She was utterly helpless, and yet her chest was the lightest it had been in months. As stupid as it seemed, it was the first time she'd held a little bit of control over the situation, and it was just enough to keep her alive.

A door squeaked, although she couldn't tell from what direction. Footsteps echoed, sounding like giants were stomping toward the cell. Her heart seized as an ash-skinned man stepped into the light. She noted quickly the red glow of his irises that perfectly matched the many braids that fell onto his shoulders and down his back.

He leered at Violet, a smirk touching his lips. "Good morning."

She'd been knocked out an entire day, maybe more. The only time magic had affected her that long before was when she'd overused her own.

When she didn't answer, he stepped closer to the bars. "I said good morning. Don't act like you don't understand me."

Violet suddenly remembered the chain around her neck, the other thing she should have played ignorant about.

"Morning." The reply fell off her tongue smoothly.

"That's better." His voice was silky, although she couldn't help hearing a sinister edge to it. "You've been out awhile. I apologize." He glanced to the left. "You shouldn't have been so rough with her. I know King Paskal would not be happy to hear that."

The mage from earlier emerged from the shadows. She muttered, "Sorry," and snapped her fingers, causing the pink glow to vanish. The man dismissed her before he pulled out a small key and shoved it between two bars. Violet couldn't see a lock, but the gate parted down the middle.

He pushed on one side, and it swung in. His shoulders drooped as Violet backed away. "I'm sorry. Perhaps I should introduce myself." He bowed before holding out his hand. "Alvin Fogg. Or just Fogg."

Violet took his hand in hers. It was warm to the touch but not clammy. "Harper." She had only introduced herself to King Paskal that way since he'd phrased his question as "miss," but Fogg was going by his last name, and they had been calling Caine and Alice by their surnames too.

He smiled knowingly. "It's a pleasure to meet you, Miss Harper. You must be starving. Care to accompany me to breakfast?"

She waited for him to pull out restraints or to make a threat, but he only stood patiently, waiting for an answer.

"All right." If it meant getting out of her cell.

He seemed pleased and stepped to the side so she could exit. He offered his arm, but she declined the physical contact. Fogg was unfazed though and only asked that she stay close. Violet walked next to him as they left the damp chamber and ascended the stairs.

"Could you please close your eyes for a moment?" he requested.

Violet did as he asked, her heart pounding as he guided her forward. She could feel a foreign energy pass over her but resisted the urge to peek.

After what felt like forever, he removed the hand from her elbow. "You can open them. Thank you."

They were back in the main hallway. *Is there a secret passage to the dungeon, then?*

She recognized the door that led to the throne room, but they moved past it, climbing another few flights of stairs. No one stopped them. People greeted Fogg as if she weren't with him. Many stayed silent, frantically trying to look anywhere else.

They entered a lavish room decorated in swirls of pale blue and green. Fogg directed Violet to a dainty table and pushed in her chair as she sat down.

He made a move to sit but spun around suddenly. "Could you give me one moment, please? I've forgotten to attend to another matter. I will only be a few minutes."

Violet stared at the tablecloth, trying to process the idea that she was alone and unrestrained. It had to be a trap, of course it was, but the door looked so inviting.

Violet kept herself seated and instead got a better grip on her surroundings. She was in what she could only guess was his bedroom. It was the type of room she expected royalty to sleep in, with its lush carpets and lacy drapes.

Another door stood on the other side of the room. The little table sat next to a large bay window. Sliding doors led to a balcony near a plush bed.

Fogg returned shortly, a man behind him with two silver platters covered in various breakfast foods. The server avoided Violet's gaze as he placed the plates on the table.

Fogg sat across from her, muttering a quiet prayer before picking up his fork, something she hadn't seen Caine or Alice do. Although intrigued, Violet kept her questions to herself.

She glanced out the window. She wondered if they were close by or if her original captors had abandoned her altogether.

"What are you thinking about, Miss Harper?"

He gestured to her food, and she dug into an egg, ignoring the thought that poison could be lingering within.

Fogg's gaze stared through her, and only then did she remember he had asked a question. "Um…"

He put a hand up. "Let me apologize again. You must be dreadfully confused. I'll answer any questions you have."

Violet didn't like this option any better. With no idea of how much intel the king's men had gathered, anything she said could be new information.

He sighed. "Maybe not. Would you prefer if I spoke instead?"

She nodded, and he continued.

"Is it your companions you're concerned about?" When she didn't answer, he said, "They aren't the allies you presumed them to be. I promise you that."

It wasn't that she didn't believe him, but she wondered if the people here were any better.

"We do want to help you, Miss Harper. Just tell me what your energy is like so we can teach you better."

Violet tried to ignore the nonsense he spun. She'd heard it already. "Can I go home?"

"Ah, unfortunately the delicate situation makes that impossible." He bowed his head. "I'm sorry."

If everyone was so on her side, she couldn't fathom why they couldn't grant that one request. Violet continued eating, pretending he wasn't there. She had more of an appetite than she'd expected and left only a few odd scraps on the plate.

Fogg led her away. They passed the stairs and entered a room at the opposite end of the hall.

"I'll come back to see you tomorrow. I'm afraid I have duties to attend to for the rest of the day."

It was a simpler version of the breakfast room. It lacked a balcony but had a wall-to-wall window in its place. It was nearly as elegant with its baby-blue decor.

"I'm staying here?" she asked.

"Yes. That cell was only temporary until we could be sure of your safety. We want you to be comfortable." He turned back one last time. "Miss Harper, you must stay in this room. For your own well-being, of course."

Violet gave him a few minutes to vacate the hall and turned the knob, verifying it was unlocked. She retreated to the bed, unwilling to push her limits quite yet.

She had only been awake for a little over an hour, and her eyes were already getting droopy. She pulled the heavy comforter over her head, not seeing any gain in forcing herself to stay awake.

~

Violet closed the curtains halfway so the sunrise's orange glow was no longer blinding her. She'd slept through the day again. The dizziness left from the sleeping magic was gone completely, so hopefully her excessive sleeping was only due to exhaustion.

Violet froze as someone knocked on the door. She let herself breathe when it was only one of the staff, another platter in hand. She sat by the window and picked at her plate. The room was above nothing but endless trees. Still, she stared into them, hoping to see a glint of ice or fire.

She pulled at the window latch, expecting it to be sealed shut, but it opened with plenty of space for her to climb out. Violet could make a mad dash for the exit. If she caused enough havoc, she would probably get out.

But go where? She needed someone who knew about the portal between their worlds.

For the moment, Violet leaned out the window, planning the easiest route down.

Chapter Twenty-One

Violet

THE ROOM WAS AS PRETTY as it was barren, and Violet couldn't use her magic as a source of entertainment without the chance of letting them know she possessed energy. She'd thrown a vase against the wall the next morning to see what their tolerance for her was, but nobody had come running. Violet had wrapped one of the more pointed shards in a cloth and pocketed it.

Afternoon finally brought someone to her door. She barely lifted her head off the table. "Come in."

Violet sat up straighter as a woman closed the door. Her pale-yellow dress swayed against the ground as she strolled up to the window. "You have a nice view from up here." The woman's green eyes, which moved slowly across the trees, had no glow.

Violet tried to place the curly auburn hair. "You're the princess." Violet had met all of the royal family now. Caine had told her about the queens untimely death many years ago.

"Yes. Do you know my name?" When Violet shook her head,

the royal smiled. "Good, we're even, then. I'm Rilla. And you are?"

"Violet," she said without thinking and quickly corrected herself, "but everyone's been calling me Harper, or Miss Harper."

Rilla's shoulders jolted as if she was going to laugh, but no sound followed. "Don't worry. I won't tell. Do you like Fogg?"

Another question so suddenly. "He's a little too friendly," Violet answered.

"He's a charmer." Rilla glanced around suddenly, as if someone had called her. "Can I ask something of you?"

"Maybe."

Rilla's lip twitched up for only a second. "If you do end up in Caine's company again, please tell him I said not to bother. It will only end in death."

"What do you mean?" Violet asked.

The princess ignored Violet, her next sentence coming out in a rush. "Well, it was nice to meet you, Violet."

She held out her hand to shake Rilla's and gasped as a cold object slid down her sleeve.

The princess bowed. "Have a good day, Harper."

Violet retrieved the item from her shirt once she was alone again. It was a thin strip of metal about the width and length of her pointer finger. She leaned toward the window to see the engraving. *First floor, second hall on right from stairs, wall under painting.*

Was that where the dungeon passage was?

The longer she held the item, the more magic she could sense. It was endlessly cold no matter how long it stayed in her hand, but it never became unbearable.

Violet hastily shoved the metal in her pocket as someone knocked again.

"Good afternoon, Miss Harper."

She returned Fogg's vibrant smile with a half-hearted wave. She'd hoped he would leave her alone for lunch, but he had already settled across the table from her.

Once the attendant had delivered their food, Fogg asked, "Oh dear, why the look?"

Violet hated that she could see genuine worry in his eyes. She hoped it was only concern. *Was the princess's visit known?* Rilla hadn't told her to keep quiet about it, but Violet felt her pocket to make sure the metal plate was tucked all the way down.

"I'm bored," was all she could say without simply screaming at him and asking what the hell else he thought was wrong.

"Ah. I'm not being a very good host, am I?" Fogg tapped his fork against the edge of the plate. "Would you like to take a look around the castle? I'm sure you'd like to know the place where you're staying."

Violet agreed without hesitation. Maybe she could find the area where Rilla's plate was directing her to.

"May I ask a question?" Violet decided to push her luck, if he was in such a giving mood.

"Of course."

"Does the king have a portal back to my world?"

Fogg waggled his finger. "Uh-uh. If you want more information, I need something in return."

"Like what?"

"A little magic. Show me anything you can do."

"Of course. I'll need a deck of cards though."

Fogg's triumphant smile was wiped away. "Pardon me?"

"I can do card tricks." Violet had a hard time stopping herself from grinning. *How stupid do these people think I am?* One comfortable night wasn't going to have her at their feet.

Fogg closed his eyes. "Miss Harper…"

"I just want to know who can use it. That's not asking too much, is it?" She let a little desperation slip into her voice, even clasping her hands in front of her. "I don't know who's telling the truth anymore. Can I at least know a little more about that?"

His eyes narrowed, and he focused on the window. "As far as I am aware, the former archmage was the only one who knew the exact details of the connection between our worlds, and he didn't leave any traces of it within the castle."

She would have to figure out how to sneak into Caine's room. He likely wouldn't have left anything out in the open, but it wouldn't hurt to see what else was there.

She tried for a little more prodding. "Is the princess here? I've met His Majesty already." Violet tried not to make a face as she mentioned the king.

"She is." Fogg squinted at her. "You won't see her though, sneaking around with that magic of hers." The last part came out in a hiss.

"What magic?" Violet asked.

"Ah… she gets into places she shouldn't." He let his features rest again. "Not that I am speaking ill of the heir, of course. Now, that's enough questions. Is there something about your magic that you want to tell me?"

Violet shook her head. "Thank you."

Fogg's eyes bore into her. Violet sipped her water, trying to rid her head of the fuzzy feeling.

Their stare down broke as the door swung open, the mage behind it not bothering to knock.

"Well, that's not very polite." Fogg met the woman who kept frantically glancing between Violet and Fogg at the door. The ire in his eyes disappeared at her harsh whisper. He turned back to Violet. "Miss Harper, I do believe we will have to postpone our little tour until later."

"Why?"

"There's an urgent—" He was cut off by someone shouting down the hall. "I must attend to something." He slammed the door shut.

Violet's anxious laughter echoed through the room. She hazarded a guess that it was Caine and Alice causing the sudden commotion. "Took you long enough." Her heart pounded at the thought of coming face-to-face with them again, but if she couldn't convince anyone in the castle to help, then they were still her best bet.

She repeated what Fogg had said about the princess as she approached the washroom door, reaching around to lock it from the outside. No keyhole was visible on the doorknob, but her cell hadn't had one either.

Violet pushed the sliver of metal against the knob. It disappeared into the handle. When it was halfway in, she turned it. The mechanism clicked, and she pushed the door open. She tested it on a locked desk drawer as well, yielding the same results.

Violet tucked the key next to her vase shard. For a moment, she allowed hope to slip into her heart.

Chapter Twenty-Two

Caine

CAINE LOOKED over the map one last time. It wasn't a good plan. In fact, it was probably akin to his idea of kidnapping Violet in the first place.

"I'm all set." Alice put their lone bag near a bush.

They had spent the last day flying on Flare, trying to get as close to the castle as possible. Every town they'd passed over must have been alerted, but it didn't matter. The king had been waiting for them since Violet had been taken.

Both mages had stayed silent as they'd flown over their hometown, landing on the outskirts of the houses. The castle was a half hour's walk from there, although they wouldn't be going on foot. They could already see a few of the familiar towers above the treetops. Caine pulled Alice close. They tested the invisibility spell in front of a town resident before teleporting themselves to the castle.

Caine groaned as they appeared in the lower level of the castle, and he dropped the spells, sliding to sit on the stone ground. Doing both spells at once made his head feel like it was going to split in two. Still, he checked their surroundings to confirm they were in the right place.

They were in the depths of the castle, close to the secret meeting room. Three dungeons resided within the castle walls, two on the east side and one on the west. This one was unknown to most of the castle's residents. If Violet was still alive, that was likely where she would be.

Alice rested her fingers on his temples, soothing the pain slightly. "How are you doing?"

"I think I'm getting sick." He'd noticed yesterday and had hoped it would pass quickly. He would be better in a few days, but this was the time he needed his magic to be the strongest. It was out of his control though. All he could do was push through it.

She patted his head. "Well, let's try to do this quickly, then I'll make you some soup."

He scoffed, surprised at himself for actually looking forward to that.

They only rested for a few minutes before slinking down the candlelit corridor. Alice led the way, adding to the flickering shadows with her own fire.

Every step thundered through the otherwise silent hall, but nobody came charging toward them, and each cell was empty. The king rarely took prisoners, but not even a guard occupied the cramped space.

The other chambers were surely more guarded than the one they were in. They only had one more chance to guess. The east one was above their heads. It would be easiest to take the stairs right up rather than trying to make it across the entire castle.

Alice stopped suddenly as a door swung open, light pouring into the area. They had to decide fast: run the other way or rush whoever was at the end of the hall. Both options certainly meant they would be found, but at least the latter meant they would have one less person on their tails.

The door shut as Alice extinguished the torches. The person at the end seemed oblivious to the overly dark hall, simply pulling out a lantern with a small pink orb floating in the center.

Caine hid the glow of ice behind his back. Frost crept up the wall they pressed against.

"Are you going to…?" Alice started to ask in a hushed voice. "I could tie him up, but he'll come after us eventually."

The blade sat on his hip, but he couldn't bring himself to draw it.

"Is someone there?" the man called, lifting his lantern.

Caine finally gripped the handle of his dagger. It was no time to be sensitive. The man didn't have a chance to scream. Alice regained her flame, and they stepped around his body. Caine cast invisibility on them again as they moved through the secret passageway and up the stairs to the next dungeon.

They peeked through the crack in the door. Only ten people filled the room, split between mages and sword wielders. "There's no way we'll make it through that."

They would have no way to hide once they started. It would be a blitz through the room and the last shot they had. They didn't linger any longer, charging into combat.

Only the first two soldiers were caught off guard, and Caine sent a wave of ice toward them, leaving large gashes along their bodies. Alice deflected fire from another direction, scorching the wall beside her. They sprinted past the next few guards, ducking under swinging blades. Caine paused long enough to send a wall of frost back, and they pressed ahead.

"Call the warden!" someone shouted.

The warden was a brawny man, well versed in both magic

and swordplay. On any other day, Caine wouldn't have worried, but they couldn't afford to deal with that right then.

Only nine more cells. Alice shouted for him to go on while she held back as many as she could. The guards recoiled at the barrier of flames she created.

Caine cursed when he reached the end of the cells. They'd guessed wrong. She wasn't there. Alice caught his exasperated glare. She opened her mouth, but the door behind Caine slammed open. He backed up. The warden had come, and he'd brought more people than they could manage.

Still, Caine held his dagger, switching it between his hands, ultimately deciding on his injured side. He covered the ground ahead with ice, but it was immediately melted by another mage. A few ran past him toward Alice, who was already pointing her sword at two attackers.

Caine eyed the warden, who rushed forward with a broadsword.

Caine switched sides at the last minute. "*Ignitia!*" he yelled, throwing a ball of fire and hoping to catch the other off guard. The warden turned on his heel as he flew past Caine, deflecting the flames and slamming the butt of his blade into Caine's already-injured shoulder.

Caine collapsed, gasping for breath as two people grabbed his arms. He immediately recognized the sticky leather magic blockers around his hands. He combed his memories for when they might have created more of them. As far as he knew, the king had decreed that none except the two Caine himself had created could exist, but these were not the rough leather he had used in a rush to get it done. Smooth cloth caused only a dull throb to course through him as he attempted a spell.

He watched helplessly as Alice's blade crashed against another, her light-rope only tripping her attacker momentarily.

She wasn't faring well, and he had no voice to bring her attention to the air directed toward the back of her legs. She was swept off her feet and fell back into the warden's waiting arms. He wrapped Alice's hands and shoved her down next to Caine. She pressed her head into Caine's shoulder, and he couldn't find it in himself to tell her it was his injured one.

The warden picked up their blades, tossing them in the corner. "His Majesty will be joining us shortly."

Chapter Twenty-Three

Alice

"CAINE? Do me a favor, and don't get us into any more trouble."

He laughed dryly. "Now why would I do something stupid like that?"

A horde of mages and soldiers stood poised around them. The king was away from the castle, and it would be a little while before he arrived. No one seemed willing to move them without his approval, so they sat in the same place as they'd been captured. Unlike Caine, Alice's hands had been tied in the front, and she made herself comfortable, head in his lap, staring up at the ceiling.

She tried not to move her injured leg too much. Someone had glanced at the ripped flesh, but apparently it wasn't bad enough for them to care. Blood wasn't gushing out, but she didn't want to open it more.

Caine saw what she was looking at and glared up at the nearest guard. "You know, His Majesty can't talk to us if we bleed out."

"Suck it up."

Alice sighed. Didn't she just ask him not to—

A mage said, "Maybe we should heal them, at least a little."

The warden cut off whoever else started to speak. "Go on then."

A mage she didn't recognize kneeled beside them. He healed the wound on Alice's leg and another smaller one on her arm before pulling back Caine's blood-soaked sleeve.

"Just stop the bleeding," Caine directed.

The mage frowned. "It looks worse than that."

"Oh please. If you can figure out what's wrong, I'll tell the king personally you can have my old position."

The mage applied a spell, reeling back when it faded into nothing. "Is this from one of us?"

"No."

"Maybe an antitoxin?"

"Doesn't help, nor do the terms."

They flinched as the warden's sword clanged against the bars. "I didn't tell you to socialize."

The mage settled for stopping the bleeding. Alice and Caine thanked him, and the mage went back to his corner, his face red as someone whispered in his ear.

With no clock on the wall, Alice guessed an hour had passed. She wiggled her hands, earning a fierce look from a guard.

No. That was Jane glaring at Alice as she lay battered on the floor. Unlike the ones who had come for them so far, Alice knew many of these people. She'd considered some of them friends, and so far, only one stranger had shown even a little compassion.

She didn't understand how everyone was so sure of the king's word. *Doesn't anyone think about the fact that he'd kept this otherworldly person with magic a secret for so long? That he was still hiding it from his citizens?* The only reason Alice even knew was because of Caine and Sparrow.

She didn't think what Caine planned to do was morally right by any standards, but what their ruler planned to do wasn't any better. *Or did His Majesty create some lie like we did for Violet?*

Alice turned a little, wiping a tear into Caine's pants leg and blinking back the rest. She glanced up, but his eyes were closed. She couldn't tell if he was conscious or not.

Alice lost track of the time until the room collectively bowed. She sat up, nudging Caine as the king stopped in front of them. He ushered all but two mages out of the room, and even they were asked to stay at the far end of the hall. Alice shrank a little under his sorrowful gaze.

"Your Majesty," Caine said without bowing his head.

Alice tried to read Caine's features. They hadn't discussed anything other than getting Violet out, assuming the only other outcome was death, but he always had some plan brewing, and Alice just hoped he wouldn't drag them farther down.

"Blackwood, Miss Willowflower." The king stopped suddenly, sorrow overtaking his features. "I am only here to ask a few questions. I cannot waive the punishment for an infraction of this magnitude." He paused again, but neither mage filled the silence. "Can Miss Harper use any magic?"

"I can't answer that," Caine said.

"Blackwood, don't draw this out more than you need to. Miss Willowflower, please."

Alice pressed her lips together and looked the other away.

The king called back his men. "Take them down to the lower level. Keep them alive until further notice."

The trip was rough. Neither of their escorts seemed to care that they were having a hard enough time sitting up, let alone traveling down the lengthy passageway.

They shoved Caine in one cell and began dragging Alice to another.

"Can we at least stay together?" Alice begged. When they continued pushing, she tried again, her voice cracking, "Please? What harm is there?"

One of them muttered under their breath and thrust her in the cell with Caine.

She gasped and stumbled into a kneel. "Thank you."

Alice shifted to face Caine, and although they were trapped behind bars, he was beaming.

"She's alive," Caine said, "and she hasn't told them."

Optimism bubbled in Alice. No one would die until they had that information. "What about Cross?"

"I think that's the chaos we need."

Violet

Violet checked her pocket one last time for the shard and key. Fogg was due to return anytime. He'd stopped by the previous evening, promising to see her for breakfast.

It had been half a day since the disturbance she assumed was her teachers. If they hadn't made it to her room by then, she would need to be the one to rescue them. Unless they were dead. If not, she would find them and pray she wasn't walking into a swift death from Caine or Alice. She wondered if they were weak enough that she could threaten them into sending her home.

She halted her pacing to answer the knock at the door. "Come in."

"Good morning, Miss Harper," Fogg greeted her, leaving the door ajar. Someone was probably waiting outside, then.

Trying to keep her voice even, she said, "Is everything okay?

What happened yesterday?"

"So curious." Violet stood her ground as he loomed over her. "Actually, that's what I wanted to talk about. Your two friends arrived. It seems they were searching for you."

Violet let the knot in her stomach untwist. "They did?"

"Yes, and it would really make a difference for everyone's safety if you would tell me what magic you have in your possession."

"No."

"Tell me."

Violet denied him again.

"Oh, for Endrel's sake!"

Violet jumped away as the man made a grab for her.

"What is wrong with you?" Fogg bared razor-sharp teeth as he snarled. "I've done everything possible, and I can't crack you. After this long, you should be on your damn knees."

Violet backed away, eyeing the door as she withdrew the vase shard from her pocket. Black smoke poured out of Fogg's jacket. He called someone's name, and a mage came rushing in.

"Hold her down. I refuse to be humiliated like this."

The mage charged forward, an orange glow at his fingertips. She swiped up with the glass, but the mage's hands were too close.

"*Glacitia*." Violet tried to speak too fast, and she screwed up the end of the word. Still, she threw the mage back with a chunk of ice aimed at his stomach. The mage slammed into the wall and fell motionless on the carpet. Two soldiers ran in but backed out of the room the second they saw Fogg.

She expected Fogg to comment on her magic use, but he only growled, "Fine, I'll take care of you myself. As far as the king will know, there was an accident."

Violet didn't wait for him to strike. She launched icicle after icicle, each hitting their target as she shouted the term over and over. Many of the words twisted on her tongue, but her sternum pounded when they hit Fogg, the ice sharp enough to pierce right through.

He looked over the shards, shrugging and yanking them out. Fogg's tone was calm, as if there weren't gaping holes across his body. "You're going to have to hit harder than that, Miss Harper."

"*Glacitia.*" She threw an ice ball large enough to make him stumble and ran out of the room, clinging to her vase shank. She sputtered as she pulled some of his smoky magic into her lungs, adding to the pain already flaring up in her chest.

Violet sprinted down the hall. She took the steps down four at a time until she reached the main floor. That had been her end goal, but she hadn't expected to have him chasing her. She ducked into a large doorway barely out of reach of Fogg's now-clawed hand.

She threw the door shut, using the weak sealing spell Alice had shown her. "*Sigilltia.*" The wood near the handle was already bulging, smoke seeping under the door.

Violet dashed to the other side of the room, but a guard intercepted her.

"She's escaped!" he shouted.

He grabbed her arms, but the door gave way behind them, and Fogg stalked forward. The guard pulled Violet with him. "Go, go, go!"

They sprinted down the hall, avoiding plumes of smoke that raced past their heads. According to Rilla's key, it still wasn't the direction Violet needed to go, but they didn't have other options. The man called for help into empty halls.

Fogg caught up to them as they came to a locked door. The guard's shaking hands were unable to pick the right key.

Shoving the keys back in his pocket, he drew his sword and pushed Violet behind him. She kept her own key gripped tightly in her hand. She didn't want to use it in front of them.

"You dare block me?" Smog overtook Fogg's body. A giant smoky figure towered over them. The only recognizable feature was his ruby eyes glaring down. He wrapped the soldier in smoke. "Stand down."

The guard dropped his sword and lay on the ground.

Violet felt for Fogg's energy, pushing away the smoke with a gust of air before it could surround her. She could make out some of his body again and aimed more ice. He deflected it this time with his vapor projectiles.

She created a frozen dome around him. It was already cracking, but Violet had enough time to unlock the door. She threw some frost behind her, ignoring the pain cramping her sternum. Hopefully he would think she'd run back the way they'd come.

Although no guards blocked her path, Violet stayed close to the walls, peeking around the corner before sprinting down another hall. She became more panicked with every echoing step, fearful that everyone was waiting in one place to ambush her.

Without a sense of where she was, Violet hoped she would find her destination by chance. She turned down another hall, waiting for two guards to pass through before continuing.

She gasped as someone whispered close to her ear, "Left down this next hall will take you to the stairs. The directions should be clear from that point. I trust you've figured out how to use the key?"

Violet spun around, recognizing the princess's soft voice but not seeing her. "Yes."

"Hurry then." A hand brushed her shoulder, and Rilla

appeared beside her. "You cannot be seen or heard. The spell will only last for five minutes."

"Thank you. The portal—"

"You must ask the mages. I'm sorry I cannot accompany you any farther." Rilla was already turning away. "Good luck."

Violet ran where Rilla had directed, coming to the stairs. A handful of frazzled guards raced by, but true to the princess's words, Violet went unnoticed.

Within a few minutes, she stood below the painting, and Violet pushed her key through the wall. She hurried through the gap that opened, waiting for a second to make sure the wall closed behind her. Her footsteps were silent going down the stairs, the sound returning once she made it to the landing. Rilla's spell had worn off then.

Violet glanced into every cell she passed. Pausing just before the last one, she inhaled deeply and stepped in front of it. Caine and Alice jumped up as she came into view.

"Violet," Alice breathed.

Although relief showed in his eyes, Caine grimaced.

The key twisted in her fingers, but Violet decided to let them out before asking any questions. If they were going to kill her, they would likely lie about it just to be freed anyway. The bars parted to the key easily, but the magic barrier remained. Violet eyed it for a moment before pushing her palm into it. Both mages looked fearful, but she didn't flinch. After a few seconds, the pink fizzled out.

"Did you break that with your hand?" Alice asked at the same time Caine said, "That didn't hurt?"

"No. You said as long as I found the energy to do it, it was possible." Violet shrugged, backing away as she formed a fireball in her hand. "Are—"

Caine cut her off. "Unless it has to do with us escaping, shut it. You can yell at me later."

"Are you going to kill me?" Violet asked.

"I'm going to if you don't shut up and walk."

She stood her ground, watching their hands for magic. "Give me a straight answer."

"No, Violet, we're not going to kill you. Don't you think if I still wanted you dead, you would be dead by now?"

Violet kept the fire in her hands. She would have to trust them. "Do you have a plan to get out?" She didn't know why she asked. Of course he did.

"Cross should be here by now," Caine said.

"Is that a good thing?" Violet asked as they started toward the exit, Alice leading the way.

"The king will be busy with his son's homecoming," Caine answered. "That should be enough of a distraction to escape."

"And Fogg's running around too. He went berserk suddenly," Violet added, dismissing her magic.

Both mages paused. "You met Fogg?"

When Violet nodded, Caine tensed. "Did you tell him anything?"

"No. Why would I? I only showed him one element and a term, but only in self-defense."

He chuckled. "Well, that's why he's mad. I'm sure being unable to delude a human didn't help his ego."

"He's a siren," Alice clarified. "His magic allows him to make people do and say things they normally wouldn't. Caine and I have always used our energy to block him."

That's what they sent him to do? He was supposed to manipulate Violet into giving herself up to them. Violet hadn't trusted his kind words, but she shuddered at what might have happened if she hadn't unconsciously prevented his attempts.

As they got to the top of the stairs, Caine said, "All right. We just need to make it outside and get on Flare. I wish I could teleport out, but I don't have the energy right now."

He ran his hand over the wall, and they stepped into one of the main halls.

They had more than just distractions. Fire flew against the walls as a sword sliced through a man's neck. Blood dripped down the other's blade before it was covered in a sheet of ice. A mage used telekinesis to wrap a castle banner around someone's neck. A handful of people shouted unknown terms. A few tried to rush at them but were drawn back into the chaotic battle before they could reach the trio. Violet assumed some were Cross's soldiers, but she had no way of telling.

They used the cover of the battle to sprint around the edge of the hall. Violet stepped over bloodied bodies, trying to ignore the people who still groaned and twitched. Only one man stood checking his own wounds at the end of the room.

Caine approached him. "Hi, Brady. Do you know where our weapons are?"

Brady drew his sword, standing up on wobbly legs.

Caine smiled as he played with a sharp icicle. "Are you sure?"

The wide-eyed guard lowered his sword and led them down some of the emptier hallways. He slowed as another person ran past, but Caine clicked his tongue.

"You're dawdling."

The guard picked up his pace, not stopping again until they made it to the room with their supplies. Brady slid to the ground, holding his injured arm, his breath coming out in huffs.

They donned their cloaks, keeping the hoods down for the time being. Alice paused as she handed one to Violet but quickly let go and turned back to the door.

Violet pulled a knife and sheath around her hip and

discarded the vase shard. Caine threw a healing potion to Brady before stepping into the hall with them.

The next room only held a few pairs of soldiers locked in battle. A mage broke away and hurled stones in their direction. Caine wrapped the mage in ice, and the rocks tumbled to the ground.

Violet found herself stepping back, letting Alice and Caine attack despite her own magic tickling her fingertips. The pain had already left her chest, but she didn't want to push herself to the point of passing out.

Alice reached for the door, but a bolt of lightning shot down in front of the exit.

Cross strode into the room. "I'm getting tired of this."

"Caine, leave with Violet," Alice said, facing the prince.

The ice Caine had prepared flickered out. "What?"

Alice's own fire grew as she hissed, "Go. We don't have time!"

A bolt of lightning flashed past their heads. Caine shuddered a little, but he was already moving toward the door, Violet close behind him. They glanced back one last time as Alice lunged at Cross.

Chapter Twenty-Four

A FEW GUARDS trailed behind Cross, swords drawn to block Alice's attack on the prince. She pushed them back with a surge of fire. Cross only brushed the flames off himself, letting his men flail.

He waited patiently as she detained the remaining two. "Caine's always sending you to fight his battles."

Alice's hair stood on end as he grew closer.

"Have you forgotten my offer?"

Alice stumbled back.

Cross cackled. "I wonder how much you thought about it. The last four months have been a bit rough, but I'm still willing to take a yes."

She stared at his outstretched hand, the same as before. "This is a waste of time, Your Highness. Thank you though."

"Wrong answer, Willowflower," Cross spat.

"*Ignitia!*" Alice conjured all the fire she could muster, letting it crawl up the walls, a singed tapestry fluttering down behind her.

Lightning cracked down, and Alice redirected it at the prince, missing his head and hitting the window behind him.

Alice drew her sword as Cross cleared the fire in his path, gathering it up to bring down on her head.

She put her hand up and let the flames curve around her. *"Ignitia!"*

The giant blast hit Cross's chest, and he flew back. Alice turned and darted through the door. She needed to put distance between them. She might have knocked him down, but she was sure Cross would have protected himself from the fire and would be chasing her any second.

Alice pushed past a guard. He yelled for her to stop, but she could hear lightning crash in the distance. *Good.* Cross was distracted. The fastest way was through the courtyard. Alice snuck through the glass door and sprinted across the field.

Caine

CAINE'S LUNGS BURNED, and Violet's labored breathing accompanied his own. They traveled through as many secret passages as possible, but most of them were contained in the center of the castle. Only a couple more halls remained anyway.

They ran into a handful of people who made half-hearted attempts to halt them. Everyone's focus was on the destruction happening in the east wing. He almost wanted to thank Cross for commanding such a large siege on the castle.

He tried to keep his mind off Alice, but all he saw was his friend on the floor, electricity pulsing through her corpse. He bumped into Violet's back as she stopped suddenly.

Todrick blocked the next door, a hawk perched on his shoulder. "The king said he'd double my payment to recapture the traitors."

Caine sent an icicle flying toward the bounty hunter by the end of his sentence. He sidestepped the attack. His bird flew out of the way as Caine sent a smaller one toward the creature.

Violet yanked Caine to the side suddenly.

"Hey!" he yelled at her, but an orange light flashed over his head.

He stared back at the masked attacker. He wondered how that person had followed them all the way to the castle without him or Alice realizing it. The mystery attacker didn't hesitate, lunging for Caine, the same bone knife raised and aimed for his heart.

He shot ice, but the person only sent it back with a flash of blue. Fire, air, frost, it all reflected at Caine. He grabbed his dagger and glanced at Violet and Todrick.

The bounty hunter caught his eye and laughed. "I just need to capture one of you alive."

Violet only dodged Todrick's blade, no magic leaving her hands. Caine didn't know what to tell her, and he didn't have time. The masked mage was set on stabbing Caine anywhere they saw an opening, and their magic was too potent for him to receive even a small scratch.

Caine shot what little ice he could toward Todrick, but it fell uselessly to the ground.

Violet

IF THE BOUNTY hunter got any closer, that would be the end of it. She would be right back in a cell. But Caine and Alice's blood would surely be splattered on the walls before they got another chance to escape.

Violet couldn't see herself living much longer either. With her magic no longer hidden, there was no buffer between her and the crown. They had everything in their grasp. The king was probably sitting up in his room, shouting orders and promising people rewards just to have her back under his damn foot.

Violet barreled toward Todrick, raising him above her with levitation and letting him slam back to the ground. Talons dug into Violet's back, and she waved a fiery palm at his summon. The bird wouldn't budge despite the flame clinging to its feathers.

Todrick managed to stand, but Violet leapt on him. She grabbed his coat, the fabric singeing under her hands. Her added weight sent him tumbling back into an ice patch that had crept off Caine's fallen icicle.

He swiped his hand up, knocking the blade out of her hand. Violet grabbed it with telekinesis before it could hit the ground. She let the knife hover above her hand for a moment before shooting it forward. It moved too fast for Todrick to dodge, implanting itself in his neck.

Violet's shriek almost matched his as she took hold of it, dragging the knife through his throat. Claws no longer ravaged her back as his summon disappeared.

Blood poured from the wound, some making it onto her face, but Todrick was still gasping for breath. Violet stared down at the knife sitting in the ragged flesh. She needed it. Caine was still struggling behind her.

Her stomach tightened as she felt the blade leave Todrick's skin. She only pulled it partially out before abandoning the task altogether. Violet jumped up and grabbed Todrick's sword instead. Even with telekinesis, Violet could only hold the heavy blade high enough to keep the tip from dragging across the ground as she staggered toward them.

Violet redirected a ball of fire back at the masked assailant and hefted the weapon up as high as she could manage. The hidden assailant cursed and extinguished her fire. They raised their hand to throw something else, but Violet swung the sword, and they ducked to the ground instead. The tip of the broadsword's blade crashed down next to their head. Violet met the masked eyes. They twitched as if the assailant were going to make another move, but they disappeared again.

Violet's magic slipped, and the sword fell to the ground, echoing in the silent room. She turned away from Caine as he took a step toward her. He didn't push any farther and walked over to Todrick. She stood alone until her breathing was not as heavy.

Violet kept her gaze away from Todrick's body as Caine handed back her bloody knife.

Only their footsteps beat against the marble floor clear of any blood or bodies. They exited through an archway into a pasture. The forest she had seen from her window was only a few yards in front of them.

Caine called Flare, and they climbed on then paused. Alice wasn't there. *Had she gotten caught on the way? Had she even made it out of Cross's grip?*

Violet kept watching the castle walls, expecting to see magic flying at their heads, but nobody came. She didn't let the thought of leaving without Alice be anything more than an idea. Violet was still furious at them both but couldn't bring herself to mention it.

Caine had to be itching to leave as well. He played with his summon's feathers and said, "If she didn't come this way, then the closest exit to her would have been through the courtyard and into the west wing."

Flare's feathers puffed out, and the bird dragged its talons through the dirt.

"Someone's coming," Caine said.

Violet could see people running toward the archway. "Do you want to look for her?"

Caine nodded, and they flew upward. Violet's head spun, but she trained her eyes on the garden below. A bright-blue spot peeked out between the foliage.

"Caine, I see her, but…"

He followed her gaze. Their comrade was lying on the stone in a puddle of crimson. Two soldiers were already dragging her away. The beat of Flare's wings drew the soldiers' gazes upward, and they started shouting for backup.

Violet wrapped one arm around Caine and buried her hand in Flare's feathers as they sped up, climbing into the air without warning. She lost track of how long they flew. The cold air slapped her face and sent hair into her eyes. She prayed that they wouldn't crash into anything or suddenly fall.

When they finally landed, Violet sat on the ground, trying to stop herself from throwing up to no avail. She pushed herself away and lay down in the grass, hoping the earthy smell would help block out the stench of blood. An ant-like bug crawled over her leg, but she didn't bother to flick it away.

She glanced up as Caine came to sit in front of her. The tears welling in his eyes made Violet notice her own rolling down her cheeks. Violet moved closer and rested her head against his shoulder. He wrapped an arm around her waist, weeping quietly. Whatever bitter feelings she had for him could be put aside, just for a moment.

Chapter Twenty-Five

Cross

CROSS PUSHED OPEN THE DOORS, familiarity washing over him. He wondered how long it had been since he'd walked those halls, into the king's quarters that had been promised to him. It didn't matter anymore. He'd garnered his own kingdom and devoted followers. He was only missing one last piece.

He motioned for the mage he'd brought with him to wait in the doorway as he entered the office.

"You're bringing good news, I'd imagine, since you've decided to let yourself in." The king of Endrel sat behind a desk, his chair facing the window.

Cross itched to swipe the items off the surface with his sword. Instead, he leaned down onto the desk. "Oh, I'm afraid not. I'm sure all three of them are long gone by now. Don't worry. The next time they come here, the result will be much different."

The stupid king had the gall to turn around with a perplexed look plastered on his face.

Cross snickered as it turned to shock. "What? You don't

recognize your own son's voice? Such a shame. Mom would be disappointed." He cupped a hand over his father's mouth.

The mage stepped forward. The king looked at the blue emblem, screaming for help with his eyes. The woman only smiled.

"Anyway." Cross hated to cut it short, but they couldn't have anyone walking in. "Like I said, the traitors will be taken care of, but you won't be here to see it."

The woman was already scorching the desk, setting fire to notes, files, and the king's sleeves. Cross removed his hand from the king's mouth, not remembering when the other one had come up to grip his father's throat.

King Paskal stumbled out of his chair, but the mage was faster. A blood puddle spread across the floor under his frosted body.

Cross laughed until tears rolled down his cheeks. "Help!" he called into the hallway, hiding the last of his smile. "The king's been killed!"

Another one of his soldiers walked in. "I'll pass on the news in a moment. We've caught one of the traitors."

Cross cocked his head. "Who? The archmage?"

"No, his assistant, but she's barely breathing."

He sighed. She wasn't going to be as much fun as Blackwood. Unless… "Keep her alive. I think she might be of some use."

The girl didn't have to be the only test subject.

PART THREE

STORM ONSLAUGHT

Chapter Twenty-Six

Violet

"BY ORDER of His Majesty Cross, I demand you—"

Violet stepped to the side as ice shot past her, crashing into the blue-embroidered guard. She could recite their little speech back to them at this point. The appalled townsfolk were becoming common as well.

Yes, there they were, the king killers in the townsfolks' very city. If only they knew what their newly appointed despot had likely done to get to his position.

This city didn't appear to have received the same shipment of guards as the last two had. She and Caine dashed through houses on foot, only hopping on Flare when they had gotten a distance away.

Violet wished all the flying would cure her fear, but she was still gasping for breath when they came to rest within a cave. She edged back out the opening to collect some firewood while Caine laid out what little supplies they had nabbed. They would last her and Caine for a few days at least.

They were settled before nightfall. She pushed air carrying the campfire smoke away, unable to deal with the familiar smell.

"Caine," Violet called across the cave.

Amber eyes flicked over for a second. "Hm?"

"We have to talk eventually." It had been two days, and the only conversation between them had been necessary for survival and not another word but that.

"Start talking, then."

"Come here."

Caine stared her down as he came to sit across the fire. He started before she could. "You want to go home."

"Yes."

"Well, I want my life back." He cut in again. "But my only friend is dead, and the entirety of Endrel thinks I'm a murderer, so we're both stuck." She opened her mouth, but he waved her off, taking a deep breath. "I've been thinking. Are you going to let me talk?"

Violet pressed her lips shut. It was supposed to be her conversation to lead, but she wanted to know his thoughts. "Fine."

"I know the original plan was a lie, but maybe it could still work. You fix the cloaks, and I'll make the portal."

She nearly accused him of planning to kill her after the cloaks were done, but he had told her plainly the first day they'd escaped that he wanted nothing to do with her magic. Maybe he really did just want to live without Cross's armies on his back. Besides, she had to pick someone to trust, and unfortunately, her only options were Caine or Cross.

"All right." She held out her hand.

He didn't take it. "No blood pact?"

"Would that mean anything?" She would do it if it meant he couldn't go back on his word.

"It's only symbolic. I've broken them."

Violet pulled her hand away as quickly as possible and hoped he would go back to his corner.

Instead, Caine stretched out next to her. "I know the ingredients by heart and where to find them. Everything should be easy to collect except for one root that takes years to ripen. There's some in the castle. I'm not sure we'll find any that are ready in the wild."

"I guess we'll have to try." She shifted away. "You still have to tell me how my magic works, why I have it."

Caine didn't answer, grabbing a piece of wood. He froze, staring at the bark before setting it aflame and tossing it into the fire.

"You owe me that, Caine."

Finally, he said, "I told you nearly the truth. I don't know where your magic came from or how the last archmage found out about it. I do know that any energy you're around, your body attaches to. The longer you stay with us, the more you're able to conjure, but you don't have enough control."

"Is that what you were trying to do when I first got here? Make me lose control?"

"We exposed you to as much magic as possible, even if you weren't conscious of it. I wanted to push you until you used it, calling you names and testing your patience." His lip twitched. "You didn't levitate that chair, I did. We thought you would leave, and we needed to scare you a bit more."

Violet reeled back. Taking a deep breath, she focused her energy on the fire, letting it flare higher. "Alice too?"

His shoulders slumped at her name. "It was…" He sighed. "It was my idea, but she went along with it."

Violet was beginning to think that was how he always grieved. Caine had sobbed the first day, and after that, it was as if nothing had happened. He balked whenever her name slipped out, but that was it. Violet tried not to bring it up regardless.

"So would any of this have happened if you hadn't kidnapped me?" *Or was I doomed from the time I was born?*

"Probably not," he answered. "Unless someone in your world also had magic, and that isn't the case. I don't think you would have ever known you had this kind of energy, and there was no way you would have accidentally used the terms either."

She stared at her hand, feeling the magic that could fly off her fingertips at any second, the same hand that had killed someone only a week ago.

"So, you took me from my home and started up all of this magic in me just so you could kill me? Why not let me practice in my own house, then?"

"We rushed there. The king was getting antsy, and I only had time to make one portal. I should have made two and trained you there, but I was so confident that the cloaks would hide our identities completely. So yes," he continued. "Part of it was because I truly had no idea how destructive your magic would be, especially if you were able to use the terms. Even with the king close to us, I was more comfortable here, where I could get to more materials for potions if need be. And some part of me didn't think it was fair to impose ourselves on your world."

"But killing me was okay?"

"I guess in my head, yeah. And I needed you unstable. You would have been too comfortable there. I wasn't sure if I could trigger your magic if you were relaxed."

Violet forced herself to stay calm, as calm as he was telling her everything with a straight face, as if it were normal.

"Why do… why did you want my magic? You seem powerful already. If it wasn't to help me, then why didn't you leave me for the king?"

Frost appeared at his fingertips. "What?"

She leaned back. "I just wanted to—"

"That is not your business." Caine's face was redder than she'd seen it before.

"Was it to stop the king from getting it or for your own benefit?"

"Both," he said through his teeth.

She stopped pushing him as ice spread out from where his palms pressed against the stone. "I'll keep watch first," Violet said, leaving the fire. As much as she wanted to know, it would be easier to keep peace between them until she could go home.

"You've barely been sleeping."

Violet laughed. "Oh, can you take a guess why?"

"We already talked about this. If I wanted you dead, you'd be dead."

She still watched the entrance, keeping him in her peripheral vision.

"Look, I understand—"

"No, you don't understand." She twisted to face him completely. "Please. When have you gone through this?"

"Fine. But you being sleep-deprived isn't going to do shit for us. Do you prefer death when Cross catches up? At least if I kill you, it'll be in your sleep."

"That was exactly my—" Violet screamed into her hands, trying to keep her magic at bay. She was going to end up hurting him. "Do you realize that you tried to kill me a week ago?"

He shrugged. "I stopped, didn't I?"

"Not really. You still kept fighting."

"You were swinging poison at me. What was I supposed to do?"

"Poison that you had held to my neck! I was a little on edge, if you could imagine."

Caine stared at the fire. "I am sorry for trying to kill you, but like I keep saying, if I still wanted you dead, we wouldn't be talking. I've had the time and the motivation."

"I know!" Violet pressed her palms together, willing her magic to stay put. "And still I rescued you. *I* rescued *you*. So, on top of having to trust you, I *cannot* take you acting like I'm being irrational."

He uncrossed his arms. "All right. Watch first, then."

Caine

CAINE RUBBED the sleep out of his eyes after Violet woke him up. She glared at him but lay down in his place without a word. He pulled his coat around him and sat at the cave entrance. He had yet to properly fix his jacket. Caine had put in a few rough stitches, but with all of his movement, a few of those had already popped. He lit a small candle, but the cave was otherwise covered in shadows. He kept glancing back to ensure Violet's sleeping figure was there.

Their deal was straightforward. He was still having a hard time believing that he was going to open the connection between their worlds once again, but there he sat, making little checkboxes on a new list.

It was a simple set of ingredients for such a complex task. The portal would be done in less than a month, if they were lucky enough to stay alive that long.

It was well known that the rogue archmage, assistant, and captive were the late sovereign's murderers. Caine didn't have to be there to guess that King Paskal's death was not a simple accident, but Cross was the only one left to take the throne.

Princess Rilla was assumed dead as well. Whether the citizens of Endrel believed their new king or not, no town would refuse his demand of excess guards and identity checks. Although all anyone really needed to see was unfamiliar vibrant eyes.

That would be good news for him, eventually. Caine would stay away from his family and hope that Cross wouldn't go after them. He could elaborately fake his and Violet's deaths. They would have to do something explosive enough to justify the lack of bodies, but it could be done.

If she could successfully change the cloaks so that their eyes were camouflaged as well, he would be safe, just a lone, single-energy mage looking for someplace to live. Alone. Caine had gotten the only person he'd genuinely liked and the family member he had restored his relationship with killed. Two people he loved. *For what? Some stupid plan that will never be executed.*

Part of him still considered taking Violet's magic, but it was a hazard for them both to keep her there, and if it wasn't his own goal, at least Alice's wish would come to fruition.

That and Rilla's message. Violet had relayed her conversation soon after they'd escaped. *Tell him I said not to bother. It will only end in death.* Both could only guess at what it meant. Of course his path would lead to death. That was why Violet had originally been brought to their world.

Rilla's message had to have meaning though. She had gone through the trouble of aiding Violet's escape. Caine would heed the princess's warning, grateful that part of the decision had been made by someone else.

~

THEY DIDN'T BOTHER TRYING to enter another town the next morning and continued trudging north.

Caine took a deep breath as if that would alleviate the constant throbbing in his shoulder. He'd done his best to wrap the wound after dousing it in another antitoxin. The gash on his shoulder was still in the last stages of healing. At the rate it was going, it would take another week. At least his sickness seemed to be leaving with the strange magic. Violet had deemed the masked mage Caine's assassin, the person seemingly after him alone.

Violet hissed suddenly. Blood seeped through the cloth she had pushed against her palm and dribbled down her wrist. She was still trying to learn restoration magic, ignoring his warning of practicing on herself.

"Do you want me to heal it?" Caine offered.

He wiped away the blood only to have it bubble up just as quickly. Whatever little nick she had cut into her palm had deepened enough to make his head throb by the time he'd closed it.

Caine barely heard her thank-you. "You're only having such awful results because you're practicing on yourself, and the term will make it worse," he reminded her again. Whether she'd listened, he couldn't tell.

Violet stared into the woods as they paused for water.

"Again?" Caine asked.

"Yes. You still can't feel it?" She drew back as if the force was physically in front of her.

He reached out a little, but nothing jumped out at him. "No. Describe it to me."

"It's dense. I thought I felt the same energy when I was on guard a few nights ago, but it was really brief. Maybe it's nerves again."

Caine focused on the forest for a second before urging her along. "Come on. We have to get someplace secure before nightfall."

As they turned down another path, a horse whinnied in the distance. He and Violet slipped behind a cluster of trees as Caine made them invisible. They stayed crouched until the ensemble passed, Caine nearly toppling over when they felt safe enough to reveal themselves.

"We have to get someplace safer." He took a few gulps of air. "I can't keep this up."

Violet scooted closer, a healing glow flashing on her palm for just a second. "Is anywhere safe?"

"The west edge of Endrel might be."

Some of it had been devastated when King Paskal had tried to fight Cross's separation, but even before that, towns hadn't been established along the west coast. Few houses spotted the land, and the plant life had flourished.

"We can stay out of Cross's grasp and collect the herbs. I just need to rest long enough to keep Flare out."

They both paused to listen, but nothing stirred the forest.

Violet helped him stand. "Let's go tomorrow, then. Hopefully they won't pass through again."

~

THEY HAD no cover other than trees, but it would have to do.

Caine tapped the tip of his blade against the stone in front of him. The night was passing slower than he would have liked. His eyes were heavy, glazing slightly when he focused on one spot for too long. He was supposed to have woken Violet up an hour ago, but Caine liked to think he learned from his mistakes.

As soon as the air shifted behind him, Caine swung around,

swiping his knife. He caught his assassin across the chest. They yelled, the magic on their hands flickering out. Caine swept a gust of wind under their feet and dropped down to press the knife against their throat. The person's hood had slipped off enough that Caine could see the edge of the mask. He flicked it up with his dagger, cutting them under their chin, but Caine could hardly stay upright when he saw the flinty blue eyes staring back at him.

"Hm?" Violet gripped her small weapon despite her half-lidded eyes. She blinked a few times at the other man and said the name that refused to leave Caine's mouth. "Felix?"

Chapter Twenty-Seven

Felix

FELIX PRESSED a hand against his chest, trying to slow the bleeding without dropping the knife. The white glow of his unused magic flashed along its edges.

Caine's gaze was unfocused. He mimicked Violet's question. "Felix?"

"Yes." Maybe if he answered them, they would stop gawking.

"Why—"

"Why what?" Felix spat.

"What are you doing?" Caine whispered.

He might as well answer since he was unable to move without irritating the wound on his chest. "Trying to kill you, Caine. As a thank you for ruining my life and murdering Holly. Everything I'd worked toward burned with the person I loved. I wish I had been home during the fire. There was a magic barrier around the house, and I couldn't help her escape."

Felix gestured to Violet, only then noticing that their group was missing a person. He really didn't like the idea of being cornered if Alice came back. He would have to move fast. Felix ignored the pain in his chest as he lunged forward, knocking Caine back into the dirt before he lost his will to fight altogether. He rolled away as frost swirled around them, but Caine didn't conjure anything more.

"Felix—" Caine started but was cut off as a ring of green light flew at his head.

Felix took a second to glance at Violet. She stood, blade in hand, but made no move toward them. When he turned back, Caine had icicles floating above his hand as he made small steps to the side. Felix weakened the energy of one as it shot toward his legs. He snapped his fingers, jumping to the side and cloaking himself in darkness.

Caine froze as his attack passed through the image Felix had left behind of himself. It would only take a few seconds before his brother realized it was nothing more than light. With that distraction, Felix ran behind Caine and raised his knife again. He created a wall of multicolored fire, pinning Caine between himself and the flames.

Felix gasped as an invisible force threw him back into a tree, and his fire extinguished completely. He tried to stand, but his head spun, forcing him to kneel. He wrapped one arm around his chest, pressing harder as blood coated his arm.

Violet sat down, too, breath coming out in pants.

Felix narrowed his eyes and pointed his knife at his brother. "Caine wants you dead."

"Not anymore," Violet said. "And I need him so I can get home."

Caine dismissed his magic. "I'm sorry."

"What?" Felix gave him a stony stare.

Caine rubbed the brand on his wrist, and Felix's fingers twitched to feel his own. He'd covered it up with both sleeves and magic, fighting most nights not to look at it.

"You know I would never want to hurt you, even unintentionally," Caine said. "Maybe you don't know." He took a shaky breath.

Tears glistened in his eyes. Felix sat up, searching his brother's face for any sign of insincerity. He had only heard Caine say sorry without a sarcastic remark behind it a handful of times, and only one of them had ever been directed toward him.

Caine's shoulders shook in quiet laughter, and Felix felt the urge to stab him again. "What now?"

"You're an awful assassin."

"Yeah, and you're an awful archmage."

"That might be true, but at least I'm doing a little better at accomplishing my goals."

Felix looked up at the sky. When they hadn't been face-to-face, it had felt like killing a stranger, but he struggled to really hurt Caine. Felix's hatred had been slipping the entire time he'd followed the group, and he'd slowly stopped blaming his brother. It had taken a lot just to go through with that last attack.

Even if he could bring himself to do it, he wasn't sure it would bring him any satisfaction. Caine would continue to be his arrogant self all the way to his deathbed, and Holly wouldn't want Felix to become a murderer. She hadn't even known about Caine and Alice's altered intentions. She'd been unaware that Violet wouldn't live through the experience. He, Caine, and Alice had figured it was best to never tell her.

"Where's Alice?" Felix asked. The mage had yet to return.

Both Caine and Violet's faces went solemn.

Caine murmured, "She didn't make it out of the castle with us."

Felix dropped the knife. Holly wasn't the only victim there, and Violet hadn't asked for any of her fate either. He couldn't see how he could be much better than his enemies if he took another life. "I'm so sorry."

"All of this is my fault, but sitting here blaming ourselves isn't going to bring her home or give us our lives back." Caine's eyes flicked down for a second. "Do you want me to heal you?"

Felix shrugged off his cloak. "It's your fault."

"I wouldn't have done it if I'd known it was you." Caine ran his thumb along the gash. "We're collecting the ingredients for the portal now, and Violet's going to fix the cloaks."

Things must have really taken a turn for the worst if Caine was bailing on his plan. Felix leaned back on his palms. The tightness in his chest had eased slightly, and he took a deep breath just to feel it.

Coming back to see his house turned to ash had already been a slice through his heart, but he hadn't been able to get near it to check for Holly's body. Even after coming back at night, the entire town had been on guard waiting, not for him but for Caine and his group to come looking.

The pressure strangled his heart and lungs. Felix had thought the only way to make it leave was to kill the cause of it all. He still ached for Holly but not as fiercely.

Felix placed his knife back in its sheath at his hip, letting the color drain from it first.

Caine had his face in his hands. "I'm so glad you're alive. I really thought I'd killed you. I'm so sorry about Holly."

"Don't cry," Felix said. He hadn't come there to comfort his brother.

"I won't."

"He sobbed enough before anyway," Violet piped in.

"Go back to sleep." Caine shooed her away.

Violet drew her knife again. "No, switch with me."

Felix tried to stand, but Caine motioned for him to stay put. "What?" Felix asked.

"Where are you going?"

"Away."

"You may as well travel with us. Our new king is bound to have you snatched up before you can blink," Caine pointed out.

"I'm not staying here, Caine. I don't want to be around you." Felix was willing to forgive his brother and apologize himself, but to travel together so soon was pushing it.

"At least stay until I get the cloaks perfect so I can give you one. Looking for ingredients should go a little faster with three people."

Felix's energy could hide him well enough, but to turn into another person entirely would be a blessing. He could wait for that.

Felix ignored Caine's smug smile as he lay down next to the remains of their fire.

Caine flinched as he reached for one of their packs. "What did you do to me?" He rolled his shoulder.

Felix tried not to taunt his brother as he removed the remains of his energy from Caine's wound.

"What is your magic anyway?" Caine asked as he healed the rest of his shoulder. "You never told me about this."

"I control light and energy, not just intense fire. Come on, you never tried to figure out why our parents called it spectral magic?" Felix chided. "I begged them not to tell you. It would be one more energy you had to be better at, especially since I'm unable to use the terms."

Of course his brother didn't comment on that. Caine refused to make eye contact.

Felix went on, feeling his magic flare up at his fingertips again. "Being a teacher isn't as time-consuming as being archmage. I had a lot of time to practice. I can't believe that as overblown and powerful as you like to act, you didn't figure it out. Violet did."

"Thanks for healing me," Caine said, lying down again without another word.

Felix did the same, trying to convince himself he could put up with his brother for a month.

Chapter Twenty-Eight

ALICE PINCHED the bottom of her already-singed pants leg, making another small burn and bringing her total up to five. That didn't take into account however many days she had spent passed out on the stone cell floor. She could do nothing about the sharp pains that taunted her stomach.

Am I meant to die here? Alice wished they would execute her, if that was the case.

She'd gotten so close to escaping. Alice had avoided using the hidden tunnels, trying to keep as many people away from Caine and Violet as possible. But as the other door had come into view, searing pain had sliced down her back from an unseen attacker's blade.

Alice had woken up to darkness, not a light present in the dungeon halls. She had been healed and locked up, but she'd seen no sign of the castle's inhabitants, if she was even in her own kingdom. All she could do was tally the days on her pants leg until someone came—or the inevitable finally took her.

Chapter Twenty-Nine

VIOLET GRIPPED Caine's cloak as Felix used his own magic to steady himself on Flare. Cold air sliced past them, branding her cheeks.

"This is going to be a long one, Violet," Caine warned.

They had stopped in a village briefly to pick up supplies and were finally heading west, away from Cross. Their shopping trip had *almost* gone perfectly. If Felix wasn't stuck with them before, the king's men getting a good look at his eyes as they fled town had put him on Cross's target list.

Their flight lasted until sunset. Violet squeezed her eyes shut in another futile attempt to let the sickness pass. All it managed to do was add to the pounding in her head.

She could barely hear Caine over the wind as he said, "Hold on."

Violet tried not to scream as they dipped down, free-falling for what felt like eons. By the time they slowed and landed, all she could do was slide off the bird and lie down. Her skin was chilled from the constant wind. The hours of flight had her breath coming out in heaves.

Felix was frantic beside her, checking Violet's energy. Caine only directed him to their bags, where he retrieved an orange vial. Violet drank quickly, unsure if she would rather have her head spinning or the sharp grassy taste in her mouth.

"I've never had anyone but you get airsick, but it should help." Caine felt for her pulse. Although she thought it was impossibly fast, he pulled away. "Don't move around too much. I don't know what other effects it will have."

"We're kind of conspicuous in an open field, aren't we?" Felix asked, setting his pouch next to Violet's.

"I know. I don't have the energy to keep Flare out," Caine said.

"I can go look for a safer place," Felix offered.

"No, stay with her."

Violet avoided Caine's eyes as he looked her over again before heading into the trees.

Felix fretted over her for a few more minutes, eventually content with throwing a blanket over her shoulders.

The sun was already dipping below the trees. Violet coaxed a small ball of light out from her palm, letting it float between them. It was yellow this time, although she hadn't done anything different.

Caine stepped back into the clearing. "There's a dense forest area where we can hide, although I haven't seen evidence of Cross's troops."

The walk to the bushy alcove was short. The warmth of a fire that soon burned removed the chill from Violet's bones as she drifted to sleep.

~

ANOTHER DAY'S flight brought them to the overgrown shore, and the following morning started leisurely. Although it rested in the back of their minds that someone could burst into their little hideaway at any moment, they took their time preparing for the day. Even though they had plenty to do, none of their party seemed ready to move, whether it was from the long flight or feeling safe for the first time in weeks.

Breakfast was accompanied only by silence. Felix moved to sit with Violet, and he persuaded her to practice his magic again since he was willing to share its full capabilities. They focused on controlling light and color first. As with healing magic, Violet was a little scared of hurting someone while trying to manipulate their energy.

Felix hovered his hand over a rock and moved it away a second later. Violet passed her fingers through the image that was left. It wavered slightly and disappeared after a few moments.

Violet mimicked his movements, trying not to think about it too much. It seemed like whenever she tried a new energy, her brain refused to accept any possibility of doing it. Maybe if he threw the rock at her head, she wouldn't have time to overthink it. Unfortunately, she couldn't manage to duplicate even an outline of the stone. Felix tried explaining it again to no avail.

As he played with a blade of grass, Felix said, "Maybe we can try getting rid of light instead. You bought candles the other day, right, Caine?"

"Yeah." Caine bit the inside of his lip. "I was thinking we could hold a commemoration for Alice and Holly, if you guys wanted to. We already have candles in there if you want to practice with those, but…"

Felix smiled at him. "I think that'd be nice."

Violet agreed. They weren't her family, but even between

training and running for her life, she'd managed to get attached to the strangers in four months.

~

THE MOON and stars shone across the clear sky. Violet helped collect marble-sized stones, which they arranged in a circle, two short purple candles in the center. One flame burned blue, the other a deep orange.

Caine shifted through the herb sprigs in their bags. "Yellow is companionship. Green's adoration. Blue, kinship. Orange, thank you."

Violet took two orange sprigs, playing with the tiny flowers dotted along the stem. Felix picked a green flower and blue leaf, Caine held two blue.

Violet checked for her necklace as Caine spoke quietly, but the translator would not pick up his words. He dropped a leaf on top of each flame. Felix's voice was laden with tears. He trembled through his sentence and added his herbs to the candles. Violet hesitated, words lost on her tongue.

Caine brushed her wrist, his voice wavering as he said, "You don't have to—"

She took his hand. "Thank you both, Alice and Holly, for aiding me in every way you could. I wish the best for you." She burned her flowers. Violet laid her head against Caine, concentrating on his and Felix's untranslated closing words.

The candle flames burned out together.

Chapter Thirty

Alice

ALICE TRIED to stand as one of the king's men unlocked her cell, but she could only pull herself up enough to kneel. The mage with the guard broke the magical barrier and stepped back. She played with a ball of water in one hand and a sleeping spell in the other.

The guard didn't bother to draw his sword as he stopped in front of her. "What were your and the archmage's plans?"

Alice pressed her lips shut. The guard swung his foot around. Alice screamed as it connected with her stomach, knocking her onto her side.

"What were your plans?"

Alice glared up at the guard as she clutched her stomach. Weak or not, she would burn him if his foot got close to her again.

"Fine. I will let His Majesty know about your refusal to cooperate."

Alice took a few gasping breaths and pressed her palm to her chest, praying that it wasn't a broken rib. She didn't have the energy to heal anything more than a bruise. The pain eased a bit. No one was getting any information out of her. She had nothing helpful to tell them anyway.

"Get up," a different mage said.

The man locked two leather cuffs onto Alice's wrists. "The king would like to see you."

Two guards dragged her down the hall and up the stairs. Alice's feet knocked against each step as she struggled to stay upright. She gritted her teeth as her knees hit the wooden floor.

"Good morning, Miss Willowflower."

Alice had meant to keep her head down in protest, but the voice did not belong to the older man she was expecting.

"Why don't you come sit? I'll call for breakfast."

She couldn't move, her chest tightening. *Where's King Paskal?*

"Come now, I don't have all day. Do you need help?"

That made her push herself off the ground. Thin leather restraints still blocked her magic, but at least they were bracelets and not handcuffs. Alice staggered across the room and collapsed into the chair.

"Ah. You don't look so well. Maybe tea to start with." Cross pushed a teacup closer to her side.

Alice picked her head up to look out the window, half expecting a war zone outside, but the sun shone over the blooming spring trees. She picked the cup up with shaky hands.

"What, no thank you?"

Alice met his gleaming yellow eyes for the first time. If she had been raised differently, crude words might have left her mouth. She only sipped her tea.

Cross picked up his own cup. "How rude. I always expect better of you."

Alice barely heard him. *Is the princess gone as well? Or are we in*

Sophonix? She could have sworn the guards were dressed in Endrel's blue.

"Your friends are alive, if you were wondering. Although I don't think they're aware of your state, or maybe they don't care."

Even if they did know, Alice hoped they wouldn't try to come get her. It had gotten them close to death already. "Where are we?"

The tea had soothed her throat significantly. It must have been laced with a healing agent, but she couldn't taste its tang.

"In Endrel Castle." Cross laughed. "Oh, that's right. You missed my coronation."

Alice nearly slammed the cup back onto the table. "Where's King Paskal?"

"Dead, as is my sister. I was so distraught after the traitors murdered my father and did away with my sister. What could I do but take his place and double the efforts to get the disloyal citizens caught?"

Alice nearly threw up the little bit of tea she'd ingested. *Had King Paskal gone down to confront them himself? Would Caine have killed the royal as a means to escape?*

"Oh, the look on your face is delightful! Who do you trust? Me? Or the people who left you to die? Anyway," Cross continued. "That's not why I called you up here. I've been informed of your refusal to talk, but I'll give you one last chance."

Cross came over to her side of the table. "Take my offer. I have given it to you three times now. Why continue to protest? You have nothing else going for you. Blackwood and his little group either don't know you're here or have abandoned you altogether."

She nearly jumped back as he held out his hand. Just the

implications of taking it made her eyes well up. She would always be on Caine's side. They had made it that far. She would let Cross think she was working with him willingly, at least to escape the dungeon. Alice shook his hand, failing to keep tears back.

"That's not enough." Cross pulled out two brass rings, placing one in her shaking palm.

Following his motion, Alice slipped it on, the cool metal burning into her skin as it shrank to fit her pointer finger. She could feel the magic emanating from it, already coursing up her arm.

Chapter Thirty-One

Caine

CAINE SHOVED the needle through the cloth a little harder than he'd meant to, jabbing himself in the thumb. He wasn't completely inept when it came to sewing, but it had been Alice's passion, and he'd always passed those tasks on to her. Caine stuck his finger in his mouth as blood bubbled at the tip. He glared over at Felix, who was laughing at the whole ordeal.

"I should make you do it yourself," Caine said.

Felix reached over. "All right."

"Go away." Caine moved the cloth out of his vicinity. "Search for ingredients."

"When she comes back."

Violet had offered to start collecting some of the ingredients and was searching in the surrounding forest for the flora that made up the bulk of the list.

"One of us should have gone with her," Caine said

The land was devoid of civilization, but that didn't mean Cross's army wouldn't search there as well. Caine had eventually handed over the list once she'd promised to stay within screaming distance.

"She's fine. We haven't seen anyone else here yet, and she has enough energy under her belt at this point, right?"

Caine couldn't be so sure. Picking up on magic and mastering it were two very different things. As much as Violet had learned, she still had little to no control, lashing out with huge bursts of energy only when she was forced to. He barely had an idea of how Violet's world worked, but if magic was nothing more than fiction there, even a little slip-up could ruin her.

It was almost laughable, the thought of her returning as if nothing had changed, but she was making that choice. It was one less thing he had to think about.

Caine matched the cloak up to a finished one. It wasn't perfect, but as long as the glamor spell stuck, its appearance was negligible. He gripped the cloth in his hands, flipping through his notebook past all the scratched-out revisions of the spell. Hopefully he'd tweaked it enough to fix the eyes.

"*Coriutia.*" Caine ducked his head as the cloak flashed a brilliant yellow before returning to burlap. He dropped the cloth, panting.

Felix was shivering beside him, but still he came closer, offering water.

"Put it on," Caine said between breaths. He cursed when he looked up at Felix. The glamour was there, but bright-blue eyes stared back. "I don't understand what I'm doing wrong. Everything works except the eyes."

Caine tried it on himself, but the problem still lingered.

"Can I try?" Felix took the hood in his hands for a few seconds. It shimmered a little, and he slipped it over his shoulders.

Green eyes replaced his blue ones, their shine dulled significantly. Caine laughed a little. "You and that spectral magic. I should have had you do that before."

"I didn't think about it."

Caine's laugh trailed off. "Violet…"

Felix pulled off the hood. "Are you going to tell her?"

"I don't know." That made her end of their deal null. He didn't need her.

"You'd better decide. She's probably coming back soon." Felix tossed the cloak over to him. "I can reverse the effect if you ask, but that's on you."

Caine felt the cloth, barely getting a sense of his brother's magic. "I can't believe…"

Felix played with a little ring of teal light. "You can just say that my energy is impressive. It won't kill you."

"Fine. Your magic is something I've never seen, and it's pretty powerful," Caine added. "But one of us is still archmage."

"Was. And look how long that lasted."

"Five years, which I ended of my own accord."

Felix cooled the ring and sent it toward Caine. "Whatever makes you feel better."

Violet

VIOLET DROPPED her collection by their bags before sitting across from the brothers. A little less than half of the list wasn't bad for their second day. Caine took the paper and looked over the items, checking them off as he did so. She waited for some snide comment about her picking the wrong plants.

He only nodded. "I think that's enough for today."

"Everything's correct?"

"Yes."

Violet cheered quietly, her body aching too much to really celebrate.

Caine's lip twitched at her little noise. He picked up a cloak. A third one had been added to the bunch once again. Caine had Violet try it on, taking it back to place it over his own shoulders. His amber eyes had turned to a dull pink.

"How?" Violet whispered.

Caine gestured to Felix. "Mr. Magic just touched them."

"Okay, once was enough," Felix muttered.

Violet gripped the hem of her tunic. "So that's it, then?"

"No. We're still making the portal."

"You're still going to make it?"

Fixing the cloak had invalidated their agreement. If the cloaks were done, he didn't have a reason to help her. Violet looked for his blade with her eyes, but the sheath wasn't around his waist.

He only nodded. "You're more of a hassle to keep here."

Violet searched his face, but his expression stayed neutral. "Okay."

Felix started for the woods. "I'm going to look for a few more things before it gets dark."

"Thank you for sending me home." Violet tried to make her smile as genuine as possible.

"What other options do I have? I can kill you, or I can keep you alive and we could stay miserable together."

She crossed her arms. "Why not kill me, then? You have what you want." She kept her hand ready in case he decided to use the frost gathering on his jacket. She was pushing him beyond his limits.

"Maybe it's what Rilla said. Alice thought it was because I got too close to you. I did try to be awful and distance myself from you, and that didn't work. I can't bring myself to kill someone

I've spent this much time with. So my new plan is the one I'd originally made up. Any more questions? Or would you like to question the validity of my morals some more, Miss Harper?"

She shook her head, and he mouthed, "Thank you." Caine moved to leave, but he stopped suddenly. "It's not like you really had a choice whether you got to go home or not."

"We made a deal—"

"From the time you were kidnapped, 'no' was never an option for you, sunshine. That's why the portal isn't done. It was never meant to be made again."

Violet's stare bored into his back, but her attention was drawn to the dry brush she was setting aflame. She doused the fire only to feel it flare up again as Caine snickered.

"You might actually be getting the worse end of the deal here. Planning on going home and bringing your body count over one?"

Violet pulled at her braid, grateful that Caine walked away before he saw the tears pricking her eyes.

Her hand slipped into her pocket, but Violet had lost her little paper somewhere along the way. It didn't matter. She was going home. No one was going to get hurt because of it, and that bastard wasn't going to make her think any differently.

Caine

HE MOVED a few yards away from the clearing, but his thoughts nagged him to go back. "Violet—"

She had moved to sit outside their camp and was either ignoring him or too far away to hear. Charred grass marked where she'd once sat.

He kept the apology on his tongue and walked back into the woods.

Chapter Thirty-Two

Felix

FELIX CUPPED a tiny red ring of his magic, trying to combat the chilly pond water.

Violet rubbed her palms together. "You're going in, right?"

He peered into the murky water. It couldn't be that deep, but the temperature made them both hesitate. "We should have made Caine do this. Can you keep the water off me?" Felix asked. "Just lift it a little bit."

"I can try."

Bog root thrived at the bottom of most ponds and lakes. It was always a pain to harvest. The plant's roots buried themselves many feet below the floor. Trying to focus on both excavating the roots and not drowning was sure to bring poor results.

Felix helped Violet push away some of the water as they searched. Lots of plant life covered the floor, but he couldn't identify a single bog root. They moved around the perimeter of the pool until one withering little plant showed itself.

Felix slid down the muddy pond basin. Frigid water splashed

at his ankles, but he didn't ask Violet to move it any more. He sloshed over to the dying plant, kneeling beside it. A little yellow ball formed at the tip of his finger, and he pushed it into the branch.

The brown spots faded back to a pale green. Felix felt along the ground and coaxed the largest root out from where it was buried. He heard Violet gasp as the full stem stretched out of the pond. Felix chopped the end of it off and helped the severed end replant itself again.

He wrapped one end of the root around a tree and let it pull him up. Violet rubbed her sternum as she released the water.

"Thank you," Felix said.

"That's gigantic."

He coiled the root, which made it look more like soggy rope than a plant. Felix hoisted it over his shoulder. They probably wouldn't need that much, but it was a good basis for other potions.

"Wait." Violet lifted another bubble of water. A generously sized fish swam frantically inside the small space. "Is this safe to eat?"

He leaned closer. "It looks like a kalptin. Do you want to catch a few more?"

~

Felix dropped the bundle of roots next to Caine, who glowered at him. "Did you take the entire plant?"

"Hey!" Violet dropped the bag of fish, trying to shoo away a tiny Flare.

The bird continued to peck at her ankle.

"Flare," Felix called the bird over.

It squawked and hopped into his cupped hands.

"Hi there."

The bird squeaked as its flame turned blue. Felix was gleeful as well and changed the flames to purple, much to Flare's delight.

He wondered if Flare remembered doing that years ago the same way he did. Caine had often left his summon to roam the house, and Felix would play little games with the overly energized bird. Strangely enough, he hadn't seen the summon at all during their most recent stay.

Felix let Flare climb down off his hand. The bird nuzzled Felix's leg before hopping over to the fire pit.

Felix prepared the bog root, peeling off its tough cyan skin with a knife and watching Caine and Violet dance around each other as they cooked the fish.

After dining, they laid out what had been collected for the portal.

Caine compared the pile to his list. "We have everything except the omnen, and days of my suffering."

"There's really nothing else that can replace it?" Felix asked as they wrapped the collection back up.

"Nothing with the potency we need. I don't even know where to begin looking."

Everyone went quiet. Although the thought of heading back to Endrel Castle was surely in their minds, no one suggested it.

"What about your house?" Felix asked, remembering the little home Caine had for himself on the outskirts of the city.

"They've probably burned it down by now." Caine shot a panicked glance at Felix.

Felix turned away from his brother, biting the inside of his cheek as images of his own house flashed in his head. He put his hands in his lap, using his magic to cloak the blue fire growing there.

"It wouldn't hurt to look," Violet said as she ran her finger down Flare's back, yanking her hand away before his beak could catch her.

"Going back to the city—"

She cut Caine off. "Is as dangerous as everything else we do. Let's just try."

"If you want to get killed on the way back to town," Caine said, yanking the clasps shut on their pouches, "then sure. We'll go back."

Felix didn't agree either way, though he wished for it to be their last trip.

Chapter Thirty-Three

Alice

ARCHMAGE WAS ONLY a position Alice had wanted before she'd met Caine. Once they'd become friends, she'd been content as his assistant. The two jobs had just as much responsibility and carried nearly the same amount of power, and Caine had treated her as much more than a secretary.

If Cross had asked her a little earlier, when she and Caine could barely stand to be in the same room together, she might have said yes, but Alice had finally settled into her role by the time Cross had offered to make her archmage of his kingdom in the making.

It wasn't a secret that he was planning on leaving his father, but she couldn't figure out why he'd wanted her. Alice had never told anyone except her aunt that she'd even considered it.

Now, an archmage's cloak lay on the bed, fitted for her. Alice had stared at it for the last ten minutes but couldn't pick it up, and she only hoped Cross wouldn't make her wear it.

He had given her directions, but she hadn't really needed them. Caine had always been transparent about what went on in the King's Assembly meetings, including the spells it took to pass through the castle walls.

She stopped before the entrance. *"Cessation."* A calming spell could only do so much, even with added strength.

She arrived last, letting Cross direct her to the seat between himself and Sparrow. Alice avoided the captain's stare.

Cross called the meeting to order. "First I'd like to announce that Miss Willowflower has joined us as archmage."

A few people gasped. Alice refused to acknowledge any of them.

Cross continued, "Of course this isn't knowledge that will leave the castle. Not yet anyway, and I do hope she can help us with the task at hand."

Alice's heart thrummed as she focused on keeping the candles on the wall from flaring up.

She listened intently to Cross's announcements. Violet, Caine, and Felix were all alive. Somehow, she felt better hearing him say it. How they'd managed to evade Cross for so long, she couldn't tell. His army was out in force, scouring every town and forest.

"Miss Willowflower." Cross leaned over so he could look down at her. "If you have anything to add, it would be most appreciated. I'm sure you of all people here should have a better idea of where your comrades are."

A laugh escaped her, and Cross's stare turned cool.

"This is funny?" he asked.

How they were alive, especially Felix for that matter, she didn't know. Nor did she care, as long as it stayed that way. "Do you want an honest answer or a helpful one? I don't know what they're doing. The plan was to either get her out or die trying." And yet she was still stranded there.

Cross's mouth twitched into a smile. "Is he sending her home?"

"I have no idea, Your Majesty."

The rest of the meeting was used for strategizing, which Alice could barely focus on. Cross didn't provide any more information on her friends, and no one was any more helpful than she was, stuttering out suggestions or politely declining an invitation to talk. Alice wanted to do nothing else but drop her head onto the table and cry.

~

ALICE STOOD with everyone else but couldn't bring herself to bow. She knew Cross had to have noticed.

"Willowflower."

"Sorry, I'm out of habit." She bowed only her upper body, never touching her skirt to attempt a curtsey.

Cross chuckled. "That's all right."

The hair on her arms rose, reminding her why she needed to show slight compliance. "Thank you, Your Majesty," Alice said.

The electricity in the air died down, relieved faces following.

As everyone was dismissed, Alice kept her forced smile and asked, "Do you need me for anything?"

"I'll find you if I do."

Alice nearly sprinted back to her bedroom. She sat on the floor, keeping her hands away from herself before she caused any burns. She wasn't sure how long she stayed like that. The knock on her door made her jump up. She went to the table in the corner before responding.

"Sparrow."

The captain waited in the doorway, playing with her ponytail. "Can I come in?"

Alice gestured to the seat in front of her. Sparrow pulled her in for a hug before resting her elbows on the table as she sat across from Alice. "I know a lot has happened, but I'm here if you need me." Sparrow wrung her hands. "You don't have to talk if you don't want to."

Very slowly, Alice explained everything to Sparrow. Nothing she said was a secret to Cross. If he was using Sparrow, it wouldn't have ill effects on her companions.

Sparrow was pretty aware of the situation herself, having received the same information Caine had from the beginning. Cross had been keeping the general close as well, given how friendly the three of them had been.

Alice still couldn't answer the question of what Caine was planning. Cross had said it'd been a week since he'd seen any sign of them. Alice feared that meant Caine had gotten what he wanted and it would be the last they heard of him.

She didn't say all that to Sparrow though, and the other woman didn't ask anymore.

Sparrow had her own horror stories to tell. Living under Cross's rule had everyone on edge doing their jobs. The stress of capturing the "traitors" was ever present. Alice could already feel the constant looming threat of his presence, but she would play along just for the chance to…

"Have you seen Alvin since you arrived?" Sparrow asked.

"No, not since before we left the first time."

"I haven't since you two got captured, and I'm too scared to ask Cross. I hope he's not dead. I know he transmogrified."

"I think Violet pissed him off. He couldn't charm her."

"Yeah, he told me that." Sparrow ran her fingers through her hair. "I knew it was bothering him, but so much was going on that I brushed it off."

"We'll look for him," Alice promised. She and Fogg had

always been cordial coworkers, but Sparrow adored him. The least Alice could do was keep an eye out.

Sparrow caught her playing with the ring, Alice's new habit. "Cross was wearing that."

"We both have one. It's to signify our agreement." That was the only way Alice could put it without vomiting.

"Why?"

"I don't know. I can't take it off." She had Sparrow tug on it. "It's enchanted, but I can't tell with what."

"I don't understand what he's doing. If he really wanted Caine to come, all he would have to do is make it known that you're alive." Sparrow sighed. "I don't know who to turn to anymore. Maybe you guys had the right idea running away with her, or maybe it made things worse." She took Alice's hands in her own. "But right now, I trust you. We'll figure something out. I don't know what, and it'll probably get us killed."

Alice squeezed back gently. "It's no different than my last few months."

"It's getting late," Sparrow murmured.

Alice tugged her up but didn't let go, intertwining their fingers. "Stay the night, then." As childish as it was, Sparrow curling up next to Alice was enough to make her feel like things were going to be okay.

Chapter Thirty-Four

CAINE RAN his hand along Flare's feathers as a silent thank you. He had trained the bird to withstand combat and long flights, but Caine hadn't pushed him to his limits before. They wouldn't have made it nearly as far without the summon.

His other hand rested on Violet's. He was acutely aware of her head pressing into his back, her arm wrapped around his waist. Her voice had been shaking before she'd even boarded Flare, but Caine didn't have a remedy for it. Felix had suggested a calming spell.

With Felix's energy focused on dimming Flare's fire to help them fly during the night, Caine had needed to cast the spell on Violet. He had hoped the need for physical touch would deter Violet, but whatever sickness she felt from being in the air must have trumped that discomfort.

She had provided him solace on multiple occasions. It was only fair he did the same. The spell worked in tandem with their energies and was having an effect on him as well, easing his thoughts of returning to civilization and helping block out images of his cabin's ashes.

Caine knew there wouldn't be a single leaf of omnen there. He couldn't tell if it was hope or blind stupidity that kept him flying. After checking his cabin, they could start scouting the forest he'd originally found it in. It grew in single stalks, but if they were lucky, another could have sprouted in its place. Felix could always help speed along the process. All they needed was a little piece.

And then Violet could go. Caine wished he could say the last couple of days had been easy. The few nights he had been on guard, dagger in hand, Violet asleep only a few feet away.

He had everything he'd wanted from the beginning. Only this ending had a few hiccups. And if one of those issues hadn't been the loss of Alice and Holly's lives, he might have been more inclined to drive the knife through Violet's heart.

He couldn't decide if it was more selfish to take what he'd been going after or to throw it away despite the sacrifices that had been made. Either way, at the moment, shoving Violet off Flare wasn't a viable solution.

They would have to stop soon. His cabin was still half a day's journey away, and all the spells had weakened them considerably. Caine landed in a cave close to the first caverns they'd stayed in. Felix slipped off, and Caine waited for Violet to follow his brother, glancing back when she didn't. He felt for her pulse to make sure she was only asleep. Carefully, he lifted her off and dismissed Flare.

Felix left in search of firewood. Caine laid Violet against the stone ground. As he stood, the sudden jolt of their energy disconnecting woke her. He saw her shiver and pulled a blanket out of one of the packs, tossing it to Violet.

She wrapped the sheet over her shoulders. "Thank you."

He gave her a half-hearted wave.

"No, for flying with me like that. I didn't even feel it."

He refused to meet her gaze. "I'm glad it helped."

~

THE CALMING MAGIC could only do so much as they flew the next afternoon, growing closer to their destination. He could see the little spot from there but couldn't tell from their height if the structure was actually standing.

Caine landed, looking only at the ground. "Is it there?"

Even at their confirmation, he glanced up disbelievingly. His cabin was in one piece.

The inside had been disturbed. The contents were obviously ransacked, every cupboard and drawer thrown open, items from the shelves strewn across the floor. The chest containing his and Alice's cloaks was gone.

But the king's men wouldn't have found anything significant there or in his room in the castle. Any information regarding the magic needed for Violet's capture had been destroyed long before. Even at the request of the king, Caine had given nothing more than vague progress reports. Only he and Alice had had any idea of what was needed past the ingredients, and they would need a capable wordsmith too.

They checked every room for any type of sensor that would alert the castle to their presence. Although the house was clear, they only gave themselves two days there before someone could catch on.

True to his memory, there was no omnen. Sudden rain meant their forest search would have to wait until the following day.

Felix offered to cook, leaving Caine and Violet to occupy

themselves in his study. They started cleaning up, but their ten-minute break turned into an hour. Each sat on either side of Caine's desk. Caine was flipping through an old potion recipe book. Violet seemed content to stare at the raindrops streaming down the windowpane.

The calendar on the corner of the table caught Caine's eye. He flipped to the current month and immediately wished he hadn't when he saw the date.

Violet

VIOLET TWIDDLED Rilla's key between her fingers as she leaned back in her chair. It had stayed safely in her pocket, although they hadn't needed a reason to use its skeleton key ability yet.

"Do you have anything I can unlock?" she asked.

Caine started at her voice. It dawned on her that he'd been humming a vaguely familiar tune to himself. She repeated the question, and he leaned over the desk, running his hand over one of the drawers until it flashed blue.

Violet pushed the metal plate into the keyhole. She tugged out the drawer, and Caine scoffed.

"Can I see that again?" He ran his finger over the key, furrowing his brows.

"What?" Violet asked.

"There's new writing."

She flipped it over. One side still had her own escape information, but the other said, "The eighth tower." She put the key on the desk and asked, "Where is that?"

"We refer to the towers of our castle by number, but Endrel only has five." He got up suddenly and went to the map on his wall. "I wonder how many Sophonix has."

Caine pulled out a large roll of paper from inside a cabinet and flattened it on the ground.

Violet sat beside him and examined the enlarged map of the two kingdoms. The map showed the inner workings of both castles as well as more detailed drawings of each town. Most scenes on the parchment looked printed while some buildings and landmarks were sketched in and noted in cursive.

Endrel's image depicted the exact contents of each floor, including the secret passageways. Cross's castle was not as fleshed out, only describing locations for the throne room and a few bedrooms. It did, however, show nine towers.

"What's in the towers?" Violet asked.

"I've never been," Caine said. "Ours have various rooms. From the sound of it, I think you stayed in one of the lower ones."

"Could Rilla and the king be there?" They weren't sure if the other royals had truly been done away with or if Cross had hidden them, but if the princess had helped them escape, maybe she had preserved her own life as well.

"It's possible." Something passed over his face. "You know what will make it really easy to get that last ingredient from the castle? And who can clear our names completely?"

"You want to go and rescue them to exploit their power."

Caine's devious smile grew. "You're looking at me as if that is the worst idea I've ever had."

"It's just crazy speculation, and there's no way we would get through that alive." If even Caine was concerned about getting into Endrel Castle, Violet couldn't see why Cross's domain would be any better.

Caine held the tip of a pen, letting it glow a searing red before pressing it to the paper. "If I had to guess, one of these is the 'eighth tower.'" He burned two circles over the tallest towers. He continued, "And there's probably a magical barrier around it. I could get through the lower wall…" He wrote a small x at the base of the castle drawing.

Violet couldn't tell if he wanted her to interject her own thoughts. Caine tapped the other side of the pen against his chin, all but ignoring her anyway.

"Let's just walk right in," Violet suggested mockingly. "How strong is Felix's magic?"

He shrugged. "We could. With the number of people Cross brought with him to Endrel, there can't be too many people left in Sophonix."

"I was joking."

He wiggled the pen, making the marks disappear.

~

THEY SHARED their plan over dinner. "I'm disowning you again," Felix said, glancing between the two of them.

"Come on," Caine said to his brother. "Violet's right. What's the harm in trying?"

"Death. We can't just charge in."

"Of course not. We made our mistakes in Endrel, and you can help us this time."

Felix narrowed his eyes at Violet. "Are you really agreeing with this?"

Violet nodded. It was risky, but staying there and searching was dangerous too. It would finally give them the upper hand, and if Rilla was there, Violet wanted to return the favor and rescue her.

Felix shrugged. "It's two to one. When are we leaving?"

Felix

THE RAIN WAS STILL POUNDING against the house as they turned in for the night. Felix stood at the end of Caine's bed, pulling on borrowed nightclothes. He was doing his best to avoid Caine, who was determined to catch Felix's eye as they stretched a new sheet over the mattress. If it weren't so problematic to put them in the same room together, Felix would have asked Violet to switch with him and slept in Alice's bed instead.

Caine gave up on having a face-to-face conversation. "You're not okay with this."

"No, obviously not, but like I said—"

"This isn't a case of being outvoted, but we have to try. You can leave. Take a cloak and go, I won't stop you."

"But then I'm sending you to your deaths." His magic would give them the cover they needed. It wasn't a guarantee they would make it out of Sophonix alive, but he would increase their chances.

"What do you want to do, then?"

"I don't know." Felix had no ideas of his own to offer, but the stakes of their trip kept growing. He had gone from giving Caine shelter to becoming a known criminal. "This doesn't seem like the solution. You don't even know if they're in Cross's castle."

"And I don't know if the plant is still growing here, but if we check tomorrow, and it's not, then what?"

If the royals were in Sophonix, then their plan would turn into a full-blown mutiny Felix didn't want to be a part of. He was always scornful of Caine's hauteur because he was archmage. Learning about the treachery that Caine had gotten himself wrapped up in had made Felix despise it more. And there he was again, stuck between his brother's bullheaded ideas and abandoning his family.

He regretted every day not telling Holly that Violet was

there to die. *Would it have helped?* His tender-hearted fiancée might have let the trio stay even then.

The bitter words were out before Felix could stop them. "This is as insane as what got us here in the first place. Maybe you should have stuck to your original plan."

"So, you're saying I should kill her?"

"I'm just pointing out that you're acting like your morals have completely turned around. People are still dead, and Cross is right behind us."

"Fine." Caine snatched his sheath off the nightstand and held the blade out to him. "You do it, then."

Felix faced him. "What?"

"Go in there and kill her. Because that's all I'm getting from this conversation. Go on and see how easy it is after spending all this time with her." He had stepped closer with every word until the blade sat dangerously between them. "Maybe be a little quieter than I was so you don't have to deal with actually fighting against a near defenseless, defeated—"

"I'm not asking you to kill anyone!" Felix waved his hand, and red fire followed. "You've done plenty of that already."

Caine flinched, stumbling over whatever he was about to say.

"I didn't mean—" Felix started.

"It's fine." Caine slid his dagger back into its sheath. "You're right." There was no satisfaction in his voice.

Caine answered the knock at the door, and Violet stuck her head in.

"I'm sorry." Her voice turned to a whisper. "I can't sleep in her room."

Felix shivered at the sudden change in temperature. Although he was just as tense, his magic didn't affect the air like Caine's, and the room had gotten unbearably cold. "You and

Felix can share my bed, if you'd like. I'll spread something out on the floor."

"I'm not kicking you out of your own bed," Violet said.

"Here." Felix peeled the sheets off Caine's bed. "Let's all lie on the floor. It'll be like when we were kids, right?"

Caine watched him wordlessly as Felix layered blankets with Violet, and eventually he grabbed some extra sheets from the closet. Felix couldn't quite grasp his expression, but the chill in the air had gone completely.

They stretched out onto the makeshift cot, enchanting one of the comforters so it was large enough to share. Felix lay between the two of them, his back to Caine.

He glanced around, only able to see Caine's glowing amber eyes staring back at him.

Felix turned away. "Go to sleep, nosy."

Violet made a little noise but shut her eyes. If Caine was still watching, he didn't know. Felix drifted off to the patter of rain.

Chapter Thirty-Five

FELIX LED THE WAY, Caine unable to dim his light orb any further. Although the glare was no longer reflecting off the thick ocean fog, it was nearly impossible to see more than a foot ahead of them.

The short conversations they'd shared had been as heavy as the air around them. Felix had gone back to his terse exchanges, and Caine had given up on talking to Violet altogether.

Violet had jolted from her sleep, heart racing, every night since they had escaped the castle. The jittery feeling never showed itself when they traveled, as there was at least a slim chance of being able to defend herself.

She couldn't see either of her acquaintances enduring it for much longer. She considered what would happen when Cross eventually swarmed them. Faced with the loss of their lives or hers, the choice was obvious. The only question was if she would be left for Cross, or if Caine would draw the blade himself.

Caine stopped them, focusing his own light on the map.

"Let's try from here."

They would have to use Flare to get across the ocean that churned between the two kingdoms. There were shorter distances, but the way they'd chosen led them straight to the mountains that lay behind Sophonix. It was just a short climb up to the castle from there—unless they got shot out of the air first.

Their flight seemed too brief, nothing except the breeze around them, but Caine was already parting the fog, looking for someplace to land. The castle was close to the shore, embedded in the rocks. The crude stone structure towered over them. They clambered down into a small cave, the morning fog disappearing with the rising sun.

Felix encased two of the cloaks in an orange shimmer. His extra magic would make them completely invisible without Caine needing to expel any energy. Felix would stay there and watch the coast so he could warn them if Cross did return.

"Be safe, please." Caine took half a step toward his brother then turned on his heel and pulled himself out of the opening.

Violet climbed up after him. Only when she put on her own cloak could she see Caine.

They walked a few feet away before he slowed his pace. "He used a lot of energy on those. I don't want to leave him like..."

"We'll be back soon," Violet reassured him.

They hauled themselves up the stones and to the wall below one of the towers. Caine teleported to the other side.

It was just as desolate inside. It might have looked normal with sunlight through the windows, but with only flickering candlelight, the stairs spiraled up into darkness. It was the first time Violet felt like she was really in enemy territory. Of all the people she'd stood against, Cross had held out the longest.

There was a fifty-fifty chance they'd found the correct

tower. If not, it was a long way to the other end.

Not a single guard blocked their way. If the royals really were there, no one was terribly concerned about them leaving. *How is the kingdom functioning without its leader? Has Cross abandoned them with his focus now on Endrel?*

A single wooden door stood past the platform at the top of the stairs. Caine tested the surface and pushed it open. The hinges creaked as it swung into an empty room.

Caine walked over to the lone window. "On to the next." He joined Violet at the door and started to push it shut.

"Wait!"

The princess appeared, jumping up from the wooden bench. She walked hesitantly toward the open door, her shoulders relaxing when Violet removed her hood.

"You did come." Rilla's brows lowered slightly. "But where are your friends?"

Caine

"I'M HERE." He had stepped out again to make sure they were alone. He tugged down his cloak and bowed. "Good morning, Rilla."

"It's nice to see you again, Caine." She glanced out the door. "You're still missing one."

"She's no longer with us," Caine supplied quickly.

Rilla shook her head. "I'm sorry. This went so much further than I expected."

"Where's the king?" Caine saw no sign of the older man.

"Dead, by my brother's hands surely."

"And why aren't you?" Caine asked.

Rilla tilted her head slightly. "You don't sound very happy to see me, Mr. Blackwood."

He hadn't gone into detail with the others about what he was going to say to Rilla, only that he was going to ask for help. Violet was glaring at him but kept quiet.

"It was only a question, Your Highness."

"I'm hiding from Cross. When I realized the nonsense in Endrel was only getting worse, I helped you all escape then left on my own."

The princess had never been too open about her magic, but he'd picked up little rumors here and there of her incredible ability to hide. He'd experienced it to some degree but had never had concrete proof. Her eyes didn't shine in the slightest, but maybe she'd hidden them as well.

"So, you hoped we would come find you?" Caine continued. "That seems rather reckless."

"I suppose it was," Rilla said. "But I also wasn't sure of your intentions, Caine."

Violet flashed the key in her direction. "The second side took a while to show up."

"Yes, I thought maybe I'd messed up the spell, or that you simply didn't understand. I was rather rushed, and I only had so much space."

"Well, of course, as soon as it appeared, we hurried here." Caine leaned against the wall. "Now if only we could get back into Endrel, I could finish recreating the portal for Violet. The last ingredient is in my room there."

"What are you suggesting?"

"Well, you are next in line for the throne. How hard would it be to dethrone Cross?"

"Mr. Blackwood—"

"Of course, that is only a suggestion, but it would be beneficial to us all."

Rilla pointed to the door. "We'll discuss it on the way."

Invisible again, Rilla using her own magic and the other two with their hoods pulled up, they started down the stairs.

After a minute Rilla asked, "What happened? I can see you both again, but your faces have changed."

Violet looked over at Caine, pulling at her cloak. "They went back to normal?"

Caine touched the cloth. He couldn't feel the enchantment anymore. "Felix!"

They rushed down the last flights of stairs, skipping steps until they got to the bottom.

Caine teleported them outside. *Not again.* It was only a handful of Cross's men, but Felix kneeled in front of them, clutching his shirt.

Caine wasn't sure who hit first. His own ice flew as Violet charged at another, a mix of magic on her palms. The two who hadn't been struck down pushed past Rilla, sprinting back toward the castle. Caine made sure they didn't get any farther. He kneeled in front of his brother.

Felix's chest heaved as he said, "I kept the spell up as long as possible."

Caine moved closer and pressed his palm against Felix's back, holding his brother in a half hug. Felix wasn't physically hurt as far as Caine could see.

"We need to leave." Rilla stood next to Violet. "How did you all get here?"

Violet answered when Caine didn't. "We flew over on Caine's summon."

"Fly back, straight across. I'll be right there."

Caine summoned Flare, sandwiching Felix between himself and Violet. He guided the bird directly across the water. He had no idea how Rilla would get across, but there wasn't time.

Felix was unconscious as they moved him onto the grass.

Violet checked for his pulse as Caine hovered over his temple with a healing glow. His brother's breathing had already gone back to normal. "He's okay."

"What about Rilla?" Violet asked.

Caine looked over the cliff. "I don't know. Should I fly back over—"

Violet stared at him as he laughed. Rilla was incredibly close, floating atop a large lime-green jellyfish below.

"Would you like help off your lily pad, Your Highness?" Caine called down.

Rilla introduced the jellyfish as Emerald and suggested they come join her. Caine was doubtful at first, but they had plenty of room to stretch out on the squishy mass.

After reviewing the map, they bobbed off into the ocean, the morning sun creating little glittering jewels in the waves around them. It would be a ways to Endrel, especially at their speed, but between Rilla's summon and her magic, it was the safest option.

Caine sat next to Felix, his eyes squeezed shut. His mind kept flashing between images of Alice and his brother, blood splattered across them both.

Felix groaned and glanced between the three of them, the ocean, and the jellyfish. Caine couldn't tell what he was most concerned about.

"How are you feeling?" Caine handed him a potion.

Felix stretched. "I overworked myself. You know what that's like."

Rilla scooted closer. She had been watching with a quiet smile. "Don't tell me your name. You were never in the castle much, but... Felix?"

He nodded as he lay down again, grimacing as his cheek touched the jellyfish. "Did everything else go well? And what in Endrel are we riding on?"

Chapter Thirty-Six

THERE WERE a few gentle knocks on the wooden doorway in between his study and the bedroom. Alice waited patiently, and he smiled up at her. "Ah, my request did make it in time."

It couldn't have. He'd just finished an afternoon meeting. If anything, this would be her second meal, but with everything going on, he hadn't had time to eat.

Alice curtsied, already an improvement since yesterday. "Good afternoon, Your Majesty."

"A very good afternoon indeed." Cross motioned to the seat across from him.

He kept glancing up, meeting her eyes as an invitation to speak, but she only smiled at her plate and played with a chunk of yam. So chipper, and yet not a word—good or bad—had left her mouth. Perhaps he would have to push her a little more.

Cross froze as she suddenly tapped her ring against his. He felt his bewilderment flash across his face before he could stop it. "Miss Willowflower?"

Alice only blinked back a few times. "Hm?"

He did his best to let his face rest again. "Feeling bold this morning?"

"I'm curious."

He leaned forward. "You must be more specific. I would hate to take your words the wrong way."

Alice giggled. "I think the rings are a little silly. Isn't it a bit much?"

Cross paused. "Well, the enchantment is there for a reason."

She snapped her gaze back to his. "Enchantment?"

"Don't act stupid," he hissed.

Alice ran her thumb over the band. "There's magic in it? I can't feel anything. What kind of enchantment?"

Her questions tumbled out rapidly. Cross hadn't mentioned it to her, but it wasn't to keep it a secret. She was their second-strongest mage. There was no way she couldn't pick up on such robust energy.

"You must have realized it doesn't come off."

She tugged on it, and he did the same, but it only twisted around the base of his finger.

Her voice shook. "I was too afraid to take it off. I assumed—"

She screamed as Cross grabbed her wrists, pulling her to kneel on the carpet.

"Alice Willowflower, you are a very smart woman. So you should know better than to test my patience."

Cross squeezed just enough to leave nail marks in her burning skin. He leaned down so their foreheads pressed together. "Let's try again. Can you feel the enchantment that is so obviously on the rings we wear?"

"No," she spat back. "But thanks for the tip."

Cross scowled and let go as the fire grew on her palms. It had to be a joke. He hadn't gone through all his plotting to have his pawn act like she didn't know her place. But if she really didn't feel it, that part of the plan was out the window. It was fine. Everything was fine. He still had a hook in her.

"Ah." He'd forgotten she still sat on the floor and was fidgeting with something in her pocket. "You're dismissed. Thank you for the company, Miss Willowflower."

She bowed wordlessly and hurried from the room.

Cross wiped some of the condensation off the windows, surprised to see a blood streak. He'd gotten cut without realizing it. Cross entered his office, retrieving a roll of gauze from the desk drawer. He reclined in his chair, reading over the kingdom's briefs as he wrapped the wound.

No one was necessarily happy that the fallen prince had become their new ruler, but that was to be expected. It didn't matter. They had no choice but to believe that he wasn't their enemy, or at least not the biggest issue at the moment. Those *issues* had yet to be neutralized.

Where are they? His army was scouring every town, and yet all he got back were failures. He really didn't want to spread searches out to the edges of the land. It would take too long to carefully search the expansive shores.

He could spare one troop for the time being. Maybe they could catch the group by chance. Even if they didn't, it wasn't too many resources lost.

Cross pulled the cloth from his finger. Breakfast hadn't quite gone the way he'd planned. Perhaps they could try again over dinner.

Alice

ALICE MADE space on her desk, pausing at the sight of a calendar, laughing a little at how much it would have bugged Caine that it was on the wrong month. She flipped to the correct date. *Has it really been four months already since we kidnapped Violet?* Alice's birthday had passed while she was in her cell…

She put the calendar away too.

Alice prepared her workspace to make another attempt at removing the ring from her finger. She worked for about an hour before someone knocked. Alice shoved glowing vials into the drawer. "Come in."

She let her heart rest as Sparrow entered. Cross had been… gifting her with little pointless visits over the last week. He never stayed long, but it happened too often.

Sparrow locked the door. "How's it going?"

"Nothing's reacting." Their plan to rile him up had given Alice a chance to collect some of his blood on tissue when he'd grabbed her. She had tested his blood and hers with everything possible. Nothing had even the slightest reaction. The ring's energy was endlessly hot, but the magic was so foreign. Alice had also tried shape shifting to let Sparrow slip it off. But even when she'd changed into a rabbit, the ring had adjusted its size and locked itself onto her paw. "How about you?"

The captain had been checking in with some of the people who had served King Paskal, in hopes that a schism was rising. "No one is bothering to argue with Cross. I can't really fault them for it, though. People have been talking about…" Sparrow fidgeted with an herb leaf.

"What?"

"You."

"Oh."

"A few people are sympathetic. Most of them are saying that you did this to yourself."

Alice slid down farther in her seat. They were right, in a way.

It was still frustrating to hear, knowing that they didn't have the full story.

"It doesn't matter." She knocked the ring against the table. "Let's focus on this." Maybe she could chip off a piece of the metal and try it that way. Alice picked up a small knife and pressed it against the ring.

She screamed and clutched her shoulders, her body seizing up in that position. That same hot energy from the ring engulfed her skin. As the pain faded, Sparrow yanked the knife out of her hands. Blood warmed her arm and dripped down the side of the chair. She had never let go of the knife and had shoved the blade into her shoulder.

"Alice." Sparrow's voice was dim past the deafening ringing in her ears. She was holding something against the wound. "Alice."

Alice pulled away, pressing a healing spell to her shoulder. The searing pain had only been present for the millisecond the knife had touched the ring, but its energy still lingered. She shivered as the last of it left her body.

Sparrow swiped a cloth over the chair, only managing to smear blood across the wood. Alice left her, silently kneeling next to a basin in the washroom and splashing water up her arm. Pink-tinted water ran down the porcelain sides.

She barely caught Sparrow asking who was at the door followed quickly by, "Your Majesty!"

"Where is Miss Willowflower?" Cross's voice was gravelly.

"I'm in here." Alice didn't know if Sparrow would have tried to lie for her sake, but she wasn't going to let her friend take the brunt of the consequences.

His footsteps stopped at the beginning of the tile floor. "What did you do?"

Alice didn't turn, continuing to splash tepid water on herself. "I was cutting herbs. The knife slipped and hit my ring."

He stared her down in the mirror. The brooding anger that normally lay in his features had been replaced with a slight frown.

Alice toweled off, reviewing each shoulder. She had a thin line on one and little crescent marks from where her nails dug in on the other. She looked Cross up and down, but there was no physical sign of the reaction he'd had.

She politely moved him out the doorway, pausing right before her desk. "Can I help you with anything else, Your Majesty?"

Cross circled his ring with his thumb. "Be careful."

Alice curtsied. "Of course."

~

News traveled through the castle quickly. From what Sparrow had gathered over the last few days, the same pain had knocked Cross to his knees. She and Alice knew the truth, but with their king showing a sudden uncontrollable weakness like that, even his own ranks were part of the gossip.

Alice was gleeful the moment after their incident. Hearing about some kind of backlash against Cross wasn't unwelcome. She was working on potions with new elation, tucking each away neatly, just as before.

Cross held no more power over her than the false title of king he had given himself. And that one truth meant they were leaving. He could tower over her and pretend there was more to their agreement if he wanted. He'd had real fear in his eyes. All Cross had done was give her a lackluster order to be mindful of the ring, and she intended to do that.

Alice planted her hands firmly on the floor and shut her eyes. She was all too aware of Sparrow's knife inching closer.

"Are you ready?" Sparrow asked.

Alice nodded. She readjusted herself only to feel the captain's arms engulf her. A few nervous giggles left her as she returned the hug.

"All right." Sparrow picked up her knife. "I'm sorry in advance." She pressed the edge into the band.

The deliberate attack against the enchantment scorched Alice's limbs. Fire crawled through her veins as she dug her nails into the carpet. They had decided on five seconds, and Alice had meant to count with Sparrow, but any words she'd planned on had been replaced with a silent scream.

Did I black out? Her head was in Sparrow's lap, the other woman clutching her tightly.

"I'm fine, Sparrow." The last of the pain was subsiding, and despite her panting, she stood without nausea.

As Sparrow drew her sword, Alice tugged a leather glove onto her right hand just in case any of the potion splashed back and tested the material to make sure it wouldn't aggravate the band further.

As she popped the cork off a red vial, the door slammed open. Sparks were already flying from Cross's fingers. He chortled. "I think Blackwood rubbed off on you a little too much. You're getting brazen. Now, what did we talk about earlier?"

Lightning obscured Alice's answer. She balled the electricity into one hand, tossing it back in his direction.

Alice whipped her light-rope around his legs. She pulled it tight, but the prince didn't fall as he lifted his hand again. Cross stopped halfway through the motion, lightning dissipating before it could leave his palm. Sparrow leapt forward, slicing

Cross's arm. Whatever control he'd had was gone. Lightning flew toward Alice.

She deflected it and slammed into Cross's upper body as Sparrow swiped at his legs, successfully knocking the man on his back with a heavy thud. She grabbed his arm, dumping red liquid over his finger.

"What are you—"

Sparrow slammed a smaller blade into his bicep, leaving it there as they sprinted for the window.

They slipped down the brick wall, Alice slowing their descent with a torrent of air as the ground approached. Once they landed, Alice lit a small fire, and they sprinted to the stables. The horse Sparrow had prepared was waiting there, stripped of anything marking it as property of Endrel Castle.

If Cross sent anyone after them, they would never know. Alice held Sparrow tightly as they galloped past trees, leaping over rocks and fallen branches.

Chapter Thirty-Seven

Felix

FELIX PEERED into the cloudy water. Even the ocean had lasting effects from their little war. Although he knew it would clear up in a few miles, his skin crawled at the contrast between their lively green float and the gray murk.

Caine kept shifting slightly closer, as if Felix wouldn't notice. Felix warned him with a silent glare before dipping his fingertips into the chilly sea.

Bluish-gray water spread from where his hand bobbed in and out. A lucid trail was beginning to form, and he drew away, some clean water still clinging to him. He flicked it at Caine, scooting away before his brother could shove him off the side.

"I could levitate you off this thing if I really wanted to," Caine threatened.

"So could I," Felix called back.

Violet faced the other way, but her shoulders shook gently.

Felix had worried about the three of them in such a confined space. However, the trip so far had been mostly silent yet not uncomfortable. Caine had apologized to him from the first night they had begun their float, for both yelling at him and nearly getting him killed again. Felix had tried to ease his concern, but Caine looked near to tears, and he couldn't do anything more than accept his brother's apology.

Violet had relaxed a little too. She wasn't really talking to them, but she no longer glared when their gazes met.

Felix wished he could believe they had all really gotten closer again. No one had discussed anything with Rilla yet, but at least it felt like something was finally going their way. That thought alone calmed his own worries, if only slightly.

The princess seemed content by herself, whispering quietly to her summon. Felix couldn't figure out how she had managed to keep it going for days straight. As far as he understood, most summons took their owner's energy to stay out. Caine was only able to keep Flare present for more than a few days when he was the size of a parakeet.

"Aren't you worried about getting caught traveling like this?" Felix asked aloud.

He could chalk up the summon to some special facet of her energy, but they were still floating along the ocean on a bright-green beacon.

Rilla ran a hand over the jellyfish. "No one can see us or hear us."

"Your energy is like mine."

"Nearly. I lack the heat and color element of your energy, but my dose was so tiny, I ended up without some traits."

Felix cut off his next question, glancing over at the others. "Dose?" he asked.

Rilla laughed at their perturbed expressions. "Ah. You're still unaware of my father's experiments. That's what Violet and I are." Rilla got quiet once again, little chuckles slipping out as she stared out into the ocean.

Caine spoke up. "What are you talking about?"

Felix tried to gauge Rilla's emotions. Her voice was calm, but for the first time, she frowned. "I don't really know anything. Violet and I are products of experiments created by my father and the previous archmage. Part of that was artificial magic. I have no knowledge of their intentions or what else has been created. The queen had been given a potion when she was pregnant to increase her magic and mine.

"I'd imagine the same was done to Violet's mother since they could transfer objects between our worlds. If I had to guess, I would say that my creation was botched, as I am not a wordsmith, and they decided to move on to Violet. It's only a guess though."

Artificial magic… they hadn't been able to come up with an explanation for Violet's power. Manmade magic had only come up once in their discussions. Neither had even seen it done let alone given to someone in another world. No one had ever had a need for it. Those not blessed with power still had plenty to do. The same was true for mages who were not wordsmiths.

"Did Violet give you my message?" Rilla asked, facing Caine.

"Yes," he answered. "Although I'm not certain what you meant."

Rilla lowered her shoulders again. "I told you to stop for your own sake, Caine. I think your predecessor died killing the queen for her magic. Violet's body and mine are capable of handling all that power because we were bred to. Your energy is strong, but your fate would be the same. Maybe. There must be more we don't know about… no one ever let me know about what was going on. I only found out by sneaking into meetings and rifling through the old archmage's things."

Felix watched Caine, but he wouldn't meet anyone's eyes.

Violet shifted like she was moving closer to them, but she turned to face the ocean instead.

Rilla leaned forward, resting on her hands. "What is it you want? I know I haven't been rescued out of the goodness of your heart, and I'm sure Violet's life is resting on the same decision. Be honest with me."

"We need the last ingredient for the portal." Violet gestured to herself. "I want to go home. And unfortunately, that relies on Caine getting the portal ingredient in your castle. Is that possible?"

Rilla smiled. "Yes, I don't think there will be too much backlash if I show myself to be alive and reveal Cross's lies. I cannot say what will happen past that, but I welcome you to retrieve what you need from the castle."

Violet regarded Caine for a half second before thanking Rilla.

~

THEY BOBBED along for another hour before the princess broke the silence. "Do you want your position back, Caine?"

"As archmage?" Caine asked, creasing his brow.

"Only if you agree to figure out everything my family created, from the artificial magic back down."

"That's it?"

"I'll clear your name on every offense—both of you."

Caine looked to Felix for his confirmation. Felix couldn't see any reason not to agree.

The final rays of sunlight were giving way to a star-filled sky. Felix couldn't fathom being able to walk down a street without fear. To be able to go see his parents again would be enough.

Violet

THE GENTLE WAVES were not enough to soothe her worries about having to take down Cross. Rilla was insistent that they kill him. Whether it was on the spot or through a proper execution, she was convinced no good could come from letting her brother continue to live.

Violet didn't contribute any more to the discussion. They didn't have much of a plan past walking in. Cross's own army might oppose them, but no one could see Endrel's citizens fighting against Rilla.

~

THEY SET their packs and cloaks down by a tree close to shore as Rilla bid farewell to her summon. The path through the woods should have been barely traveled, but many fresh hoofprints marked the dirt. Felix set a spell over their items to keep them safe and coaxed a vine to coil itself around his arm.

Violet kept wanting to pull the cloak's hood over her head. She had no reason to hide, but she missed its comfort. Her heart raced faster as the castle came into view.

Two guards stood at the large fence at the back of the wall. Rilla walked with her head held high and stepped up to the front.

"Good morning." She dropped into a full curtsy. "We would like to speak with His Majesty."

Chapter Thirty-Eight

Caine

BOTH GUARDS STARED BACK at them, openmouthed.

One of them fled into the garden, leaving the other to stutter, "Your Highness." His head snapped back. "That was one of Cross's soldiers. I think the king is in his room. There was an issue last night, and—"

Someone inside screamed.

The guard drew his sword. "I'll tell as many people as I can get to that you're here, but whatever you're doing, do it fast."

Caine counted the windows on the upper floor when they got to the wall, pressing his hand to the stone under the fifth one to reveal a secret passage. They sprinted through the corridor, emerging into one of the main halls.

Evidently, news of their presence was already there. Felix caught a ball of fire, turning it green as it rested in his palm.

"Wait!" A young mage threw her hands up—Avery, if he recalled. "I didn't know it was you. Cross's goons keep coming through here."

"Where is Cross?" Rilla asked.

"In the king's room, as far as I've heard, Your Highness."

Violet turned to the princess. "Are you coming with us? This doesn't work if you die."

"Of course." Rilla motioned them forward. "I think you'll keep me fairly safe."

"Let's split up," Caine suggested. "Felix and I will stay ahead of you to try to keep things controlled."

If Rilla was insistent on coming, they would at least be able to minimize the chances of her getting attacked and let as many people as possible know that she was alive and helping them.

Avery piped in, "I'll come too. Your word isn't the most trustworthy right now, Mr. Blackwood, and we have orders to kill you."

"Fantastic," Caine muttered. "Thanks. Go on ahead. We're right behind you."

As Caine turned back, Violet threw her arms around him. It was only for a moment, and he didn't have the chance to return it. She did the same to Felix.

"Be careful, okay? Don't be so reckless."

Caine felt himself smiling before he could stop it. "I'm not sure I can do that, Miss Harper." He looked over his shoulder one last time. "You be safe, too, Violet."

Caine risked teleporting once. Avery recruited another mage, who regarded them skeptically but was still quick to dash up the stairwell.

As they reached the top of the stairs, a swordsman grabbed the hilt of her blade but didn't draw it. "Avery?"

"Hi, Tanya. They're with us." Avery pointed to Caine and Felix. "Princess Rilla is here. We need to tell people and get rid of Cross's men."

"I can't just take your word for that."

They all turned as a scream pierced the air. "Cross's men are

—" A body flew into the wall behind them, landing crumpled on the floor.

"Can you trust me at least?" Avery conjured fire as someone ran at them. "We don't have a lot of time here."

Tanya drew her sword. "If I see you attacking anyone on our side, I'm coming after you both."

Caine changed his frost into air, knocking the mage who charged at them off his feet. Only when he could confirm the mage was an enemy did he drive an icicle through his chest. With everyone adorned with Endrel's blue, he would have to be careful with his deadlier attacks. Mistakes were inevitable, but he could prevent some of them without too much risk.

He moved forward with his brother and Avery as the younger mage called over and over, "They're with us. The princess is here."

Caine jumped back as Felix grabbed a swordsman around her waist with his vine.

She struggled in its grip. "I'm with you!"

As Felix dropped her, she lunged blade-first. Caine threw up a wall of ice as Felix threw yellow flames at her back.

Caine kept his ice raised, but the room had gone quiet. Only allies stood with them among the dead and detained. Even with Cross's takeover, the Endrel residents outnumbered Sophonix, and despite a few apprehensive looks, no one moved against Caine or Felix.

"Mr. Blackwood!" Avery called from in front of the next stairwell.

One more floor and they would be on Cross's level.

Violet

RILLA KEPT up with Violet's quick pace, still giving the others time to scope out the next floors.

Violet held her knife tightly, hoping she would only need magic. It was less personal to toss fire across the room.

Rilla made them invisible, which for the most part let them sneak past a few skirmishes unnoticed. By the second floor, Rilla had to drop the glamour, weak from their lengthy trip there.

Violet lifted a swordsman into the air as his blade swiped close to her head. He flailed in midair before she released her levitation spell and dropped him to the ground. An Endrel mage encased the fallen foe's hands in rock and dragged him to sit with the rest of Cross's apprehended soldiers.

Blood slicked the stairs as they reached the third floor. One swordsman sprawled across the tile. Caine and Felix waited at the top, slightly bloodstained but otherwise unharmed. They had already been through that hall, the path clear to the king's room. Caine pushed through first and met an unlocked door. Each readied to attack.

Cross lounged on top of a desk as they entered. Leaning back on his palms, he said, "Come now. This isn't really a fair fight, is it? Four against one?"

Violet searched the room, but he was right. No one stood at the king's defense.

Rilla stopped beside Violet. "Are you going to step down peacefully?" the princess asked.

Her brother laughed. "No."

"I'll have no choice but to take your crown forcefully."

"Why, because I want to take what's mine? Do you know how long ago I was promised her power? And a wordsmith at that." Cross sneered. "The vessel was picked at random, but evidently we ended up with the most uncooperative person possible."

Rilla opened her mouth, but Cross held up a finger. "I've failed to mention your dear assistant is here, Caine. I did have her working as my archmage, but unfortunately, that had to come to an end." He cackled. "Oh, you poor things. You think I'm lying. Malissia, could you bring our guest out?"

The side-room door opened, and a mage walked out, Alice in tow. He shoved her to the floor.

"Alice," Caine stammered, his magic flickering out for a moment.

"Hi." Blood and dirt stained her torn dress. She leaned back against the desk, half a smile on her lips.

"You want to know what this ring really does, Miss Willowflower?" Cross knocked a brass band against the wood. "Our blood pacts are useless, but this bonded us. My life is tied to yours, and the second my energy is gone from existence, so are you. That seal you poured on it last night means nothing."

Everyone froze but Alice. "Kill him, then. Kill me."

"Is my death worth hers?" Cross asked. "Why don't you ask my dear sister?"

Rilla's hands were gripped tightly in front of her. "I won't take an innocent person's life, and I refuse to ask this of any of you."

"I'm not that innocent," Alice said, sitting up.

Caine kneeled and grabbed Alice, but it was only to cut off the flames she had in her hands.

Cross called again, and a few of his men joined them from the room Alice had been in. The king darted straight for Violet. She cringed as Cross beckoned to her.

"Why don't you come do what you were made for?"

Violet tightened her grip on her blade but didn't know

where to hit. She wouldn't let Alice die. She dodged lightning, looking for a nonlethal opening.

As frost hit his back, Cross shoved Violet through the door and put up a wall of electricity between himself and Caine.

Violet barely caught what he shouted before the barrier went up. "*Inpulstia!*"

Is that the word for...?

She sent air at his feet. He only stumbled for a moment and shot a bolt of lightning at her face. Violet gasped as she caught it between her palms. Her heart swelled as the electric pulse tracked down her arms and into her shoulders. The unwelcome pressure of her energy was gone as the electricity rested in her palms, wrapping around her hands but never shocking her.

She spread her fingers out, and the bolts followed, scattering throughout the room. A gentle hum coursed through her as she conjured the energy on her own, letting it cover her hands again. She flicked it toward Cross and dashed forward.

Violet tried to bring down the electricity blocking the door as Cross aimed waves of white-hot lightning at every side of her.

"*Inpulstia!*" Violet shouted as she balled up his energy, letting it grow to three times its size and shooting it at his head as she tried to run past him.

He just barely caught the attack and threw it to the ground. Cross charged at her, keeping sparks on his hand as he grabbed her arm and shoved her against the wall next to the lightning barrier.

Violet shrieked, fighting to hold onto her weapon as electricity pulsed up her arm. She pushed against the energy, forcing it to stay in one spot above her elbow. The heat burned under Cross's grip, electricity eating away at her skin. She had to hit him. Her knife slid into his chest. Cross's cackling came out in heaves as he dropped to one knee.

Violet cursed. Too much blood was already seeping out. Without thinking, she put a hand over the wound.

The word for healing, what is it? What is it? "Santia."

The blood stopped as the gash shut completely. Cross raised his hand, but Violet grabbed the nearest blunt object, a hanging wall lantern, using her telekinesis.

"*Motia.*" She slammed it against his head.

Blood dripped into Cross's eyes as he stumbled away, and Violet successfully took down the electricity barrier. Someone's arms were around her before Violet could collapse. Her head was so heavy, like her temples were being squeezed between bricks. Still, she slid away from the person to kneel on the floor, cradling her charred arm. Her already-heavy breaths turned to hyperventilation as she saw it had been burned to the bone.

Caine sat with her, wrapping one arm around her waist as he pressed a glow to her wound. "You're all right. *Santia.*"

The skin was already tightening. She cried into his shoulder, refusing to watch her disfigured arm heal.

Rilla said behind them, "Detain Cross. You have something that will cut off his magic, right? He's to stay alive but contained. Caine Blackwood, I officially reinstate you as archmage of Endrel Kingdom. I will enlighten my citizens about what they need to know concerning the current situation. What you reveal to your families is at your own discretion."

"Let me rest a bit, and I'll finish healing it," Caine whispered to Violet before bowing his head to Rilla. "Thank you, Your Highness."

The princess stopped to press a hand against Violet's back, lowering her voice. "Thank you, Violet. Please, Caine, create the portal when all of you are rested."

He nodded. "I will."

Violet looked at her throbbing arm again. Bone still showed through in a few places. Burnt skin and muscle looked as rotten as it smelled.

Caine took a deep breath and pressed his fingers to it again.

Chapter Thirty-Nine

Violet

VIOLET COULDN'T FIGURE out why her head continued to throb.

The previous day had ended as well as they could have hoped. Cross was successfully locked in the hidden dungeon, his magic cut off and made so he was unable to bring any harm to himself. Sparrow was found lying in one of the cells, beaten nearly to death. Alice briefly explained their attempted escape and how Cross's guards had been waiting for them.

Fogg was in the dungeons, too, and Rilla only asked that he was given food and water.

Felix and another mage were with the captain and Alice in the office next door, healing them slowly. It had taken Caine and a second mage an hour to restore Violet's arm. Her skin was still marred in some spots, but the pain was no longer present. She let it be, allowing them to focus on the other injured castle residents.

She sat in the corner of Caine's study, pretending not to watch him work. He had a glassy orb floating above his desk. It dripped silvery colors, although a puddle never seemed to form underneath. Each time he pushed an herb past its surface and into its center, the drip changed its hue.

Caine had given Violet a healing potion, but it hadn't fixed her ache. She'd hoped sitting still would calm her, but she was only getting antsier. Violet didn't know where else to go. Her imagination was coming up with every awful scenario it could.

Caine sat down suddenly, his head in his hands as pain spread across his face. Only then did Violet realize how faint he looked. He had been prodding at what she guessed was the portal since that morning, whispering ancient words she hadn't learned.

"You don't need to hurt yourself to finish that. I can wait."

Caine flinched at her voice. "I'm fine."

He wasn't though. She'd been through enough with him to recognize the fatigue in his cracking tone.

Violet had taken note of the tea caddy when she'd been exploring earlier. As she heated water, Caine rested his head fully on the desk. She thought he was asleep as she set the cups on the coffee table, but he made his way over to the couch, pushing himself into the far corner.

Violet put her cup to her lips, the liquid burning her tongue. When she put down her cup to attend to the stinging, Caine reached over and placed two fingers on the porcelain until steam stopped pouring out.

"You're going to break a cup like that, forcing it from hot to cold," Violet said.

"I used to. These ones are enchanted now."

The humor was missing from his tone, and Violet was disappointed that it was gone.

"Caine."

He looked up only long enough to show acknowledgement.

"I..." Violet shook her head. She couldn't bring herself to say everything was okay. It wasn't. Something else was running around in her mind. "Do you really think my magic is stable enough to go back?"

"You have more control than you started with. I think you'll be fine."

"I'm just worried." Violet sank farther back in the couch. "I don't even know what I'm going to tell anyone."

"You were kidnapped. It's the truth."

Violet changed the topic. "How long is it going to take?"

"I'll be done in a few days—unless I keep getting distracted."

Violet stuck her tongue out at him, and he returned the gesture. She left, hoping to clear her head by talking to the others, as he sat back at his desk. It would be her last few days with them anyway.

~

VIOLET SPENT her last week in the castle as Caine created the portal. A little uneasiness lingered in their conversation, but Violet almost wished they had been more standoffish. It would have made leaving easier.

She checked her eyes one last time before joining Caine and Alice in his study. Felix had removed their luster completely and shown her how to do the spell herself, although Violet hoped his magic would hold.

"This is for you." Caine retrieved a small, neatly wrapped box from his desk drawer, holding it out to her. An envelope was attached to the bottom. "Don't open it until you're back in your world, all right?"

Violet shifted it in her hands, but nothing gave away its contents. "Thank you."

"Don't thank me. I haven't done anything for you."

Violet glowered for a moment but couldn't bring herself to say anything harsh.

Alice handed her a pair of black leather gloves. "They're made with a magic blocker," Alice explained. "You'll be fine, but just in case."

Caine pushed the finished orb against the wall. Violet stared into the brilliant colors, glancing back one last time. She could still feel their arms wrapping her in a tight goodbye.

Squeezing her eyes shut, Violet stepped through the portal. She gasped for air as the frigid magic gripped her insides, forcing her forward.

She lurched out the other side, keeping her little presents safe as she fell into her apartment. She stared into her living room, not believing it. After four long months, she was finally home. Violet let the gift box float above her hand. She had her magic, and she was home.

"Crystal?" she called into the house, garnering no response. It was still bright outside. Maybe she was at work.

She rushed into her bedroom, moving the few things left on her dusty bed and lying on her mattress. In her own bed again. She would tell someone she was back in a moment. She couldn't see her phone nearby anyway, and curiosity was urging her to open the letter.

Longing tugged at Violet's chest as she read the familiar handwriting:

I probably haven't apologized to you properly up until now. You were tormented for our own gain, and I can't say sorry enough. I know it means nothing. I tried to kill you, and that can't be forgiven. I don't really know if anything good came out of our interactions, but I did come to like you, even if I haven't made it terribly obvious. If by any chance you do want to see us, this orb is a portal that will serve as a permanent connection between our worlds. There are instructions for both using it and destroying it on the back of this letter. No matter what you choose, you're the only one who can see this box and its contents. I do not intend to create another one of these again. We've made enough decisions for you, so I leave this in your hands.

Acknowledgments

This story has been five years in the making, and I am so happy and proud to see it published. Of course, I could not have done this without the help and support from everyone around me. Thank you to my family, especially my mom, brother, and aunt. They have encouraged me from the start and can probably recite the first few chapters without looking. Thank you, Angie, Amanda, Irene, and Lynn for working with me to edit my manuscript. Thank you Bailey for bringing my cover idea to life. Thank you Matt for helping me refine my blurb. Thank you to my brother for taking my photo. Thank you to all of my beta readers for the feedback you provided me. I am so grateful for all of you.

About the Author

Keira O'shea a writer, reader, and cat lover. She lives in Connecticut, where she is studying psychology. *Incantations* is Keira's debut novel. You can visit her at keiraoshea.com.